'Damn you

I cannot leave   carriage and ce

She opened her mouth to tell him just what she thought of his top-lofty attitude, but changed her mind when Betty seized her hand. 'Please, Miss Lydia, don't let him leave us here; it will be dark soon and I'm afeared. . .'

'I fancy I am the lesser of two evils, Miss Wenthorpe,' he said with a smile which infuriated her. 'And I promise to keep my baser urges in check.'

Dear Reader

We welcome back Gail Mallin who offers DEBT OF HONOUR set against the brooding backdrop of the Lake District, and in DEVIL-MAY-DARE Mary Nichols gives us Lydia, who walks a tightrope of possible disgrace. Our American offerings are STARDUST AND WHIRLWINDS by Pamela Litton set in Texas 1873, and AUTUMN ROSE by Louise Rawlings gives us seventeenth-century France. Happy New Year!

The Editor

Born in Singapore, **Mary Nichols** came to England when she was three, and has spent most of her life in different parts of East Anglia. She has been a radiographer, school secretary, information officer and industrial editor, as well as a writer. She has three grown up children, and four grandchildren.

Recent titles by the same author:

THE PRICE OF HONOUR
THE DANBURY SCANDALS

DEVIL-MAY-DARE

Mary Nichols

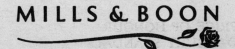

MILLS & BOON

MILLS & BOON LIMITED
ETON HOUSE, 18–24 PARADISE ROAD
RICHMOND, SURREY, TW9 1SR

All the characters in this book have no existence outside the imagination of the Author, and have no relation whatsoever to anyone bearing the same name or names. They are not even distantly inspired by any individual known or unknown to the Author, and all the incidents are pure invention.

All Rights Reserved. The text of this publication or any part thereof may not be reproduced or transmitted in any form or by any means, electronic or mechanical, including photocopying, recording, storage in an information retrieval system, or otherwise, without the written permission of the publisher.

This book is sold subject to the condition that it shall not, by way of trade or otherwise, be lent, resold, hired out or otherwise circulated without the prior consent of the publisher in any form of binding or cover other than that in which it is published and without a similar condition including this condition being imposed on the subsequent purchaser.

*First published in Great Britain 1993
by Mills & Boon Limited*

© Mary Nichols 1993

*Australian copyright 1993
Philippine copyright 1994
This edition 1994*

ISBN 0 263 78244 1

*Set in 10½ on 12 pt Linotron Times
04-9401-78529*

*Typeset in Great Britain by Centracet, Cambridge
Made and printed in Great Britain*

CHAPTER ONE

LORD WENTHORPE paused on the top stair with his hand on the polished wood balustrade, wondering what had put the notion into his head to go up to the old schoolroom floor; he had not been there in an age, not since Lydia and Tom were knee-high to a grasshopper. He had only ventured into this wing of his considerable mansion then because Nanette had upbraided him for not taking an interest in his offspring's education. Dearest Nanette—who would have thought that the darling of the Parisian stage would make such a splendid mama? He stopped to remember and then wished he had not. The memories were painful, laughter and tears, happiness and unending sorrow. But life was like that. He sighed and turned to retrace his steps; let the memories stay locked away.

The sound of merriment came from a door along the corridor which was not quite closed. Tom, down from Cambridge with his friend, Frank Burford; they were no doubt playing some prank on Lydia. Would they never grow up? He had glimpsed Lydia from his bedchamber that morning, long before most ladies would have dreamed of rising, galloping across the park with poor Scrivens so far behind her as to be useless to help if she took a tumble. Not that she would, he was confident of her horseman-

ship, but he could have sworn she was riding astride.
He could ask the groom of course, but Scrivens was
loyal to his mistress and he would not put him in the
position of having to tattle on her. When would she
learn to behave like the lady she purported to be?
Eighteen — no, he corrected himself, nineteen, and
still behaving like a schoolroom miss, and that in
spite of acting as his housekeeper for the last six
years. There were plenty of young ladies of her age
already married. He ought to be thinking of getting
her a husband. She was not wanting in sense and
had no difficulty making decisions and giving instructions to the indoor staff; she would make some
young blade a fine wife, so long as she managed to
quell her tendency to mischief.

It was his fault, of course; he had let her grow
wild with only her brother for company, while he
mourned the passing of their mother. If his darling
Nanette had still been alive, Lydia would not now
be something close to a hoyden. He had prevaricated
too long. Resolutely he moved towards the schoolroom and pushed the door open.

Lydia, in pink satin breeches, yellow stockings,
brightly striped waistcoat topped by an old-
fashioned coat with huge patch pockets and enough
silver lace to bedeck a field marshal, not to mention
a hugely knotted neckcloth, was mincing up and
down in front of the two young men, who sat on the
schoolroom chairs watching her. She stopped in
front of them to make an elegant leg which made
the white powdered wig she wore slip sideways over
one ear to reveal her own dark hair. She righted it

and then put up the quizzing glass which dangled from a ribbon round her neck and peered short-sightedly through it. 'Demme,' she said, affecting the voice of a pink of the *ton*. 'Demme, if I don't teach you young pups some *manners*.'

The young men hooted with laughter.

'Miss Wenthorpe, if you don't make a most fetching dandy, I'll consume my best beaver!' cried Frank.

Lydia took another turn up and down, stopping to twirl the quizzing glass, then added, 'You think I am *man* enough for you, sir?'

'I've got it!' cried Tom triumphantly. 'Manners maketh man.'

Lydia dropped her pose and laughed. 'You'd never have guessed if I hadn't given you a hint.' She looked up and saw her father in the doorway. His frown told her she was in for a scolding, but she was by no means subdued; her papa's scoldings were only ever of the mildest and nothing to be afraid of. 'Papa, we were playing charades.'

'So I perceive.' She did, indeed, make a very passable male. She was tall for a woman, long-limbed and slim-waisted. She had high cheekbones and strong, dark brows and her violet eyes, so like her mother's, gazed back at him without the least sign of being cowed. 'Go and change out of that frippery into something more becoming a daughter of mine, and come to me in the bookroom,' he said gruffly, disappointed not so much in her as in himself. He turned to the young men who were scrambling to their feet. 'Could you not think of something more manly to do? A gallop perhaps.'

'Sir, it has been raining, all day,' protested Tom.

'The rain has ceased. A brisk walk to curb your high spirits before dinner, I think.'

The young men exchanged meaningful looks and left the room with alacrity, leaving Lydia to face her father. 'In ten minutes, miss, in the bookroom,' he said and turned on his heel.

Lydia, indignant that he should be so up in the boughs over something so innocent, marched off to her room to remove the offending garments. Charades was a game they had played ever since they had left the cradle. Had not Mama encouraged them in it? Had she not kept a huge basket full of costumes for that very purpose and showed them how to use stage make-up to produce almost any face they desired? Mama herself had often played a male when there were not enough men to take all the parts in the little plays they produced. Papa had always been indulgent, so what had put him into such an ill humour now?

Within the stipulated ten minutes she presented herself at the library door and knocked. Her father's voice bade her enter and she crossed the threshold to stand before him, hands clasped in front of her blue cambric skirt and her head, now neatly arranged in classic-style ringlets, downcast so that all she could see of him was his shining top boots and well-fitting buckskins.

'Sit down,' he said, indicating a straight-backed chair on one side of the hearth.

She obeyed and lifted her eyes to his. 'It was only charades, Papa.'

His craggy features softened; he could not remain out of humour with his daughter for long. 'I know, and though you may see no harm in it and I own I would not have done so myself a few years ago, we must remember you are no longer a child and must begin behaving like a lady and not a hoyden.'

'Yes, Papa.'

'It is not as if you and Tom were alone; young Burford was a witness. . .'

'But I have known him since he was in leading-strings and his mama used to bring him to play with us in the nursery.'

'Nevertheless, he is a young man, a personable, lusty young man, and you must be aware of that.'

'I was not — I did not think. . .'

'No?' he smiled. 'But the time has come for you to learn how to go on in Society. You must come out and start looking for a husband. . .'

'But, Papa, I have met no one I like well enough.'

'Nor will you if you remain in Suffolk.'

'Leave Raventrees! Oh, Papa, I don't think I could bear it. . .'

'You will do as I say.'

'But you have not left the country for years, ever since. . .' She stopped, not wishing to hurt him by reminding him of the reason he had lived in seclusion for so long.

'Nor do I intend to. I have been thinking. Your aunt Agatha can bring you out.'

'Aunt Aggie!' she exclaimed. 'But she is. . .'

He smiled briefly. 'She is old and somewhat eccentric, but she is acquainted with everyone of any importance and she knows how to go on. Besides, I can think of no other who would do it.'

'Am I that bad?' Lydia whispered.

He chuckled. 'Not so incorrigible that you cannot be taught correct behaviour and how to display to best advantage. And that,' he added severely, 'is not in dressing up like a popinjay. You are a beautiful young lady, Lydia, a trifle on the tall side, but there must be some eligible bachelors who are taller. . .'

'Is that all that matters?' she cried. 'That he should be tall?'

'And have a decent background, with a good title and a fortune to match yours. I would not wish him to be too old, either, nor too free and easy with the ladies, for your sake. . .'

'That seems to me to be something of a high order,' she said. 'Supposing Aunt Aggie finds such a one and I say we will not suit?'

'You will not be coerced, my dear, you have my word, but I beg you to consider carefully before you reject a promising suitor. Marriage is a far better state than spinsterhood, I can assure you.'

'Has Aunt Aggie agreed?'

'Not yet, because I have only now thought of it. I shall write to her tonight. As soon as I have her reply, I will order Wenthorpe House to be opened and Tom can escort you to London. It won't do him any harm to acquire a little town bronze.'

Lydia was downcast, not only because she was to leave her beloved home, but that she was to be parted from her over-indulgent papa, but no amount of arguing would make him change his mind, and two weeks later she found herself being driven post-chaise with Tom and her maid for company, while everything she held most dear receded further and further behind her.

The heavy rains of the previous few days had left the roads in a shocking state and they were thrown from side to side as their coachman and postilion negotiated the potholes. By the afternoon of the second day Betty, who always travelled badly, was sitting in the corner looking whey-faced and Tom was wishing he had chosen to ride alongside. 'I'll be relieved when we stop for the night,' Lydia said, righting herself after having been thrown across the carriage almost into her brother's lap. 'I shall be black and blue at this rate. Why could we not have waited until the roads improved? It is still very early in the Season.'

He smiled. 'You know Papa; when he gets an idea into his head, nothing will serve but it must be attended to without delay.'

'I have never known him so impervious to reason. All over a simple game.'

'Oh, it was not the charades so much as his own conscience which smote him. You know, it really is time you were taken in hand. . .'

'Not you, too,' she said. 'I would have thought you would have understood.'

'Most assuredly I do, but I also realise that my little sister. . .'

'Not so little,' she said with a wry smile.

'Very well, my not-so-little sister must grow up and, if she does not, spinsterhood is not a state to be envied.'

Her protests were lost in a great swaying and creaking of springs, followed by a terrifying sound of rending wood accompanied by the shouts of their coachman and the screaming of the frightened horses. She was catapulted on to the opposite seat and then the whole carriage slid over sideways and she found herself sitting on one of the doors with Betty, screaming at the full extent of her not inconsiderable voice, on top of her. Tom found the door which was immediately above their heads and hauled himself out.

Lydia extricated herself and stood up. 'Are you hurt, Betty?'

The maid's shrieking subsided to sobs as she endeavoured to right herself. 'Oh, we should never have come; we should have stayed at 'ome where it's safe.'

'You said you wanted to come,' Lydia said, concluding from this that her maid was unhurt. 'I gave you a chance to stay at Raventrees.'

'What, and leave you to the mercies of a new maid who don't know your ways? I ain't so unfeeling.'

Lydia smiled. 'Then don't look so dismal. At least you are not now being rocked to death and we shall have to stay somewhere hereabouts until the carriage is repaired and that will give you time to recover.' As she spoke she put her head out of the door.

The carriage lay on its side with one of the

uppermost wheels still spinning; their boxes had been thrown from the roof on to the muddy road and one of them had sprung its straps and deposited lace-trimmed garments into the water-filled hole which had overturned them. One of the horses had freed itself from the traces and was galloping across a field while Tom endeavoured to free the others who struggled against their harness. Watkins, the coachman, bent over the inert form of Scrivens who had been riding postilion. She looked forward and then back the way they had come but the road, which divided fields of newly sprouting corn, was empty; there was not a building or another traveller in sight.

'Bend over!' she commanded Betty. 'I must get out and see to Scrivens.'

Reluctantly her maid complied, and with a great heaving and a shocking display of petticoats Lydia stood on her maid's bent back, hauled herself out of the carriage and jumped down on to the road, leaving Betty wailing, 'What about me?'

She ran to where Scrivens lay in the ditch beside the road and knelt beside him in the wet mud. 'Is he badly hurt?'

'I don't think so, Miss Lydia, he's got a rare hard head on 'im,' said the coachman, who was feeling over the inert body for broken bones. 'See, he's coming round.' A groan and a fluttering of eyelids from the unfortunate servant seemed to bear this statement out. 'Now, miss, if we was to help him up. . .'

Betty, who had somehow managed to scramble

out of the coach, came running across the road, trying to hold her skirts clear of the mud, which was more than her mistress had attempted to do. 'Oh, is he hurt?'

Scrivens, by this time, was in a sitting position and shaking his dazed head, but appeared not to be badly injured. Lydia left him in the care of her maid and returned to her brother, while Watkins set off across the field to catch the runaway horse. Tom had freed the remaining three and was looking down at the broken wheel and splintered axle of the coach, scratching his dark head.

'What's to be done?' she asked him.

He looked up at her. 'I shall have to ride one of the horses to fetch help.' Adjuring her to watch over their belongings, he flung himself on the postilion's mount and set off for the nearest village, where he hoped to procure a conveyance to bring them on and to arrange lodgings, for assuredly the coach could not be mended before nightfall. Watkins returned leading the errant horse and Lydia and Betty began gathering up their belongings and pushing them back into the broken trunk.

'They are ruined, that's what they are,' Betty grumbled, holding up a pair of frilly nether garments. 'They'll never come clean.'

'At least no one was badly hurt,' Lydia said, snatching them from her and bundling them in with the rest before the two men could see them. 'We could have all been killed. I wonder how long Tom will be? It will be dusk soon and I do not fancy being set upon by highwaymen. I wish I had asked him for his pistol.'

'Oh, miss, you don't think. . .' The sudden sound of an owl hooting in the trees beside the road made Betty fling herself behind her mistress with a cry of alarm.

'Don't be a little goose,' Lydia said. 'There's no one there.' She stopped speaking as the sound of horses and crunching wheels came to their ears, and this was followed by the sight of a travelling chaise coming round the bend behind them at a spanking pace. It was drawn by a perfectly matched pair of bays and Lydia stood and watched its approach with a gleam of admiration in an eye accustomed to evaluating horseflesh. When the equipage drew to a halt beside them, it became obvious that, although the horses were of the highest order, the coach was even older than their own and certainly more ramshackle. She was wondering what ninny could bear to harness such prime beasts to such a vehicle when its occupant flung open the door and jumped into the road. He was very tall indeed, something she almost always noticed first in a man, being so tall herself, and what with that and his long, aquiline nose it seemed as if he was looking down on them with a loftiness which was belied, however, by the twitch at the corners of his firm mouth. He swept off his tall beaver, revealing brown curls cut short in the latest style, and bowed over a leg encased in mustard-coloured pantaloons and polished hessians. 'Your servant, ma'am.' He looked about him for her escort, but, perceiving none but the servants, turned back to her. 'May I offer you assistance?'

Lydia hesitated, for what assistance could he offer except to take them up, and she was reluctant to agree to that, not knowing him from Adam. He might be a highwayman, a ne'er-do-well, a thatch-gallows of the worst sort — anything. 'Sir. . .' she began, uncomfortably aware of her muddied skirts and that her bonnet had slipped down her back on its ribbons and her hair had come unpinned. 'Sir, I do not know you.'

'As there is no one else to do it, let me introduce myself,' he said, taking her right hand in his and raising it to his lips, without taking his glance from her face. To her consternation, she found herself looking straight into his eyes. They were nut-brown and had a depth which seemed to draw her down into them, like a whirlpool pulling a fallen leaf into its vortex, powerless to resist. They seemed to say, Here I am; escape me if you will. Disconcerted, she tried to pull her hand away, but he held it fast. Then he smiled and the extraordinary sensation faded. 'I am Jack Bellingham,' he said, releasing her. 'Marquis of Longham, second son of the Duke of Sutton. . .'

'How can you be a marquis if you are only a second son?' she put in, still feeling weak.

He gave a ghost of a smile. 'Because, ma'am, my elder brother died a month back on the hunting field.'

'Oh, I am sorry.'

'And now you are assured of my credentials, will you allow me to help you?'

'Assured?' she queried, her common sense returning. 'Just on your say-so, that is poor assurance. You could have said you were the Prince Regent and I none the wiser.'

He laughed. 'Have you ever met the heir to the throne?'

'No.'

'Then I forgive you.'

'For what?'

'For the insult. His Highness is somewhat older and a great deal fatter than I.' He paused to walk round their overturned coach and inspected the broken wheel, while she endeavoured to set her bonnet to rights and brush the mud from her clothing with a kid-gloved hand. 'I doubt you will ride further in this vehicle this side of a se'enight, certainly not tonight. . .'

'My brother, the Honourable Thomas Wenthorpe, has ridden one of the horses to fetch help,' she said with as much dignity as she could muster. 'He will be back directly.'

'How long since he left?'

'Half an hour, perhaps a little longer.'

'Then he cannot possibly be back before dark; the next village is ten miles away and I doubt he will be able to hire a conveyance immediately, certainly not one to take all that.' And he pointed at the two large trunks, one of which would no longer shut and revealed rather more of her most intimate apparel than she liked. She felt herself colour, but he appeared not to notice and went on, 'Of course, if you prefer to take the greater risk of being left by the roadside, I will continue on my way. I am in a great deal of haste.'

'Then you had best go on, my lord. I have servants with me.'

'Damn your scruples, girl,' he said. 'I cannot leave you. Get in and cease your protests.'

She opened her mouth to tell him just what she thought of his top-lofty attitude but changed her mind when Betty seized her hand. 'Please, Miss Lydia, don't let him leave us here; it will be dark soon and I'm afeared. . .'

'I fancy I am the lesser of two evils, Miss Wenthorpe,' he said with a smile which infuriated her. 'And I promise to keep my baser urges in check.'

'I am afraid one of my servants has been hurt. . .'

'Badly?'

'I do not think so, my lord, but I do not like to leave him.'

He looked across at Scrivens and, perceiving that he was now on his feet and dusting himself down, said, 'He can ride with my driver. Now, are you coming or not?'

Lydia looked along the road for signs of Tom returning and then across the darkening fields, where the hedges and trees were beginning to throw sinister shadows, and decided he was right. 'I did not mean to be ungrateful,' she said. 'I should be most obliged to you if you would take us up. . .'

'Certainly I will, but not your luggage; there will

be no room for it and, besides, I do not wish my chaise to go the way of yours.'

'Watkins will stay by our belongings and wait for Tom, if you will be so kind as to convey me and my maid and Scrivens to the next posting inn. No doubt we will come upon my brother on the way,' she said, too polite to make a reference to the incongruity of the magnificent bays and the scuffed old coach, though her curiosity was almost overwhelming. 'I have a small overnight bag, if that is not too much trouble.'

While Scrivens, who would not for the world have complained that his head ached and his shoulder was so painful he did not know how to haul himself up there, took his place beside the driver, their rescuer leaned into the overturned vehicle, pulled out her bag and marched off to his own carriage with it. He put it in the boot and turned to hand Lydia up. Afraid of sensations she did not understand, she was reluctant to give him her hand again, but it would have been churlish to refuse, so she allowed him to help her into the carriage. As soon as Betty had seated herself beside her mistress, he took the facing seat and called to his driver to proceed.

When they had safely negotiated the blockage in the road and were once more on their way, Lydia sought to express her gratitude for his help and began an explanation of how they came to be on the road and why their coach was not as roadworthy as it should have been. 'It has not been out of Suffolk for years,' she said. 'And our coachman knows the roads around our home so well there has never been

the least chance we should fall into a hole.' If she
had hoped that this statement might persuade him
to similar explanations, she was wrong; he appeared
not to wish for conversation. He had obviously
discharged his duty as he saw it but that was as far
as he was prepared to go; polite exchanges and
confidences were no part of it. Very well, if he
wanted to be a stiff-neck, so be it; they would soon
be off his hands.

She turned to watch out of the window for Tom,
but mile succeeded mile and they met no one. Surely
they could not have missed each other on the way?
'Do you know the road well, my lord?' she asked.

He came out of a brown study to answer her.
'Tolerably well.'

'Then how much further is it to the posting inn?'

He smiled suddenly and his grim expression lightened so that she became aware of the humour
behind his hazel eyes. 'I am poor company, Miss
Wenthorpe, I realise that, but be assured I am as
anxious to arrive at my destination as you are.'

'And what is your destination?'

'Ultimately London, but for tonight a good bed
and a change of horses.'

'Have these already been bespoken, my lord?'

'Indeed yes, my man came on ahead. And you?'

'Arrangements were made before we left home,
though I collect we were meant to go a little further
before nightfall, but what with the bad roads and the
accident. . .' She paused for another look out of the
window for her brother. 'I do hope Tom has been

able to find somewhere for us to stay while the carriage is fetched and repaired.'

'Ah, your brother. . .'

The tone of his voice brought her up sharply. Surely he did not think she was travelling unescorted and had invented a brother? Or did he think Tom was not her brother, but her lover? If he thought that of her, what else was he thinking? Oh, how she wished she had braved the darkness and waited by the damaged coach. 'I do hope he has not encountered some difficulty,' she said, trying to remain calm.

'You will soon see; we will be at the King's Head in a matter of minutes.'

And if Tom is not there, she thought, what then? What would she do? What would the Marquis do? She glanced sideways at him beneath the brim of her silk-ruched bonnet while pretending to be looking out of the window. He looked decidedly uncomfortable trying to keep his long legs tucked out of the way of her skirts, but apart from that he seemed entirely composed. His well-fitting coat of blue superfine seemed not to need padding at the shoulders and his waist had no need of stays. She supposed him to be about thirty, though it was difficult to tell because his features were tanned and there were tiny lines running from the corners of his eyes, as if he had spent long hours out of doors screwing up his face against the sun, but he was certainly old enough to be married and have a brood of offspring. She fell to wondering what kind of a husband and father he made — probably very cool and distant, except when roused to anger. She did not think she would care for his anger, though perhaps it would not be any worse than his present indifference. He had resumed his thoughtful expression with his chin resting on the folds of his impeccable neckcloth between the points of his collar, almost as if he had forgotten she was there. What was he thinking of, apart from what a devilish inconvenience she was to him?

It was not so much the inconvenience of having unexpected passengers which had put Jack in a browse but the notion that fate had taken a hand in his affairs and was conspiring to prevent him reaching his destination. His own travelling carriage had overturned the first day out from home and, though his horses had not been injured, thank God, he had been obliged to buy this antiquated coach to continue his journey. And now to find himself not alone in this particular misfortune was the outside of enough. He only hoped the vehicle was sturdier than it looked and would convey them all safely to the next posting inn and even more sincerely trusted that his passenger was telling the truth and there really was a brother to take charge of her; he had enough on his hands as it was.

As Captain Jack Bellingham, he had returned from service with Wellington's army at the end of the war, expecting some respite from continual fighting, only to be faced with another kind of conflict at home. In the six or seven years he had been out of the country his father had grown prematurely old and even more inclined than before to take refuge in the bottle. He had let the estate go to ruin. And his heir, Jack's elder brother, far from helping to set matters to rights, had made them worse by drinking, womanising and gambling. His death on the hunting field when in his cups had left Jack, who had never regarded himself as a future duke, as heir not only to extensive land and property but to all the debts and problems as well.

One of these latter was a neighbour called Ernest Grimshaw who had taken advantage of the general neglect and encroached on woodland which most certainly belonged to the Longham domain. He had cut down any number of fine trees and sold the timber so that, where before the war there had been a fine stand of oaks, larch and elm, there was now nothing but an ugly scar of stumps and bracken, and, what was worse, the game had naturally disappeared with the trees. The man had had the temerity to show him some ancient map on which the wood was clearly marked but the devil of it was that it was not shown inside the Longham boundary. He had defied his lordship to turn him off or deprive him of the not inconsiderable revenue the timber provided. Jack was on his way to meet the lawyers, but he had a feeling in his bones that he was going to need all his wits about him to win through. It would have been easier and certainly a great deal cheaper to have let the fellow get away with it and concentrated on the rest of the estate, but that was not Jack's way; he would be blowed if he would let some land-thieving cit get the better of him.

It was not that he was particularly in want of

funds; his personal fortune, inherited on the distaff side, was more than adequate, even setting aside the fortune in gold and jewels he had brought out of France with him. It was plunder, of course, but, since he had found it in a French sergeant's knapsack after the battle of Toulouse and it had obviously been plundered by him in the first place, the finding of its original owner, so his one-time batman and now his valet had told him, would be well-nigh impossible, even if he or she were still alive. He ought to be grateful to the unknown Johnny Blue-coat and lose no sleep over something which, in Tewkes's opinion, was a stroke of good luck. Jack intended to make a push to discover the true owner of the cache, but that would have to wait upon the business with Grimshaw being satisfactorily concluded.

He had said nothing of it to his father, who would, he was sure, take the same view as Tewkes, that anything acquired on a battlefield was a fair prize and meant to be used. His father, who had never cared a straw for his younger son, was, now that he was the heir, insisting on him marrying and continuing the line. Jack had had little time and even less inclination to marry while he was a serving soldier; following the colours was not something he would subject any wife to and leaving her at home seemed to defeat the object of the exercise. He had seen too many marriages fail because of long separations to take the risk. He was home now and, while he owned he ought to be thinking about marriage, to do so simply to produce an heir went against the grain. He would not stand in line, fawning over eager débutantes, just to please his profligate father. He grinned as the old coach jolted over a particularly bad rut; arriving in town in this dilapidated conveyance would certainly not endear him to the fortune hunters. He smiled to himself; if he were to allow the gossipers to think his pockets were to let, he might gain the breathing space he needed.

He lifted his head to find Lydia surveying him with wide violet eyes and a tiny twitch to the corners of her mouth which might have been the beginnings of a smile. In his experience young ladies usually fell into a swoon or burst into floods of tears when confronted with a mishap of this magnitude; that she could smile made him feel a deal more comfortable. 'We are slowing down,' she said. 'You will soon be rid of us.'

Chastised, he said, 'I apologise, Miss Wenthorpe, I am afraid I am poor company. Please forgive me.'

'Oh, it is I who need forgiving for the intrusion.' They were pulling up in the yard of an inn and the driver was shouting to one of the ostlers who had run out to meet them. 'If we can find my brother, I am sure he will add his thanks to mine.'

But Tom was nowhere to be seen. On enquiring after him, she was told that he had been there but as there were no spare horses or carriages of any sort he had gone to a farm along the road in the hope of borrowing a cart.

'A *cart*?' She could hardly believe it and she knew that the Marquis, who stood immediately behind her, was laughing at the picture thus created in his mind of her and her maid sitting atop their luggage on a farm cart! 'Whatever was he thinking of?'

'Better than walking,' the innkeeper said, with a shrug. 'And he could bring on your luggage, not to mention the broken wheel to be repaired.'

'Eminently sensible,' commented the Marquis. 'But we did not meet him on the road, so where is he?'

'The horse he rode was lame and he had to walk to the farm — all of two miles further on, it be — and if the farmer were not at home or the cart loaded and needing to be unloaded it would take time. Ten to one he's still there.'

'Could you not have lent him a horse?' Lydia asked.

'Ma'am, we have no spares, as I told the young gentleman.'

'I thought I saw two looking over their stalls in the stables when we came into the yard.'

'They are bespoke for his lordship.'

'Oh.' She turned to the Marquis. 'You have taken the last two horses. How are we to go on?'

If this was a hint to relinquish the animals to her, he did not take the bait. 'I'll lay odds your carriage wheel will not be ready by tomorrow,' he said. 'And by the day after your own horses will have been rested.'

'One of them is lame; you heard the landlord say so. What about the ones you brought today?'

'They go back to Longham,' he snapped. 'I do not leave prime cattle like that for any Tom, Dick or Harry to spoil.'

'But we must go on — my aunt is expecting us tomorrow evening at the latest; she will be very worried if we do not arrive.'

He did not see that it need be any concern of his but he could no more abandon her now than he could when he'd first come upon the overturned coach, especially as her brother, if he truly was her brother, seemed to have left her to manage on her own. Confound the pair of them! 'I will deem it a privilege to convey you and your brother on tomorrow,' he said, then, turning to the innkeeper, 'Have you a room for Miss Wenthorpe?'

It seemed the Marquis had also bespoken the only spare room but he gave it up with every appearance of cheerfulness, saying he would do very well on a settle in the parlour. By the time Tom arrived, it was quite dark and Lydia was being entertained by her rescuer to an excellent supper of fish in oyster sauce, boiled beef and apple flummery.

Tom was cold and wet and dismal and not inclined to be gracious when he discovered that Lydia had arrived in the village in comparative comfort, had washed and changed, and was sitting unchaperoned in the dining-room with a man to whom she had not been introduced. It really would not do, and he told her so in no uncertain terms when, at last, they left the dining-room to retire for the night and he was able to speak to her alone.

'What would you have had me do?' she retorted. 'Sit under the broken carriage and freeze to death while you took your time bringing a *farm cart*? His lordship has been kindness itself. . .' Kindness was

not really the right word, she decided; he had been
vastly entertaining, sarcastic and charming by turns,
while remaining unfailingly polite. He had been
solicitous for her comfort and sent the inn servants
scurrying to please her, and then sat without speaking for several minutes watching her eat, as if he had
never seen a woman with a hearty appetite before.
Her concentration on her plate had not been so
much hunger as a reluctance to raise her head and
find those searching eyes on her.

'You need not have dined with him,' Tom said,
unconvinced. 'It is hardly the thing. He is a
stranger.'

'But he gave up his room for me, and a very fine
room it is too; I could not be so ungrateful as to
refuse his company, and we were not alone—the
dining-room was full.'

'We should have gone on to Watford where our
rooms were booked.'

'How?'

He had no answer and gave her none, but turned
to grumbling that he had been obliged to dine on
left-overs and was to sleep with Watkins and
Scrivens above the stables and if he did not catch his
death of a chill then he would be more than surprised. She made light of his catalogue of complaints, saying he would feel more the thing after a
good night's sleep and, taking her leave, went up to
her bedchamber where Betty was waiting to help her
undress.

It was a squeeze for them all to pack into the
Marquis's chaise the next morning, even though they

left Watkins and Scrivens behind to see to the repairs of the coach and follow on when these had been completed and the horses rested. Tom, still sulking a little, sat beside his lordship facing Lydia and Betty and it seemed to Lydia that the Marquis was having even greater difficulty with his long legs. By the time they stopped for nuncheon they were all glad to get out and stretch their cramped limbs. The inn was the one where she and Tom would have stayed the previous night but for the accident, and their fresh horses were waiting for them; but now, of course, they had no carriage to harness them to. Tom was all for riding one of them but he would not leave Lydia alone in the carriage with the Marquis, especially as they were approaching London and might set the tongues wagging with unfavourable gossip about her before she had even set foot on its flags. It would not be a very auspicious start to her come-out. Jack, seeing and sympathising with his dilemma, decided he, too, would prefer to ride, even if the mounts were a couple of mediocre carriage horses and he was hardly dressed for it, and thus the calvalcade entered the metropolis and pulled up at the door of Wenthorpe House in Portman Square.

Mrs Agatha Wenthorpe, widow of Lord Wenthorpe's younger brother, had arrived from her own home in Edgware a few days previously and had immediately set about opening up the house, which had remained unoccupied, except for a handful of servants, for years. She had engaged more staff, ordered all the windows opened and fires lit in every room. The dust-covers had been removed, the

carpets beaten, floors scrubbed, furniture polished
and flowers brought in and arranged in vases on
every table and ledge big enough to receive them so
that overriding the lingering fusty smell of disused
rooms was the scent of soap and beeswax, narcissi
and pansies.

It was some years since Lydia had seen her aunt
and in that time the lady had become even more
eccentric in her appearance. She was sitting in one
of the small downstair parlours with her feet on a
footstool by the fire, reading one of Miss Austen's
novels through a very thick quizzing glass, when they
were announced, but rose quickly to greet them. She
was a short, dumpy woman, made even broader by
the caging she wore in her very old-fashioned gown
of coffee-coloured brocade with its wide over-
sleeves. Her face was heavily powdered and a patch
on her cheek disguised an ugly pockmark. On her
head she wore a startling red wig. Lydia had loved
her as a child and she saw no reason now to change
her opinion. She hurried forward and allowed herself to be embraced. 'Dear Aunt, such an adventure
we have had,' she said, after Mrs Wenthorpe had
released her and held her hand out for Tom to kiss,
which he did, thankful that she could not see his
smile at her extraordinary dress.

'Aunt, may I present the Marquis of Longham?'
Lydia said, turning to Jack who had been prevailed
upon to come in to meet Mrs Wenthorpe. 'He has
been a prodigious help, for without him we would
have been delayed for days and days.'

'Indeed? Then I must add my gratitude to my

niece's,' she said, putting up the quizzing glass and eyeing him up and down with great candour. 'You will stay for supper?'

Jack, without a trace of discomfort, bowed low over her plump, bejewelled hand. 'Alas, I have pressing business, ma'am.'

'Then you must call when you are not so pressed. We cannot let you go unthanked.'

'I have been sufficiently thanked, ma'am,' he said. 'And now that Miss Wenthorpe is safely in your hands, I must take my leave.' He bowed again to Mrs Wenthorpe and then to Lydia and, with a, 'Good evening, Wenthorpe,' to Tom, left the room.

'Well!' said Aunt Aggie, letting out her breath in a long sigh. 'There's a top-lofty male if ever I saw one. He could not get away fast enough. What have you done to him, Lydia?'

'I, Aunt? Why, nothing. I do believe that is his usual manner. I really think he did not want to rescue us and now he is glad to have us off his hands.'

'Why should he not wish to help? Is there something wrong with him?'

'I hardly know, Aunt, but his carriage was worse then ours. If it had not been drawn by the most beautiful pair of bays I have ever seen, I would have taken him for an impostor. And, you must admit, his manners leave much to be desired. . .'

'I expect he took a leaf out of your book,' Mrs Wenthorpe said in mild rebuke. 'But we can soon put a town polish on you and then you will have any number of offers. Tomorrow we must shop for clothes. . .' She stopped because Lydia had barely been able to conceal a smile at the thought of her outrageously dressed aunt Aggie selecting clothes for her. 'I do not pretend to be all the crack myself and I am too old to change my ways, but I know someone who will see that you are dressed properly. I shall take you to my great friend, Lavinia Davies. Tonight we will sup quietly and go to bed early, for we have a busy day ahead of us.' She turned to Tom. 'What had you planned, young man?'

'Oh, I shall amuse myself, never fear,' he said. 'A visit to Weston's for a new suit of clothes, a few hands of cards at White's, a ride perhaps. And don't you think we had better buy a new town carriage? Even supposing our travelling chaise can be repaired, it is as old as the ark. Not having ridden in it since before I went to Cambridge, I had not realised how old-fashioned and unsound it was. It is hardly suitable for town use; Lydia cannot go to balls and routs in it, nor to the park, and expect to be noticed by the *ton* — unless it be for being a frump.'

'I am not a frump!'

'I did not say you were, but I am sure that is what the Marquis thought when he saw you looking as though you had been tumbled in the hay. And as for our equipage. . .'

'Damn the Marquis!' his sister said with feeling. Was that why he had looked at her so hard and long?

'Lydia!' Mrs Wenthorpe was shocked into reaching for the glass of claret at her elbow. 'That is not the language of a lady.'

'I am sorry, Aunt, but if I have to weigh up every man I meet with nothing but marriage in mind, then I would as lief not marry at all.'

'But you must, child! That is what you are here for and why I am here, to make sure you come out in a manner fitting your station and wealth and to make sure you are not gulled by unsuitable offers.' She smiled and laid a hand over Lydia's. 'You will enjoy it, my dear, and I am sure you will find someone to suit before the Season is over.'

'And if I don't?'

'Then I will have failed your dear papa, and so will you.'

Lydia fell silent on the subject. It would do no good to argue and she would have to pretend to be enjoying herself, even flirt a little, but that did not mean she was committed. Unless, by some miracle, she fell in love, she would put off making a decision; that was — and she smiled to herself — if anyone offered for her, which was not at all a certainty. She was too tall and not especially beautiful and she was certainly outspoken, none of which would endear her to would-be husbands who, for the most part, only needed a breeding machine. It was not that she was against marriage and having children, but she had, in her growing up, had plenty of time to observe the disastrous marriages of her acquaintances and compare them with the loving relationship of her own parents, and nothing less than that would do.

CHAPTER TWO

THERE could not have been a greater contrast between Mrs Wenthorpe and the modishly attired Mrs Davies, but neither seemed to pay any heed to that, and after a cosy exchange of the latest *on-dit* they took Lydia to visit a dressmaker where Mrs Davies bespoke dresses for morning wear, for walking and for carriage rides, dresses for assemblies, for breakfasts, for the opera, for balls, and a dark blue velvet riding habit with a jacket frogged in the Polish style, to be worn over a white silk shirt with ruffles at throat and wrist. From there they went on to buy a tall beaver hat with a curly brim and a peacock feather to go with the riding habit, bonnets, caps and shawls, underlinen, mantles and muffs, shoes, dancing slippers and half-boots of crimson jean.

Lydia sincerely hoped the expense her father was being put to would be worth his while and was beginning to feel guilty that she had no intention of allowing herself to fall into the marriage net simply because he though it was time she was wed. If he wanted grandsons, let Tom produce them. The idea of Tom as a father was so amusing, she was still laughing when he joined them for luncheon at three o'clock, having taken a leaf from her book and decked himself out in the latest fashion.

'Why do you laugh?' he asked, affronted. 'These

pantaloons are the latest thing and I spent a devilish long time tying this neckcloth.'

'It isn't that,' she assured him. 'You look bang-up. I was wondering if you might enter the marriage stakes instead of me. After all, you are the one who has to produce Wenthorpe heirs, not I.'

'But you are the one Papa has fixed his mind on and you ought not to disappoint him. The whole thing must be costing him a prodigious amount.'

'And I wish that it did not,' she said. 'I do not like being groomed like some thoroughbred to be paraded in the selling ring.'

'Oh, my dear, it is not at all like that,' protested Aunt Aggie. 'You will enjoy it and I am persuaded you will be the belle of the Season and have any number of offers to choose from. It is the young gentlemen who are being paraded, not you.' She rose from the table and smiled at them both. 'Now, as I have not spent such a fatiguing morning in years, I shall go and lie down. Tom, you will look after your sister.'

'But Aunt, I am going to choose a new carriage.'

'I'll come too,' Lydia said, rising quickly. 'It won't take above a minute to fetch a bonnet and mantle.'

Since her aunt did not object to this, a footman was sent to bring a hackney to the door and brother and sister set off for Mount Street, where the coach-builders, Robinson and Cook, had their premises.

Tom was torn between ordering a barouche which would have been suitable for Lydia and her aunt, and a high-perch phaeton, a showy vehicle which had enormous wheels and high seating which was known to be unstable in inexpert hands. He wanted to show off his driving skill and Lydia, who considered herself a good whip, was also tempted, but she knew her aunt would disapprove on the grounds that young ladies who drove high-perch phaetons were considered fast. While they were thus debating, the Marquis of Longham arrived on the same errand.

He was wearing splendid riding breeches of soft buckskin and well-cut riding boots which emphasised his long, muscular legs. His corded coat with its high collar covered a yellow brocade waistcoat and a neckcloth of moderate dimensions; the whole effect was discreetly modish. Greeting them cheerfully, he bowed over Lydia's hand and then, with those hazel eyes twinkling with mischief, looked about him at the vehicles on display, some of which were only half complete, and enquired if it had not been possible to repair their carriage after all.

'Not at all, my lord,' Lydia said, affecting a haughtiness which was so unlike her that Tom turned to her in surprise. 'A travelling chaise is hardly the thing for town; even you must admit to that. We have come to bespeak a light carriage.'

'Surely not this one?' his lordship said, pointing at the high-perch phaeton Tom had been admiring.

'What is wrong with it?' Lydia demanded, annoyed that he should question their judgement. 'It looks a very handsome carriage to me.'

'Oh, no doubt of it,' he said calmly. 'But surely you were not intending to buy it for yourself, Miss Wenthorpe?' He looked her up and down as if measuring her up for the vehicle in question, though, in truth, he was thinking how attractive she looked and how the colour of her costume set off the deep colour of her eyes.

'Why not?' She was so stung by his attitude, she forgot her attempt at hauteur. 'I'll have you know I'm considered to have a sound pair of hands on the ribbons.'

'That I do not doubt,' he said, appraising her with one eyebrow lifted higher than the other, which made her think he was laughing at her. 'But have you considered your aunt's feelings? She will have to accompany you when you go out and I hardly think someone of her years would find it to her liking.' He did not add that he thought the worthy matron would find it extremely difficult even to climb into its seat without an undignified push from behind, nor what the gossips would say if Lydia were seen driving it.

'And I'll wager the truth is that you are determined to have the vehicle for yourself in order to cut a dash in Hyde Park,' she said, knowing he was right about her aunt and annoyed that he should have the effrontery to point it out to her. 'Let us not disappoint you. I dare say we can manage with a barouche.'

'Why not a park phaeton?' he suggested, without denying her accusation. 'It is light enough for you to drive, if that is what you have in mind, and not too dangerous if handled sensibly. If you wish, I'll undertake to teach you to drive it.'

If this was an effort to placate her, it had the

opposite effect; she could drive as well as most men
and not even Tom would presume to suggest she
needed lessons. 'I am sure your lordship has more
pressing business,' she murmured, stifling her inclination to tell him so. 'We would not wish to impose
on you.'

Anyone but the Marquis of Longham, she told
herself, would have recognised the put-down for
what it was, but he simply smiled and said, 'Not at
all.' Then, deciding he would get nowhere with her,
he turned to Tom. 'How say you, Wenthorpe; will
you consider this one? It is wide enough to seat
three at a pinch and low enough slung not to turn
over in a tight corner.'

Tom accepted the offer of help with alacrity and
the two men began a long discussion about the
merits of the carriage in question and the colours in
which it should be finished, and, the deal being
done, arrangements were made to collect it two days
later.

'In the meantime,' his lordship said, 'may I offer
to convey you home?'

Tom agreed at once without consulting Lydia,
who had been silently watching the Marquis's handling of the transaction and secretly admitting to
herself that Tom, left alone, would not have done
half so well. Not until they were once more on the
street did she realise that the conveyance was the
self-same coach which had brought them to London.
She had already been ungracious and could not
compound that by refusing to get into it, and thus

they arrived at Wenthorpe House in the same ram-shackle way they had the day before.

The arrival of Tom and Lydia with the Marquis in attendance had not gone unnoticed the first time it had happened. It seemed incomprehensible to the ladies of Society that Miss Wenthorpe, who was so obviously in London looking for a husband, should turn up in that skimble-skamble state and should have for an escort a man whom no one knew. That he was handsome and dressed in the pink of fashion none disputed, but his mount! Did one ever see such a broken-backed mule? And as for the carriage, it was twenty years old if it was a day. Surely Wenthorpe was not that pinched in the pocket? If he was, the tattlers did not see how his daughter could be safely brought out. And to compound everything by driving about town in that self-same vehicle was enough to set the neighbourhood tongues wagging even more furiously.

Servants, tradesmen, not to mention candlestick-makers and chimney-sweeps, were sent far and wide to find out what they could. They returned with the intelligence that the horses had been hired and the carriage belonged to the Marquis of Longham, the only surviving son of the Duke of Sutton, who, like their present monarch, was as mad as a hatter. As for Lord Wenthorpe, as far as could be ascertained, there was nothing wrong with his credit and Miss Wenthorpe stood to come into a considerable por-tion on her marriage.

'That, of course, would account for Longham dancing attendance on her,' they said over the

teacups, having heard accounts of the profligate
ways of the Duke of Sutton and his elder son and
assuming the younger was cast in the same mould. It
was their duty to rescue her from this mountebank.
And if their informants should be wrong and the
Marquis was not a spongeing toadeater but a man of
consequence, then all the more reason to detach him
from Miss Wenthorpe and speedily attach him to
their own daughters. They were prepared to expend
any amount of time and energy on the project. And
thus it was that so many invitations poured into
Wenthorpe House, Lydia and her aunt were hard
put to it to decide which to accept.

In spite of this, Mrs Wenthorpe held to her
original view that Lydia ought to try her wings at
small functions and not come out in a blaze of glory
at a high-stepping affair, where one false move, one
little slip could ruin all their plans. 'Besides,' she
said, with a twinkle in her eye, 'keep 'em waiting,
that's what I say. Make 'em dangle a little.'

Her aunt's choice of phrase did nothing to make
Lydia feel any better about coldly setting out to
catch a husband, but if she had to, then she would
take her time. Accordingly, they accepted invitations to quiet little suppers and tea parties, drove in
the park in the new phaeton, drawn by a pair of
greys which, though not up to the Marquis's bays,
were creditable enough to win admiring glances,
made up a party to visit Vauxhall Gardens with Tom
and Frank Burford as escorts, were seen at the
theatre and the opera, were almost squeezed to
death in the more popular routs and generally con-

ducted themselves with genteel reserve. In the course of three weeks they had made the superficial acquaintance of almost everyone who was anyone, but no young man had been singled out, so that it became a kind of game to be noticed by the nubile Miss Wenthorpe.

Occasionally the Marquis of Longham was seen in Lydia's company, but always within a party, and his behaviour gave the tongue-waggers no cause to think he was making any progress with her if that was his intention. Indeed, Lydia herself was inclined to think him too high in the instep by far and, though always polite, she would not go out of her way to show him any favouritism. When he chose to unbend and make himself agreeable, then so might she, but until then she would keep him at a distance.

It was the only thing on which she and her aunt disagreed, for Mrs Wenthorpe had, on closer acquaintance, taken a shine to the young man and enjoyed his company, especially as he did not appear to think her dress anything out of the ordinary. In fact he had, on one occasion, complimented her on her looks. 'And he was not funning me,' she asserted over nuncheon one day. 'He is the very embodiment of good taste and sensitivity.'

'He's bought a bang-up rig—prime cattle and a spanking new curricle,' Tom said enthusiastically. 'He let me take the ribbons the other day and felicitated me on my handling of them.'

'You mean he did not go back and buy the high-perch phaeton after all?' Lydia asked, choosing to ignore the fact that the Marquis had not actually said he intended to buy it.

'Apparently not,'

'Then I was right. He pretended to want it only to prevent us from having it.'

'And glad I am he did,' Agatha put in with a twinkle in her myopic eyes. 'Can you imagine me riding as high as the house-tops in one of those?'

'Do you know his circumstances, Aunt?' Tom asked. He saw in the Marquis an entry to the *ton* and invitations to places that young ladies like his sister had no idea existed, or, if they did, spoke of them behind their fans with bated breath and a sense of daring. He liked the cut of Longham's jib, his self-assurance, his air of command and he had every intention of modelling himself on this aristocrat with the long nose and the haughty bearing. 'Has he taken you into his confidence?'

Mrs Wenthorpe smiled enigmatically. 'If he had, I would not break it to satisfy your curiosity, young man. All I know is that he is a soldier, or he was, and highly thought of by Wellington, so I suppose he must have been a good one, but since the peace he has been little seen in Society. His father, the Duke, is a buffle-head without a feather to fly with and his brother was a dissolute rake and he will have his work cut out to bring everything to rights.'

'Well, I take no note of the gabble-grinders,' Tom informed them cheerfully. 'He ain't one to shout the odds about his affairs, plays his cards close to his chest, but that don't mean he's dished up. But if he offered for Lydia. . .'

'That would be an entirely different matter,' his aunt said. 'Then it would be my duty to make enquiries. . .'

'But as he has made no such offer,' Lydia put in with some asperity, 'and I would not accept him if he did, we need not trouble ourselves about him.'

Her aunt sighed. 'He is not likely to offer when you give him so little encouragement.'

'I am not going to lick boots to find a husband, Aunt Aggie, and I am sure Papa would not expect me to.'

Mrs Wenthorpe smiled. 'No, but he might hope that you would make just a little push, my dear.' She smiled suddenly and her blue eyes lit with mischief. 'No matter, it is still early in the Season.' She paused to pick up a gilt-edged invitation card to a ball to be held at Thornton House, Park Lane on the following Friday week. 'Let us see what this brings forth, for everyone who is anyone will be there.' She tapped the card against her chin, pretending to think. 'Now, who shall be your escort? I think Longham, don't you?'

'Frank Burford has already asked me,' Lydia put in quickly.

'Frank?' Tom repeated. 'You haven't been such a ninny as to agree?'

'Why not?'

'Oh, Frank is a capital fellow, I'll allow,' he said. 'But you may as well have stayed at home and saved Papa a deal of blunt if you are going back to Raventrees on his arm. You've known him since he was in short coats.'

'I'm comfortable with him and, as he has been so good as to ask, I have accepted.'

'I hope you have not held out any false hopes, Lydia,' her aunt said, rising from the table. 'It would be most unfair of you.'

'Not in the least,' she said cheerfully, putting down her napkin and following her aunt from the room. 'I know he has a penchant for little Miss Thornton, but so far she has not deigned to notice him.'

'Miss Thornton!' exclaimed Tom, deciding that as there were no other men with whom to smoke and drink he might as well join his sister and their aunt in the withdrawing room, where they settled themselves to await the arrival of the tea tray. 'She's a little above his touch, don't you think? I cannot see her mama agreeing to that match.'

Lydia was inclined to agree with her brother when, ten days later, they took their turn in the long line of guests waiting to be received by Lord and Lady Thornton, and realised what a lavish affair it was. And all in the cause of marrying off their daughter.

The ballroom was filled to capacity and noisy enough to have been a battlefield. The orchestra which was tuning up on a dais at the far end of the room could hardly be heard above the din of people greeting acquaintances, being introduced and exchanging the latest *on-dit*. The heat from the gas lamps was already intense and ladies' fans were much in evidence, not only for cooling purposes, but for whispering behind.

'What a squeeze!' said Frank, resplendent in a yellow brocade coat and matching satin knee-breeches, tied above his white silk stockings with ribbon bows. He looked a little ridiculous, Lydia thought, but not for a minute would she have hurt him by letting him know her thoughts, any more than she would have wounded her aunt by commenting on her lavish rose satin *décolleté* ballgown with its wide panniers, a fashion at least a generation out of date.

Tom pushed his way through the crush and found a seat for his aunt before wandering off to find himself a partner for the cotillion which was then forming, and Frank led Lydia on to the floor. She was engaged for every dance after that by a multitude of young men, to all of whom she was charming, laughing and thoroughly at ease, aware that she looked her best in the cream silk gown Mrs Davies had helped her to choose. The very simplicity of its high waist and softly falling skirt displayed her slim figure to perfection and its not too low neckline and puffed sleeves set off pale shoulders and a throat encircled with nothing but a rope of beautifully matched pearls. Her hair was drawn back in a Grecian style with a top-knot and ringlets woven with more pearls. Nothing could have been a greater contrast to most of the other gaudily attired young ladies with their beads and feathers, rubies and emeralds.

It was late in the evening when she spied the Marquis of Longham, standing by himself just inside the door as if he had only then arrived. His pose was

nonchalant, and Lydia, who was dancing a Chaîne
Anglais with the Honourable Douglas Fincham,
youngest son of the Earl of Boreton, was forced to
admit to herself that his figure was made for tight
jackets and close-fitting pantaloons. Not long
before, these would not have been allowed at a ball,
knee-breeches being the accepted dress, but now
only Almack's stuck to the old ways, and here was a
man for whom the new fashions must have been
made. His long-tailed black evening coat was exquis-
itely cut to his broad shoulders and narrow waist,
while his black pantaloons served to outline muscular thighs that drew a sigh of admiration from many
a débutante. Lydia told herself severely, but not
very honestly, that she was immune.

'For someone who don't have a feather to fly with,
he's in prime twig,' commented her partner, who
considered himself no end of a fine fellow. He was
very young and extremely chubby, like a round
young puppy. His shoulders were padded and his
waist corseted and his collar points scratched his
cheeks whenever he moved his head. His enormous
cravat was tied into an intricate pattern of loops and
folds, while across his pink and yellow striped waistcoat hung a multitide of chains and fobs. Beside the
elegantly clad Marquis, he looked a veritable maca-
roni. 'But it don't signify,' he added. 'Everyone
knows his father is batty and has lost his fortune.'

'Where did you hear that?' Lydia asked, forgetting
her determination never to listen to gossip.

'It is common knowledge,' he said airily. 'His

creditors will be hammering on his door before the Season is out, unless he can find himself an heiress.'

'And I think you would be wise to refrain from such scandal,' she said sharply, making him redden from the wilting points of his collar to the roots of his fair hair. 'He might call you out for it.'

'Why, I set no store by Canterbury tales,' he said, speedily recovering from this rebuke, having little imagination and an extraordinary idea of his own worth. If a young lady gave him a put-down, it only meant that he should try the harder to engage her attention.

Correctly judging his character, she set about teasing him so that by the time the dance ended and he returned her to her aunt he did not know whether to be elated or resentful. Aunt Aggie was in lively conversation with one of the dowagers who sat in regal splendour along the side of ballroom, making sweeping and quite scandalous statements about all and sundry, but she was attentive enough to look up at her niece with a humorous quirk of her brow and a flutter of her fan behind which she was heard to murmur, 'A veritable pea-goose, my dear. Do send him about his business or he will cling like a leech.'

Lydia stifled a giggle but she was saved having to take her aunt's advice because Douglas drifted off, and she joined Tom and Frank who stood near by waiting to claim their partners for the next dance. Frank had already stepped forward to stand before Miss Thornton, when Lady Thornton pushed herself between them and drew the Marquis towards her daughter.

'Well, of all the put-downs!' Lydia exclaimed, feeling very sorry for the dejected Frank, as he turned away to seek solace in the card-room while Amelia Thornton, pink of face, set off with the Marquis. 'Lady Thornton is making a fool of herself with her daughter besides, throwing her at every unmarried man in the room from old Lord Winters who is sixty if he is a day to Douglas Fincham who was only yesterday taken out of short coats; the only thing they have in common is a title — or the expectation of one — and a fortune. As for the Marquis of Longham, I thought he had more sense than to be used in that fashion.'

'He could hardly snub the poor girl by refusing,' Tom said, reasonably. 'That would have made matters worse.'

'I feel sorry for poor Miss Thornton, for she will not be allowed to make up her own mind,' Lydia went on, her own sense of justice making her admit Tom was right. 'I'll wager if I were to present myself as an eligible man, Lady Thornton would have me stand up with her.'

Tom turned to stare at her. 'I say, Lydia, you wouldn't dare,' he said, then added, as he saw the gleam in his sister's eye, 'You wouldn't, would you?'

'Why not?' The sight of the Marquis of Longham dancing a quadrille with Amelia Thornton and showing every sign of enjoying it made Lydia feel as if it was she and not Frank who had been snubbed, and filled her with an illogical desire to do something entirely reckless.

'You'd never pull it off,' he said. 'Lady Thornton

will see through you and then you will be sent home to Raventrees in disgrace, and what will Papa do with you then? No, no, you cannot.'

'*Cannot*?' she queried, raising one arched brow. Ever since they had left the cradle, Tom only had to say she would not dare to do something than she needs must do it. 'Will you take a small wager that I cannot, Thomas? Shall we say twenty pounds?'

He stared at her for a moment and then laughed. 'You're on! Twenty pounds say you cannot hood-wink Lady Thornton into accepting you as a man and allowing you to dance with her daughter.' He paused. 'You'll have to gull Miss Thornton as well or she will kick up a fuss before you have taken half a turn about the room.'

'Naturally, everyone must believe it. I shall let Miss Thornton into the secret when the dance is ended.' She smiled, her boredom vanishing in this new challenge to her acting ability. 'I'll need a title and a name which is credible but not too easily discounted. It had better be French; their nobility is in such a tangle since the Revolution, no one will suspect.' She paused, then laughed. 'I know, we will use Mama's name. How does Comte Maurice de Clancy sound to you? I am the only son of a French *émigré* who came to England to escape the Terror when I was but a babe, which accounts for my being able to speak both languages perfectly. Oh, how glad I am that Mama insisted on speaking French to us! And if I assume an accent, it may help to disguise the fact that my voice is somewhat high.' She sighed.

'I am very much afraid I shall have to be a very effete suitor.'

'But you need a fortune, and how is that to be contrived? You can be sure Lady Thornton will want to know about that before her daughter is allowed to stand up with you.'

Lydia thought for a moment. 'Jewels smuggled out by my parents during the Revolution, caskets of the stuff, gold too, and none of it trusted to a bank. Given that piece of nonsense, the tattlers will do my work for me, then it will be enough if I give the appearance of being well-breeched. Her ladyship will never be able to disprove it before my wager is won.'

'When is this deception to take place?' her brother demanded. 'It must be done publicly, you know, and I must see it with my own eyes.'

She laughed, realising the occasion had to be right; she could not expect to deceive her aunt, however short-sighted she was, or Frank Burford, who had already seen her dressed as a man. 'I will tell you when I am ready.'

They were interrupted by the Marquis who, having returned Miss Thornton to her mama, was now bowing in front of Lydia and claiming the waltz. She smiled a mischievous little smile which both intrigued and alarmed him and allowed herself to be led on to the floor.

She had spent hours in the schoolroom learning the steps of the waltz with her brother and such friends who lived in the neighbourhood of Raventrees, though she had never danced it on a crowded ballroom floor, but she need not have worried, for her partner was expert and was so tall that he made her feel small and feminine, an unusual sensation for her. They moved as if moulded together and she hardly noticed that he was holding her closer than the regulation twelve inches.

'It is a refreshing change to dance with someone without being tickled under the chin by a feather head-dress,' he said, referring to the fact that her head was on a level with his shoulder and not the middle button of his waistcoat.

'And I to find I am not looking over my partner's head,' she responded quickly. 'You know, one of Papa's criteria for a husband for me is that he should be tall.'

He was slightly taken aback that she should be so outspoken about it but recovered himself quickly. 'What other requirements would a suitor need before he could approach the eligible Miss Wenthorpe?' he asked. 'A title, perhaps? And a fortune?'

She laughed, knowing he was bamming, but she was her brother's sister and if she had allowed a teasing to bother her she would have had a very unhappy childhood. 'Plain Mr is a title of sorts and a guinea might be a fortune to some poor beggar, so I suppose I could reasonably say yes to that.'

'And handsome?'

'Handsome is as handsome does.'

'And should he be head over heels in love with you?'

'Oh, that above everything,' she said, turning her

head to laugh up into his face. He was regarding her
with a slightly lop-sided smile and a light dancing in
his eyes which disturbed her. It was as if he had
thought of some jest but was unsure whether to
share it with her. 'You do not agree with that, I see.'

'On the contrary,' he said. 'I concur whole heart-
edly. Do you think you will find such a one here?'

'Probably not,' she said. If her wager were to
succeed it would have to be done when his lordship
was absent, for he would, she was certain, see right
through any disguise; he seemed to be able to look
right into her heart and make it beat so fast she
could hardly breathe. She was beginning to regret
the impulse which had made her throw out such a
challenge. It was madness. She smiled to herself.
Mad and bad and heaven help her if she failed!

'A penny for your thoughts,' he offered, as they
whirled round the floor in perfect unison, with his
hand comfortably about her waist.

'Oh, no, my lord,' she said, colouring. 'Not even
for a golden guinea.'

He laughed, so that the dowagers closest to them
looked up with startled expressions and then began
to whisper among themselves that Miss Wenthorpe
was far too forward and it would be her just deserts
if no one offered for her except that scapegrace
Longham, who would undoubtedly make her miserable. 'Then I must remain in ignorance, for I have
no intention of bidding any higher.'

'I perceive, my lord, that you always consider
carefully before you lay out your money.'

'Now, I wonder what you can mean by that observation?'

'I collect you were going to purchase a high-perch phaeton.'

'Was I? Then I changed my mind. It was an unnecessary extravagance.' He was enjoying the exchange, teasing her and titillating her curiosity. If she passed on what he had said to others, the town would soon believe he was mean-spirited as well as down on his uppers. Serve 'em right, he thought. He would not have his bride chosen for him by gossips or avaricious mamas, and if Ernest Grimshaw were to hear that he was without the blunt to pursue his case, then so much the better. 'Would you join me for a drive in the park one afternoon?'

'But how can I do that if you did not buy the phaeton?' she queried, lifting her eyebrows at him and proving that she, too, could tease. 'Surely you do not intend to drive me in that old coach of yours? I am still black and blue from my last outing in it.'

'It's that or nothing,' he said, trying in vain to keep a serious face. 'Do you dare?'

'My lord, you should know I never refuse a dare.'

'Then I will call for you the day after tomorrow. Shall we say at two?'

Oh, she should never have been so rash, she decided, as she lay sleepless in the early hours; it was almost as if the two glasses of champagne she had consumed had bemused her senses. Accepting the Marquis's dare was enough to put her beyond the pale, but the wager with her brother was almost criminal and certainly cruel. She began to wonder how she would feel if she were Amelia Thornton and such a prank were played on her. Mortified and humiliated were the words that came to mind. No, she could not do it and she would tell Tom so. If it cost her twenty pounds, then so be it.

But her brother was nowhere to be found when she rose towards noon and went in search of him. His bed, she discovered, had not been slept in and his valet vouchsafed the opinion that Mr Wenthorpe had gone on to play cards after escorting her and her aunt home after the ball; Barber had been told not to wait for him, so he could not be sure. Forced to wait for Tom's return, she decided to go for a ride and, ordering her horse to be saddled, she went to her room, changed into the blue velvet habit, perched the beaver on her curls and made her way to the stables, determined to gallop off her fit of the blue devils.

The day was fine, with a promise of spring, and Hyde Park was full of horses and carriages, barouches, phaetons, curricles, tilburys and gigs, each one containing its share of fashionable ladies, demi-reps and débutantes, together with their escorts, all wanting to be noticed, and the pace they were setting was slow, if not actually stationary. Riders were also out in great numbers on high-stepping thorough-breds, neat little cobs and hired hacks. She saw Lord Longham sitting astride a huge black stallion, engrossed in conversation with a modishly dressed lady in a barouche across the railing which divided the Row from the carriageway. They were laughing together, oblivious to others around them. Lydia reined in; she was in no mood to exchange polite nonsense when all she could think of was that foolish wager. He looked up and their glances met and held. Disconcerted, she wheeled her mount away and cantered off.

Finding herself in what might pass in the metropolis for open country, she set the horse to gallop with Scrivens vainly trying to keep up. 'It won't do, Miss Lydia,' he called after her. 'It won't do. At 'ome in Raventrees it don' matter, but in London. . .' When she returned home she was in a much better humour and even the scolding her aunt gave her for being late for nuncheon failed to dampen her spirits.

It was Tom who managed to do that. She met him on the stairs on her way to change out of her habit. His face was grey from lack of sleep, his hair was tousled and his cravat tied so carelessly it resembled nothing so much as a dishcloth. 'Tom, have you been up all night?' she demanded.

'Got caught up in a game at White's,' he said.

'Oh, Tom, you haven't lost a great deal of money, have you?' She looked directly into his face, but he could not meet her eye. 'Oh, you buffle-head! What will Papa say?'

He caught her hand and pulled her into his room, where he shut the door firmly. 'It ain't that much and he need never know.'

'How much?'

He hesitated, then mumbled, 'Five hundred.'

'Five hundred!' she squeaked, shocked to the

core. 'How could you possibly have let it happen? Did you give them vowels?'

'Yes. I promised to pay by the end of the month.'

'How? Your allowance will never cover it.'

He smiled sheepishly. 'No, but I thought of a capital hum. I wagered five hundred that you would persuade Lady Thornton you were an eligible bachelor and would stand up with Miss Thornton at a ball.'

'You did what?' She sat down heavily on the bed, hardly able to believe her ears.

'You can do it, you know you can,' he went on, unperturbed. 'It's only like playing charades.'

She was almost angry enough to slap him. 'Who did you make this outrageous bet with?'

'Douglas Fincham. I have either to give him five hundred guineas by the end of the month or you have to become a man for an evening.'

She stared up at him. 'Oh, Tom, Tom, what have you done?'

'It was your idea in the first place, or I would never have thought of it.'

'It was a cork-brained idea. I changed my mind almost at once and decided to pay you the twenty pounds and forget the whole thing.'

'But Lydia, you can't,' he said in anguish. 'It will ruin me. I shall never hear the last of it. I shall be ostracised.'

'Serve you right.'

'Oh, Lydia, you can't mean that. I've got you out of any number of scrapes in the past. . .'

'Childish pranks,' she said with asperity. 'They

were not like this at all.' She paused as the impli-
cation of what he had done came to her. How could
she face everyone if it became public knowledge that
she fancied herself as a man? She would lose what
friends she had and the Marquis of Longham would
be confirmed in his belief that she was the most
outrageous hoyden in the country. She would never
be able to look into those searching eyes again. 'Did
you enter it in the betting book for all the world to
see?'

'No, for it would not do for it to become public or
Lady Thornton might hear of it. It was a private
bet.' He stood looking down at her, unable to
believe that she was prepared to renege on a wager;
such a thing was unheard of, either for her or for
him or anyone else who valued their reputation.
'That don't mean it don't have to be honoured,' he
said. 'Besides, Fincham. . .'

'You could not have chosen a worse person to
gamble with,' she put in sharply. 'He will never keep
his tongue between his teeth if you do not pay up.'

'Do you think I don't know that?' he said
miserably.

'We can't let it come to that.'

He brightened considerably. 'You'll do it?'

'I have only to deceive Lady Thornton?' she
queried, her heart sinking. 'I may take Miss
Thornton into my confidence?'

'No, you have to convince everyone and that
includes Miss Thornton,' he said. 'And you have to
complete the dance and leave undiscovered.'

'Supposing I cannot do it?'

'Oh, you can, you know you can. Oh, Lydia, do this for me, I beg you.'

'I don't see why I should make a fool of myself so that you may not make a fool of yourself,' she said. 'You must tell Papa.'

'Lydia, I'll die sooner than do that. Please. . .'

'How many other people know of this wager?'

'Only Frank Burford and a steward at the club.'

'Frank?' she queried. 'Is he in it too?'

'Well, you know old Frank. He must needs put his stake in.' He smiled suddenly. 'He has already seen you in disguise, don't forget.'

'In the schoolroom! That hardly counts and, besides, I had costumes and make-up there.'

'What costumes and make-up do you want? I'll undertake to obtain them for you. It would not do for you to be seen buying such things.'

'I don't know, I shall have to think about it. How am I to disguise curves I should not have and fill out those places where I am lacking. . .?'

'A tight waistcoat, padded shoulders and a little more fullness in the breeches. I am sure you can contrive.'

'Does it have to be a ball or will a small supper dance suffice?'

'It was not stipulated.'

'Then we will aim for a quiet evening where the lighting is likely to be more subdued than at a grand affair and the fashions need not be so up to the mark.'

'Then you will do it!' It was surprising how his weariness left him and his face came alight at the

prospect of this burden being lifted from his
shoulders. 'Oh, Sis, I knew you would. You've saved
my bacon.'

'Only if I succeed.' It was madness to contemplate
it, she knew, but if she could pull it off and the
young Comte de Clancy was afterwards to disappear
never to be seen again no harm would be done and
Papa need never know what a young fool his son
had been. 'I ought to have a rehearsal,' she said.
'Somewhere where we are not known.'

'I heard there is a fair on the Heath; what say you
to that, two young men out for a lark?'

'Oh, very well,' she agreed, entering into the spirit
of it now the die was cast. 'But how shall we get out
of the house?'

In the event it was not difficult, because Mrs
Wenthorpe decided to retire early after the exertions
of the previous evening and as soon as she was safely
in her room with a late-night drink of chocolate
Lydia hurried to Tom's room, where she borrowed
one of his suits of clothes and took it back to her
own bedchamber.

There was very little difference in their height
although he was broader than she was. A little
padding in the shoulders of the frockcoat and a sash,
half hidden by the waistcoat, to pull in the waist of
the pantaloons soon put that right. That done, she
surveyed herself in the long glass and then began on
her face. Lampblack was used to emphasise her
brows and make them thicker and the dregs from
her coffee-cup used to darken her complexion. Pads
of cotton stuffed into her cheeks made her face seem

rounder and would also help to change her voice.
Then she pushed her hair up under a wide-brimmed
felt hat and decided she might do in a poor light, but
in daylight or in the bright lights of a ballroom she
would have to improve the make-up. She would not
be able to change her hair colouring with dye, which
she would have liked to do as an extra precaution
against being recognised, because she would afterwards have to reappear as Lydia Wenthorpe, so she
would have to wear a wig.

Tom called to her from the other side of her
bedroom door and she ran to open it, standing
before him, quizzing glass in hand. 'How do I look?'

'Bang-up,' he whispered in admiration. 'Not even
Aunt Aggie would recognise you.'

'I hope she may not see me. Are you ready?'

'Yes. We'll hire a rumbler down the road.'

The night was dark and the gas lamps shed a poor
light, which suited Lydia, and they took care not to
linger when they came under their yellow glow. A
hackney was found and in a very short time they
were deposited on the outskirts of the fair and were
soon swallowed up by the mêlée of people, old and
young, male and female, gentry and artisan, who
had come to enjoy themselves.

They attracted no attention as they wandered
between stalls which offered a huge variety of goods
from sweetmeats and mussels, to poems and broad-
sheets proclaiming the latest news. Prize-fighters,
stripped to their waists, defied anyone to take them
on, slack-rope walkers tottered precariously above
their heads, barkers shouted for custom to view the

bearded lady or the two-headed sheep. All around them were jugglers, fire-eaters, performing dogs and fortune-tellers.

'Shall you have your fortune told?' Tom asked. 'If you can fool a fortune-teller, it would be a capital test.'

'Should I?' It had been so easy up to now and being lost in the crowds was certainly of little use as a test for her disguise. 'You'll wait close at hand?'

'I'll be right outside.'

Thus reassured, Lydia entered the tent where a gaudily dressed gypsy, all dangling earrings and bracelets, sat at a table. 'Sit ye down, young feller,' she said, indicating a chair opposite her and whipping the cover from a glass ball on the table. 'Which is it to be, the crystal or the palm?'

'The crystal.'

'Cross my palm with silver. A tanner will do but if you really want to know the future a fore-coach-wheel would be the least of it.'

Lydia dug into her pocket and extracted a half-crown and put it into the gypsy's open palm.

'Ah, my lovely,' the old crone said. 'I do not need a crystal ball to tell me you are not what you seem.'

'Oh?' Lydia raised one blackened brow.

'You would have me think you are a young gentleman of fashion. . .'

'And I am not?' Lydia queried, keeping her voice huskily low.

'No, barely out of the schoolroom, you are. Your clothes are too big and no doubt belong to an older brother and your voice is scarce broken. Slipped your leash for a night, is that it? I do not think I care to take your money, for your future lies in a spanking from your papa and that needs no second sight.'

Lydia gave a low chuckle, determined not to let her pose lapse. If the old hag thought she was dealing with a boy, at least she was halfway to her goal. 'What can you tell me that does need a crystal ball?'

The gypsy put her hands around the glass and peered into its depths. 'That's strange,' she said. 'It is all misty, nothing is clear; it is as if someone were trying to deceive me. This I do not like.' She looked up with bright boot-button eyes. 'But this I do see — a fortune in gold and jewels, and a tall, dark man who is not pleased. Beware of trying to deceive him, young miss.'

'Miss?' she queried, taken aback.

'Thought you'd take me for a fool, did ye?' the old woman cackled. 'But it takes more than clothes and bootblacking to hoax a Romany princess. Do it for a wager, did ye?'

'Yes, yes,' Lydia said, afraid of the gleam in the woman's eye. 'I meant no harm. I can see you are, indeed, very clever and I will remember what you say about the tall, dark man.' With the gypsy's cracked laugh ringing in her ears, she ran from the tent and straight into the broad chest of the Marquis of Longham.

CHAPTER THREE

STARTLED, Lydia stifled the Oh! she had on her lips
and changed it to a husky grunt, as he took a step
backwards and looked down at her. 'Look where
you're going, boy.'

'*Pardon, monsieur.*' Why had Tom not seen the
Marquis and waylaid him, or tried to warn her? If it
was his idea of a test for her disguise, then it was a
very dangerous one. 'My fault entirely.'

The Marquis was regarding her in the same lop-
sided way he had used at the ball and she was afraid
he had penetrated her disguise. Oh, what a fool she
had been to suppose she could get away with it! He
was far too perceptive and if he recognised her now
the whole masquerade would be at an end for she
would never dare to repeat it in their own social
circles. She was swamped by a feeling of relief at the
thought of not having to do it, followed immediately
by the dread of what Douglas Fincham would do.
Tom was a fool and she was an even bigger one.
And she would rather anyone but the Marquis know
it.

'No harm done.' He touched the curly brim of his
tall beaver and strode away to be lost in the crowds.

She let out a huge sigh and turned to look for
Tom. He was standing on the edge of a knot of
people watching a boxing match and had his back to

her. She went to stand beside him and nudged his arm. 'Fine look-out you turned out to be.'

He turned and grinned. 'Oh, it's you.'

'Who did you think it was, Lord Longham?'

'No, why?'

'I just bumped into him.'

He seemed unconcerned, as he craned his neck to see the end of the bout. 'Did he recognise you?'

'If he did, he did not say so.'

'There you are, then!' He began pushing his way through the spectators to reach the front as the fight ended with the amateur challenger being carried off unconscious. The barker began haranguing the watchers for a new challenger. 'Who'll go a round with the champion?' he shouted. 'Who fancies themselves at the fisticuffs?' One round, that's all, one round and still standing and twenty yellow Georges will be yours. Come on, ain't there a fighter among ye?'

Tom pushed his way to the front and had his hand on the rope before Lydia realised what he intended. She pulled on his coat-tails. 'No, Tom, he'll kill you.'

While Tom turned to remonstrate with her, his opportunity was lost because another contender had climbed into the ring. 'Let's go home,' she said, more unnerved than she liked to admit by her encounter with the Marquis. 'I've had enough for one night.'

'After this bout,' he said, turning back to the ring and gasping with surprise because the man who was stripping off his coat and waistcoat was none other than Jack Bellingham. 'Oh, this will be a rum 'n and no mistake.'

He would not leave and they were so near the front that Lydia could see every bruise the protagonists inflicted on each other and hear every grunt of pain; she found herself wincing and wishing she could look away, but she could not take her eyes from the two men, one huge and thick-set with cropped hair and a thick bull-neck which disappeared into massive shoulders, and the other, as tall as his adversary, but whose broad shoulders tapered to a slim waist and hips and whose long, supple legs were serving him well as he moved lithely about the ring. Jack Bellingham had boxed before, that much was evident, and he was giving as good as he got as they weaved and ducked and threw punches while the crowd yelled their support and Tom cried, 'Go to it, Jack! Send him to grass!'

The heavy pugilist, frustrated that he could not get the early knockout he was accustomed to, began to slow as the crashing punches with which he floored his less experienced challengers were, for the most part, knocked harmlessly aside. But the Marquis was not having it all his own way and Lydia winced and had to put her hand to her mouth to stop herself crying out whenever the fairground pugilist landed one of his ox-felling blows and Lord Longham's head rocked back with a sickening crunch. The round seemed never-ending and both boxers were visibly tiring when the crowd began to yell, 'The bell! Ring the bell, he's done it!'

But the barker was reluctant to do so, hoping his

man could still floor the challenger and save him his
twenty guineas. The fight went on, with both men
becoming more and more exhausted until Lydia was
sure they would fall together in a heap and neither
be declared the winner, in which case the challenger
would leave empty-handed. In the midst of her
concern for him, she fell to wondering why he had
gone into the ring in the first place. He was surely
not short of twenty guineas, nor could he possibly
enjoy being punched black and blue. And Tom had
thought he would have a go! How glad she was that
he had been prevented, but if the Marquis won her
ninny of a brother might even now fancy his chances
on the next bout. She pulled on his arm. 'Tom, let's
go.'

He turned to her, grinning. 'What a mill! I ain't
going before the end. Wait for me beside the gypsy's
tent if you've no stomach for it.'

She turned and was trying to push her way out
when the spectators, furious at the delay, began a
concerted rush towards the barker, shouting again
for him to ring the bell. Realising his danger, he
complied and Lydia looked back to see Jack's hand
raised in triumph. He was hoisted on to the
shoulders of the nearest spectators, among whom
her brother, grinning from ear to ear, was promi-
nent. Tom was not in the least concerned about her,
nor the fact that she was being buffeted about by the
exultant mob. If he brought the Marquis over to
her. . . Oh, how could he have forgotten their
predicament? She felt herself go hot all over and was
sure that sweat was trickling down her forehead and

face, making tracks in her make-up. She could not face the Marquis a second time. She forced her way out of the crowd and found a hackney. Climbing in, she bade the driver wait and sat inside trying to compose herself while the spectators, knowing the entertainment was over for the night, dispersed in great good humour.

She sat on until Tom appeared with Lord Longham at his side and began to look about him for his 'cousin'. Shrinking back into the shadows of the hackney, she heard him say, 'I left him here somewhere, told him to wait, had to come and offer my felicitations before I left. What a mill! Where do you train? Oh, drat Maurice, where can he be?'

'Tired of kicking his heels and gone home perhaps?' The Marquis sounded weary, as well he might. The flickering light round the booth was poor, by Lydia was surprised to see no outward evidence that he had been in a gruelling fight, apart from a slight pinkness around his left eye and a cut on his right brow which sported a plaster. 'If it's all the same to you, Wenthorpe, I'll take this hackney and get off home myself.'

'What?' Tom sounded vague. 'Oh, yes, of course, take it; I shall have to stay and look for L. . . Maurice.'

Lydia could not let that happen. 'Tom!' She sat forward, glad the fairground lights were being snuffed out. '*Mon Dieu*, where 'ave you been 'iding?' She pretended a prodigious yawn. 'Do come 'ome; I am dead with *l'ennui*.'

Tom's face lit with relief and he grinned.

'Maurice! What a capital fellow you are to hold the last cab.' He turned to Jack. 'Will you join us?'

If she had hoped the Marquis would refuse, she was disappointed; he accepted cheerfully. She shrank to the opposite side of the carriage and pulled her hat down as Tom got in beside her and squeezed up to make room for the Marquis.

'My cousin, Maurice, Comte de Clancy,' Tom said, by way of introduction. 'Jack Bellingham, Marquis of Longham. You should have waited, Coz, for it was a capital fight and the Marquis stood up for the round and earned his twenty pounds. Had it not been the last bout, I would have made a challenge. . .'

'Poof,' she said, affecting the voice of the Comte. 'You Engleesh, I will never comprehend why you like so much the fighting.'

The Marquis laughed easily, though he must have been aching in every limb. 'That is why we win our wars.'

There was an uneasy silence until Tom said, 'My cousin has lately come from Canada; his father, my uncle, was French, you know. He took his family there at the beginning of the war to escape serving Bonaparte. He died there and so did his wife, but now the war is over Maurice has returned to claim his land and fortune. He came to England to see lawyers. . .'

'I hope he may have luck with the lawyers,' Jack said.

'You 'ave 'ad trouble with the law, *monsieur*?'

Lydia put in, feeling she ought to make some contribution to the conversation.

'A trifling matter,' he said, then, to her consternation, added, 'I am sure we have met before.'

She was about to deny it, when Tom dug her in the ribs and muttered, 'Gypsy tent.'

'*Mais* I 'ave thought that also,' she drawled. 'I am not sure for there is not light enough to see.'

'It is your voice, I think,' Jack said, and Tom stifled a chuckle and turned it to a cough.

'Ah *je me souviens*,' she said. 'We — how do you say? — bumped outside the gypsy tent, *n'est-ce pas*?'

'Of course.' He seemed to accept that. 'And did you learn anything of value from the fortune-teller?'

She gave a low chuckle. 'If the 'ag speaks true, I will 'ave once more my fortune. She spoke of gold and jewels, and a dark man. I am to beware of 'im.'

'Did she say why?' Tom asked.

'*Non*. The crystal does not tell much for 'alf an Engleesh crown.'

Having said as much as she intended to on any subject, she lapsed into silence and Tom took up the conversation by asking where the Marquis lodged. On being told he had rooms at Albany, he ordered the driver to go there first, saying he would then drop his cousin off before going home himself. When the Marquis offered to share the cost of the hackney, Tom said it was his pleasure; after all, his lordship had furnished him with excellent entertainment and it was the least he could do.

As soon as Jack had been deposited on the steps of his apartments and they were on their way again,

Lydia turned on her brother. 'Tom, how could you bring him to the cab? He of all people. . .'

Tom turned towards her. 'Of all people,' he repeated, grinning. 'Do you mean to say you have developed a *tendre* for the fellow. . .?'

'Of course not,' she said, so quickly that he was not in the least convinced. 'But we did travel to London in his coach. He has seen more of us than anyone. Why did you have to bring him out to me?'

'You would have left him to make his own way home, I suppose, after he had gone that gruelling round.'

'He did not have to go into the ring. I can't think why he did.'

Tom laughed. 'Like you, he is a devil-may-dare; he cannot refuse a challenge.'

'Then he must take the consequences.' It was not like Lydia to be unsympathetic to others' suffering and she felt more like ministering to his lordship's injuries than blaming him, but she was still shaking from the encounter and her narrow escape and her sharp tongue hid a multitude of tangled feelings she could not put into words, not the least of which was the sincere wish never to have set out on such a foolish escapade and never, never to have tried gulling the Marquis. If he ever found out, he would never speak to her again, and somehow the prospect of that filled her with melancholy. 'Oh, why did he have to be at that fair?'

'It was he who told me about it; said he might flex his muscles. . .'

'You knew he would be there! Tom, don't you care that he might have seen through my disguise?'

'You needed a good test, did you not? Besides, he saw me collecting my winnings; I could not have crept off without speaking to him.'

'Your winnings? Oh, Tom, you did not bet on the outcome?'

'Naturally, I did.'

'How much did you win?'

'A pony.' He smiled. 'Not enough to pay Fincham off if that is what you are thinking.'

'Oh,' she said, for that is exactly what she had been hoping. 'All the same, the more I think about this scheme of yours, the more worried I become. Someone, if not his lordship, is bound to see through my disguise and expose me. I shall never, never live it down. I think you should tell Papa. He will be angry but he will pay your debts.'

'Oh, sis, you are not turning traitor on me, are you? I cannot tell Papa. The last time he bailed me out, he gave me such a set-down, you've never heard the like — as if he had never lost a wager in his life! — and he said if it happened again he would cut off my allowance and make me live at home until I had repaid the whole.'

'He did not mean it.'

'Yes, he did. Rusticated by my own father; how could I endure that?'

'A great deal easier than I would live down passing myself off as the Comte de Clancy.' She paused, smiling in spite of herself. 'Why Canada?'

'If the Comte de Clancy had been in England

since childhood, he would be known to someone, wouldn't he? No one as rich as he is supposed to be would be a stranger in Society. And he would have lost that dreadful accent you have saddled yourself with, so Canada it has to be.'

'And my fortune is still in France? Where exactly?'

'Oh, we shall think of somewhere. It is to the good that we met Longham. When others set the tale off, he will naturally affirm he has already heard it from the horse's mouth, so to speak.'

'Tom, I cannot do it.'

'You must.' He paused and seized her hand. 'Lydia, you cannot see me in such dire straits and do nothing to help me. I promise you it will never happen again, only do it, this once, please.'

The cab had drawn up at the door of Wenthorpe House. 'And is the Count lodging with you here?' she asked, making no move to get down.

'Yes.' He paused. 'Oh, lor', no, for if anyone were to call and ask for him. . .'

'Quite so. Now do you see what a spider's web we are weaving for ourselves? We shall be caught in our own trap.'

'A hotel.'

'A reputable hotel would deny the existence of a fictitious guest and a disreputable one would hardly endear the Count to Lady Thornton.'

'I know!' he said, eyes shining. 'The Count is lodging with Frank Burford. He can be trusted to make excuses for his not being at home if anyone should call.' He jumped down on to the flagway. 'I'll go in first and make sure the coast is clear.'

Tom had instructed his valet not to wait up for him and had ordered the door to be left unlocked against his return, so that there was no one in the hall as they crept indoors, lit the candles placed in readiness on the table and went up to bed.

'As soon as the whole dreadful sham is over, the Comte de Clancy will leave for France and will never be seen again,' she whispered. 'I want your word on that.'

'You have it,' he said, giving her a brotherly peck on the cheek as they reached her bedchamber. 'He can come to an untimely end, for all I care.'

Lydia slipped into her room without disturbing her maid and made ready for bed, carefully hiding the male clothes in the back of her wardrobe so that Betty would not find them when she came to wake her, then she climbed between the sheets, blew out the candle and shut her eyes. But it was hopeless to expect to sleep; she tossed and turned, thinking of every kind of mishap which could reveal her deception to the whole world.

It would not have been so bad if the masquerade were to be enacted out of doors, simply to have some sport with Tom's contemporaries, but to deceive an innocent young lady and at a ball where knee-breeches or pantaloons had to be worn was the outside of enough. Quite apart from the clothes, she might forget herself and say or do something out of character; she might be taken ill or have an accident and a doctor sent, for who would know immediately that she was not what she pretended to be? Oh, there was no end to the dreadful possibilities; not least was the chance that someone would recognise her, particularly the Marquis of Longham, because he had a way of looking at her with eyes which seemed to see right into her soul. Just why she should feel that so keenly she could not fathom, unless Tom was right and she really was developing a *tendre* for the man. No, it could not be; she hardly knew him, and he had done nothing but look down his aristocratic nose at her ever since they met. The idea was unthinkable. Oh, she could cheerfully strangle her brother and that pimply Douglas Fincham, and Frank Burford too! But it was Frank who, in some measure, came to her rescue.

He arrived next day, long before the proper hour for morning calls, and asked to see Tom. He refused to leave, even when told that Mr Wenthorpe was undoubtedly still asleep; he would, he said, wait for him. The footman, with a sigh which was meant to convey his disapproval of young men arriving on doorsteps before the streets were aired, went off to tell Tom's valet to rouse him. By the time the young man had put in a bleary-eyed appearance, Lydia had come downstairs and taken Frank into the breakfast-room.

'Frank Burford, I suppose you think I should make you welcome,' she said with an outspokenness which came of knowing him since they were both children. 'Let me tell you I am surprised at you encouraging Tom in this cork-brained idea and I have been thinking I will not do it.'

'You will ruin everything if you let us down now,' he said, looking pained. 'You can do it; you know you can.'

'I should have thought you had more care for Miss Thornton's feelings than to wish to humiliate her.'

'I do not want to humiliate her, only her stiff-rumped mama, and if that makes her think twice before throwing her daughter at every plump-pocketed dandy in town, then so much the better for my hopes. I have had a bang-up notion. . .'

She sighed. 'Not more, Frank, I beg of you.'

Tom came in at that point; his hair had been hastily combed and he looked only half awake. 'It's devilish early for morning calls, Frank,' he said and then, seeing his sister, 'And you are going too far to receive a gentleman alone. What will Aunt Aggie say?'

'Aunt Aggie never rises before noon, you know that, and as for Frank being a gentleman, I can think of other things to call him which are not so polite. . .'

'Children, children,' Frank said. 'Do stop your brangling and hear what I have come to suggest.'

'Have you had breakfast?' Tom asked him, helping himself to ham, eggs, oysters and muffins from the chafing-dishes on the sideboard. 'Take something and sit down. What about you, Lydia?'

'I'm not in the least hungry. I would rather hear what Frank has to say for himself, for I am heartily disgusted with him, and you too.'

Tom laughed. 'By the bye, Frank, did you know

you had a Comte Maurice de Clancy lodging with you?'

'Who?'

'Comte Maurice de Clancy,' Tom repeated. 'He has lately come from Canada where his parents took him in '94. They have died and now the war is over he has come to England to see lawyers with a view to recovering his substantial lands and fortune in France.'

Frank looked puzzled. 'I have never heard of him, so how can he be lodging with me?'

'Oh, everyone will soon have heard of the charming young Comte,' Tom said airily. 'He is slight of stature and some might think effeminate, but, considering he has been brought up out of Society, he is the catch of the Season for some fortunate mama.'

The light dawned on Frank's features and he laughed aloud, slapping his thighs and saying, 'Oh, what a hum! What a Banbury!' Then, wiping his eyes with a lace-edged handkerchief plucked from his sleeve, he added, 'Now, do you want to hear my idea?'

'If we must, we must,' Lydia said with resignation.

'A costume ball. If the Comte is invited to a costume ball, then Lydia can wear something. . .' he paused, embarrassed '. . .something a little less. . . less tight than pantaloons or breeches.'

'Will that serve?' Lydia asked, as a ray of hope lightened the darkness of her foreboding.

'Nothing was said against it, so I don't see why not, as long as you are perceived as a man.'

'Who is to give such a ball?' Tom asked. 'And how can we be sure the Count will be invited?'

'I've already asked the doting parent,' Frank said, referring to his widowed mother. 'She has agreed, only stipulating it is not to be a squeeze. Fifty couples at the most, she said. I will invite the Comte and undertake to present him to Lady Thornton. What could be simpler?'

It was madness, all of it, and Lydia's head was in a spin, but she could see no way out of her dilemma without discrediting her brother and Frank, though she hated deceiving honest people, particularly Miss Thornton and Mrs Burford who must be led to believe she was entertaining a French count as a house guest. 'I suppose Miss Lydia Wenthorpe must develop the headache and cry off accompanying her brother to the ball,' she said waspishly. 'And then she must creep out of Wenthorpe House without a soul seeing her, make her way across to Park Street and then creep into Burford House, all ablaze with lights and surrounded by carriages with their grooms and drivers, and make her way up the stairs past everyone waiting to be greeted, in order to descend them again as the Count de Clancy, a young gentleman who has been his hostess's guess for at least a se'enight! I am persuaded nothing could be easier!'

'Oh, do not be such a cross-patch, Lydia,' said her brother. 'You will not be alone; Frank and I will be there.'

'And that odious Douglas Fincham too, doing his best to expose me.'

'Do you take us for a pair of widgeons? No, if he

does that, the wager is off and he knows it. No interference from him, that was a condition.'

'It would serve better if Miss Wenthorpe came to the ball and became unwell after she arrived,' Frank said, his brow creased by unaccustomed thinking. 'She would then be found a bedchamber where she could rest and recover. Switching clothes and reappearing a little later as the Count would be easy.' He looked at her appealingly. 'When the deed is done, all you have to do is change back, return to the ballroom and say your headache has gone. The Count leaves for France, I collect my blunt and Tom his vowels, all right and tight.'

'And what do I do when I am denounced?' she demanded with some asperity.

'No one will denounce you,' Tom said. 'And you will have the satisfaction of knowing yourself to be the best actress in London, and earning my undying gratitude. I would do the same for you if the shoe were on the other foot.'

'Pretend to be a girl, you mean?' she queried, lifting one finely arched brow and smiling in spite of her annoyance with him.

'No, no,' he said quickly. 'I meant by coming to your rescue when you are in a scrape.'

This was so true, she immediately bit back the retort she had on her tongue and stood up, saying she meant to go out riding and they could do as they pleased for she had said and heard all she was going to hear and say on the subject of the Count for the rest of the day and the night too if she could contrive it.

The ride did nothing to ease her troubled thoughts and neither did the morning calls she subsequently made with her aunt. She felt even worse when she sat down to nuncheon and Mrs Wenthorpe looked at her in concern and asked her if there was anything troubling her. 'Only you do not look quite the thing,' she said. 'If you would rather not go to the opera tonight. . .'

'No, no, Aunt, I am perfectly well,' she said, wishing she could unburden herself but knowing she could not do anything of the kind. 'I have a little headache, that is all; it is nothing.'

'Then go and lie down, child. I shall go and visit Lady Courtney without you.'

'I think I would rather read in the garden. I fetched Caroline Lamb's *Glenarvon* from the library.'

If Mrs Wenthorpe thought that this was a strange way of curing a headache, she did not say so; her niece was perhaps in the throes of her first attachment and if that were so she hoped the object of it was the Marquis of Longham. She did not believe half the tales that were being circulated about him and he would be just right for her. She needed someone strong and as wilful and full of spirit as she was or she would be bored to death. Not that Mrs Wenthorpe would dream of interfering; she believed in letting nature take its course, just so long as the gentleman was suitable. Not in the least strait-laced, she would have smiled with satisfaction if she had been at home to witness the events of the afternoon.

Lydia was descending the stairs with her book in one hand and her parasol in the other when she heard the front doorbell jangle. She paused on the half-landing while a footman went to answer it and, though she could not see the caller, the voice she knew. 'I believe Miss Wenthorpe is expecting me.'

In all the business over the Comte de Clancy, she had forgotten the Marquis's challenge, but he evidently had not. He was being admitted now and having a tricorne hat taken from him. It was not just his hat which made Lydia open her eyes in surprise, but the rest of his clothes. He was dressed like a common coachman in a heavy brown overcoat which had at least five capes and huge flap pockets, and which was so long that its skirts fell below the tops of his boots. He was such a comical sight that she could not suppress a laugh, making him look up at her.

'Miss Wenthorpe, good afternoon.' He attempted to make a leg but the heavy coat impeded him, then, realising she was not dressed to go out, he added, 'You were expecting me?'

She walked slowly down the stairs towards him, gripping the banister rail while she fought to regain possession of her senses. Had he recognised her the night before? Why did the sight of him make her feel so guilty, so exposed, so utterly contemptible? 'I. . . I did not think you meant it. . .'

'Meant it! Surely you did not think me so wanting in conduct as to renege on an invitation?'

'No, of course not,' she said quickly, taking hold of herself. Who was he but a pocket-pinched ex-soldier, no one to fear at all. 'Why are you wearing that ridiculous coat, when the weather is already over-warm for the end of March?'

He grinned. 'I thought it would be just the touch.'

'And from that I may assume that the vehicle you have waiting outside is that monstrous travelling chaise and that you intend to drive it?'

'Of course,' he said, bowing again and smiling broadly. 'Had you forgot my challenge? I shall understand if you should wish to cry off.'

Lydia could well have backed out at this point but the little devil-may-dare inside her urged her on. 'Poof!' she said, wondering why this remark should make the Marquis suddenly look startled, as if she had uttered something profound. 'If you wait while I change into something more suitable I will show you whether the Wenthorpes do not dare!' She paused, looking thoughtful. 'My aunt is out; do you think my maid will suffice as a chaperon, seeing you will be on the box and not sitting inside with me?' Before he could answer she laughed softly. 'I am afraid the poor girl will hate it; she stands far higher on her dignity than ever I do.' Leaving Jack staring after her, she hurried upstairs to change.

Betty was in her mistress's room, busily putting away discarded clothes and making a heap of those needing to be cleaned. She readily abandoned her task when told she was going to accompany her mistress on a carriage ride in the park and helped her into a skirt of a plain blue weave and a caraco jacket frogged in silver. While Lydia put on her hat with its sweeping feather, the maid fetched her best

pelisse and bonnet. It was not until she saw the
Marquis and then the vehicle in question that she
realised that this was some sort of hum. She hung
back. 'Oh, Miss Lydia, you never mean to ride in
that thing *again*!'

'Indeed I do. Now get in. If you sit back, no one
will see you.'

But it was soon evident that Miss Wenthorpe
herself had no such reservations. Might as well be
hung for a sheep as a lamb, she told herself, sitting
forward in her seat and smiling, her violet eyes
brimming with mischief. They made their way
towards Hyde Park with the Marquis sitting on the
box, flicking his whip and weaving the coach in and
out of the traffic just as if he had been driving the
latest bang-up rig. Fully expecting to find herself in
the daily parade of phaetons, curricles, landaulets
and gigs to be found there, Lydia realised, after they
had turned into the park, that this was not to be.
They turned aside on to a quiet lane where there
was no one to be seen except a couple of urchins
chasing a mongrel and a single gentleman rider who
reined in and looked at the carriage as if it had come
from another age, which, indeed, it had. The lane
became rather bumpy and, though the Marquis
drove well, it took all his concentration to keep the
coach on the road.

'Oh, miss, wherever is he taking us?' Betty wailed.
'I thought we were going to drive in the park.'

'We are in the park,' Lydia said sharply, not
wanting to admit that she was also puzzled.

'He is carrying us off to have his evil way with you. Whatever shall we do?'

'Don't be a goose.' All the same Lydia put her head out of the window and called up to the box. 'My lord, do please stop.'

It was a minute before he could bring the coach to a standstill, but he managed it, to the admiration of the solitary rider, if no one else, and then turned to look down at her. 'My apologies, Miss Wenthorpe, I had not realised that this path was so rough.'

'Turn round at once and take us home.'

'It cannot be done,' he said with a hint of a smile. 'This old coach needs half an acre to come about and if we leave the path we may well overturn. If we go on to the trees ahead of us, we shall find oursevles at the end of the Ride and can turn there.'

'Then please do so.' Furious with him, she withdrew her head and they moved forward again. If he was trying to teach her some kind of lesson, she had no idea what it was, but it did occur to her that if he had really meant to humiliate her he would have driven the coach straight along the Ride where they would have been seen by all the occupants of the fashionable carriages who were daily to be seen there.

Two minutes later he pulled up in the shade of the copse of trees, where a spanking new curricle harnessed to a very fine pair of chestnut horses was standing empty. A servant, lolling against a tree, jumped to attention as soon as he saw them arrive. The Marquis sprang lightly from the box-seat and came to open the door and let down the step for

Lydia to alight. 'I felicitate you on your courage,
Miss Wenthorpe,' he said, smiling broadly and holding out his hand. 'And now you shall have your
reward. Come.' He led her over to the curricle and
handed her in before taking off the coachman's hat
and coat and revealing himself in buff-coloured
pantaloons, a magnificent coat of mulberry superfine, a striped silk waistcoat, and a cravat mathemat-
ically knotted around a high starched collar.
Throwing the discarded coat and hat at his man,
who caught them deftly, he picked up a tall beaver
from the seat of the curricle and clapped it on his
head. 'Tewkes, be so good as to escort Miss
Wenthorpe's maid home and put the coach away.'

Ignoring Betty's protests, Tewkes climbed on the
box of the coach and turned it back the way it had
come while his lordship, smiling perversely, took his
seat beside Lydia. 'Now, let us put matters to rights,
shall we?' he said, picking up the ribbons and turning
into the carriage ride.

'And how much did you wager that I should do
it?' she enquired mildly, as they were bowled along,
bowing this way and that at the other carriages with
their illustrious and modish occupants.

'Wager, Miss Wenthorpe?' he asked innocently.

'Yes. Do not try and gull me into believing you
had nothing on the outcome.'

He laughed. 'You know, Miss Wenthorpe, I never
thought of it. When I made the dare I had meant
only to drive a little way with the coach blinds
drawn, just to show you that it does not do to take
up rash challenges. . .' He turned his direct hazel

eyes on her, making her shrink inside herself with guilt. Was he looking at her and seeing the Comte de Clancy? 'But I soon saw that would not serve, for never did I see anyone less mortified by the prospect.'

'Thank you, my lord,' she said, bowing to Lady Jersey who acknowledged her graciously. 'But a dare is a dare, after all.'

'And you would not have cared?'

'Did I look as though I did?'

'You do not mind being thought a trifle. . .' he paused, smiling '. . .eccentric?'

'Not in the least. It would not be the first time.' He could make of that what he liked, she thought, Comte de Clancy and all.

'Nevertheless, I could not parade you in front of the *ton* in that dilapidated vehicle, whatever the dare,' he said. 'So I hit on the idea of taking a roundabout way where we would not be seen until now.'

'It was kind of you, but unnecessary. And I am still lacking conduct, for you have sent my chaperon home.' She pretended to sigh, but could not suppress a smile. 'Aunt Aggie will wash her hands of me.'

'No, she won't, for if anyone should mention seeing you I shall own that it was entirely my fault because I hoaxed you.'

'But why should you do such a thing?'

'A wager, you said so yourself. Everyone gambles; it is the accepted thing. . .'

'But I collect you do not approve of gambling,' she said.

'I have seen many a good man ruined by it. And ladies, too. Do smile at Lady Hertford, my dear; she will think you in the suds because of something I have said. You are a gambler yourself, are you not?'

'Only for fun with Tom sometimes.' Oh, she was getting in deep and the more he said, the more worried she became. 'And not for money. Well,' she added truthfully, 'only a very little.'

'Then it must be for the joy of creating a mull.'

'Now, why should I do that?'

'From boredom, perhaps?' He touched his hat to Lady Sefton. 'I am persuaded there are times when you envy your brother.'

'Envy Tom? How, my lord, have you come to that conclusion?'

'Men have a much livelier time of it than ladies, do they not? They are not so bound by convention. They come and go as they please, they can gallop if they've a mind to and don't need chaperons.'

She decided to ignore his reference to having seen her galloping. 'But they have responsibilities, is that not so? They must protect and provide for their womenfolk and worry about managing their estates, and politics and waging war and coping with their labourers, who must be treated firmly but fairly. At least, that is what Papa would have me believe.'

'And do you?'

'Naturally I do.' She smiled mischievously. 'I am a dutiful daughter.'

'From that I may deduce you do not feel restricted and are enjoying your come-out Season?'

'Of course.'

'Then, knowing the risks, why did you not do the ladylike and refuse to drive out with me?'

'That would have been a dishonourable thing to do after accepting your challenge.'

'Exactly my point,' he said, with satisfaction.

She changed the subject hurriedly; he was getting too near the bone. 'Why have you kept that disreputable coach?'

'Oh, I might yet find a use for it,' he said airily. 'But I shall not ask you to ride in it again.'

He would never ask her to ride in anything with him again, she decided, if the coil she had got herself into ever came to light. She longed to confess, but wondered what he would say if she did. Would he laugh and think it a capital rig or would he condemn her forever for the hoyden she had protested she was not? She had a sinking feeling it would probably be the latter.

She looked up to see a yellow-painted landaulet with the hood down approaching them, bearing two ladies she knew very well. One was Frank Burford's mother, a lady of ample proportions dressed in a hideous purple mantle with wooden cherries nodding under the brim of her bonnet, and the other, severely dressed in grey jaconet, was her companion, Miss Whiting.

'Why, Miss Wenthorpe!' Mrs Burford called as the coaches drew level and stopped within two feet of each other. 'How are you?'

'I am well, thank you, Mrs Burford. Allow me to introduce the Marquis of Longham.'

'Longham,' she said, peering through her glass at

him. 'Know you, don't I? Son of the Duke of Sutton, if I'm not mistaken.'

The Marquis bowed and smiled. 'Yes, ma'am.'

'Knew you and your brother when you were both in short coats; how many years ago must it be? No, we will not go into that. I was sorry to hear of Edward's death; such a shock to the Duke, I imagine. Give my condolences when next you see His Grace. He was a friend of my late husband, don't you know? How is he keeping?'

'Tolerably well, ma'am, but afflicted with gout. It keeps him in the country. . .'

'It's gout, is it?' She had heard otherwise. 'To be sure, that's bad enough, and I'm sorry, but it's better than being touched in the attic, like the poor king.'

Lydia, aghast at the tactlessness of the woman, turned to look at her escort; his jaw had tightened and his smile had faded a little, but he gave no other sign that the barb had gone home. Mrs Burford prattled on, unaware of the tension she had created. 'It must be prodigious hard stepping into your brother's shoes so soon after returning from Waterloo and then to have to take over the estate from his grace, when by all accounts it has been sadly let go.' Hardly drawing breath, she continued. 'You will come to my costume ball, will you not? It is to be on the first day of April; such an appropriate day for dressing up, don't you think?'

'Indeed, yes, ma'am.' Jack's expression remained immobile.

'Give me your direction and I will see you are sent an invitation. It will be an intimate affair, just a few

friends to whom we can introduce the Comte de
Clancy. The poor boy knows so few people in
London. . .'

'The Comte de Clancy?' queried the Marquis, and
Lydia knew with heart-stopping certainty that if he
had been going to refuse the invitation on account
of Mrs Burford's veiled insults he would not do so
now. He would go simply to satisfy his curiosity. If
he had not seen her mortified by the prospect of
parading in the old coach, he could, if he chose to
turn and look at her now, see exactly that; her
cheeks were bright pink and there was a light in her
eyes which was almost terror.

'Yes, do you know him?' asked Mrs Burford.

'I have made the young gentleman's acquaintance,
ma'am.' He turned towards Lydia and again she
received that penetrating look. 'I collect he is cousin
of yours, Miss Wenthorpe.'

Her mouth was so dry and her heart pumping so
furiously, it was an effort to speak, but she managed
to murmur an affirmative.

'He is to be Frank's guest for a few days,' Mrs
Burford went on. 'It is better than lodgings or a
hotel, especially as all the best ones are beginning to
fill up at this time of year, though why he cannot
stay at Wenthorpe House I do not know.' She
heaved a sigh which made her many chins wobble
above her heaving bosom. 'Our family don't go in
for these cork-brained family feuds, I'm glad to say.
Agatha Wenthorpe ought to feel ashamed of herself
for prolonging it. I am in two minds whether to
invite her. Do you think they will bury the hatchet

for one evening? I should hate to be the cause of
any ill feeling for the boy; Agatha has a cutting
tongue when she decides to use it.' She paused only
long enough to draw breath. 'But she is Miss
Wenthorpe's chaperon and I cannot leave her out
without leaving Miss Wenthorpe out and Frank
would never hear of that.'

Lydia felt she ought to make some reply to this,
but her head was in a whirl and she could think of
nothing which would not complicate matters even
further. Frank had obviously returned home and
regaled his mother with a much embroidered story
of how the Count came to be in England, and until
she saw him again she had no idea what it was. And
now she had colluded in the whole charade by
agreeing that the Count was a relative, and it had all
gone beyond the point when she could back out.

She became aware that his lordship had taken a
card from his cardcase and was handing it to Mrs
Burford, who tucked it into her reticule. 'I shall look
forward to seeing you at Burford House,' she told
him with a smile.

The coaches drew apart to go their separate ways
with Lydia so immersed in her troubles that she
could barely bid the other ladies good-day. Frank
and Tom had both promised her they would not
invite the Marquis to the ball, but how were they to
know Mrs Burford would do it for them? Oh, what
had she let herself in for?

She stole a glance at her escort. He was looking
severe, but whether it was because of Mrs Burford's
insults to his family or because he knew the Comte

de Clancy was not all he seemed she could not tell. She tried to close her eyes and her heart to the feelings which assailed her; pleasure in his company, for there was nothing dull or ordinary about him and he seemed to understand her — too well sometimes; and a wish, which she would not for the world have openly admitted, to be held high in his esteem. She suspected that beneath his outwardly haughty manner was a caring man who would always be loyal to his friends. On the other hand, she had no doubt that he would make a deadly enemy! She was reminded of the gypsy's warning to beware a tall, dark man and shivered a little.

He turned to smile at her, making her insides quiver like a blancmange. 'Are you cold?'

'Not at all.'

'Then what is wrong?'

'Wrong?' she queried, falsely bright. 'Why should anything be wrong?'

'I don't know,' he said, so gently that she felt like bursting into uncharacteristic tears. 'But something has upset you and I don't believe it has anything to do with riding in the old coach. You were perfectly at ease until we met Mrs Burford.'

'There is nothing wrong, my lord. I cannot think why you should say such a thing.'

He stopped the carriage and turned towards her. 'I say it because I feel it,' he said softly, taking her hands in his. 'And you are shaking. Are you afraid of me?'

She dared not look up into those limpid eyes or she would be lost to all reason; instead she stared

down at his strong brown hands, holding hers so
tenderly, and that was nearly as bad. 'No, my lord.'

'But you are troubled.' He paused, waiting for her
to answer, but when she did not he added, 'I wish
you would tell me why.'

'I. . .' She stopped. If only she could confide in
him, but that would only give him a disgust of her.
He was one of those rare people who did not gamble
and he preferred ladies who behaved like ladies. She
took a deep breath and made herself look up to
meet his gaze. 'There is nothing in the least troubling
me and you are making people stare at us. Please
drive on.'

'As you wish.' He picked up the reins and they
continued on their way in silence, both feeling hurt
and dejected and neither knowing the reason.

CHAPTER FOUR

LORD LONGHAM was such an unconscionable time taking his leave after bringing her home that Lydia began to think he was delaying on purpose to discomfort her. He knew she was worried, he had said so, and he imagined it had something to do with Mrs Burford's remark about a family quarrel and he was curious, especially as he had met the Count out with Tom the evening before and there had been no evidence of a family quarrel then. She stood, bonnet and gloves in her hand, wishing he would go away instead of smiling and making himself agreeable to her aunt. And now Aunt Aggie was inviting him to stay and take some refreshment and if he accepted then the subject of the Comte de Clancy was sure to come up. She dared not look at him and held her breath for his reply.

'I regret, ma'am, that I have another engagement,' he said, with a smile which captivated Mrs Wenthorpe and filled her niece with apprehension. 'But give me leave to call again.'

'Any time, my lord, any time,' her aunt said, offering her hand, which he took and raised to his lips.

'Your servant, ma'am.' He turned to bow over Lydia's hand and the mocking smile he gave her seemed to say, I have not done with you yet; I shall

ask you again and again until I am satisfied. Aloud
he said, 'Miss Wenthorpe, your servant. May I have
the pleasure of your company again soon?'

'I am much engaged,' she said, wishing he would
leave so that she could go and find her brother. And
that young man would know the length of her tongue
when she did. 'Will you go to Mrs Burford's costume
ball?'

'If you are going to be there, Miss Wenthorpe,
then I would not miss it for worlds,' he said, and
finally took his leave.

She ignored her aunt's scold at her coolness
towards him when he had been nothing but amiable,
and, murmuring that she was going up to change,
she hurried from the room and tracked Tom down
in the library, where he was lounging in one of the
armchairs, reading the *Morning Post*.

'What family quarrel, pray?' she demanded, without preamble. 'What Mrs Burford thought of me I
cannot think, for I sat in his lordship's curricle with
my mouth open like a fish out of water when she
said the Count was staying with her on account of
some disagreement in the family.'

He looked up at her, standing in front of him with
her eyes blazing and her cheeks pink with annoyance. 'Do come down from your high ropes, Lydia;
you will surely alert Aunt Aggie that something is
afoot if you go about in such a bubble. Sit down.
What did you say to Mrs Burford?'

She refused to sit. 'There was nothing I could say,
though she must have wondered at it. What Banbury
tale have you told her, Tom?'

'I? Nothing at all. It was Frank. You see, when he asked if the Comte de Clancy might stay a few days, she naturally asked why he could not come to Wenthorpe House. The Count is supposed to be our cousin, after all. Frank could think of nothing but a quarrel between his parents and Aunt Aggie and Aunt Aggie's determination never to speak to any member of the de Clancy family again.'

'Oh, Tom, he ought not to have brought Aunt Aggie into it. What she will say when she finds out I shudder to think. A scolding will be the very least of it.' She sat down suddenly in the chair opposite him. 'Tom, we must forget the whole thing; we are getting in too deep. There will be more questions we cannot answer and more stories until we have got ourselves into such a bumblebath there will be no getting out of it.'

'Fustian! It is too late to back out now. Mrs Burford is expecting the Count, bag and baggage this afternoon.'

'No, Tom, no. It is over a week to the ball; I cannot stay there in disguise all that time and don't you think Aunt Aggie will notice my absence from here?'

'We have thought of that. The Count is in London on business, so he will spend a great deal of his time with lawyers and such like; he will hardly be at home at all.'

'And what about evenings and at breakfast?' she asked with some asperity.

'The Count is an early riser and will be out of the house long before his hostess makes an appearance, and he will be out most evenings. He is intent on seeing all the plays and operas, visiting Vauxhall Gardens, not to mention the gambling hells. Frank says his mother will not find it the least remarkable that she never sees her guest. And he will ruffle up the bed and leave linen for the wash to allay the servants' suspicions.'

'But Mrs Burford will meet the Count when he arrives. If she should recognise me straight off. . .'

'She won't. I have acquired a whole box full of clothes, stage make-up, wigs, beards, everything you need; so, you see, I have not been idle while you have been amusing yourself with Longham.'

'Amusing myself! I was never so discomfited in all my life.'

'Ah!' he said, knowingly. 'That is the nub of it. It is the Marquis of Longham who occupies your mind, not your poor brother.'

'Nothing of the sort!' she snapped. 'But he dropped more than a hint he knew I was up to something and then we met Mrs Burford. . .' She paused. 'What else has Frank told his mother?'

'Only enough to satisfy her curiosity. The Count has come to London to see lawyers about his fortune and his lands. He has not been in England long enough to set up his own establishment or acquire things like horses and carriages, and would not want to, not having decided if he will stay in this country.'

'It gets worse and worse,' she said, her heart sinking into the jean half-boots she wore. 'I can't do it.'

'Course you can. It ain't as if we are doing any harm. . .'

'No harm!' she squeaked. 'One falsehood after another, a veritable Canterbury tale becoming more and more involved. Hoist on our own petard, that's what we'll be. It will be on the lips of every tattle-monger in town and my reputation and prospects will be ruined.'

'I shall be ruined if you do not,' he said sharply. 'You don't suppose Fincham will keep his tongue between his teeth, do you?' He paused and when she did not answer went on, 'Come, dearest of sisters, you can do it on your head. 'Tis only a little charade, after all, and Frank and I will be on hand to protect you.'

She was not at all sure that either could be relied on to do that, but neither did she see how she could back out when Mrs Burford was expecting her guest that afternoon. 'I shall go with you to Park Street,' she said tersely. 'But if Mrs Burford shows the slightest suspicion, we will confess it all a prank and take our leave.'

He laughed with pleasure and, jumping to his feet, pulled her up and whirled her round. 'Oh, I knew I could count on you. The clothes and make-up are in the attic; thought it best not to leave it in your room. We'll have to carry it to Burford House ourselves; can't involve the servants. I've told Aunt Aggie we are dining with Mrs Burford and as she don't like Frank's mother above half she don't care a groat that she is not to come too. She says she will dine in her room.'

Lydia spent the remainder of the afternoon with her aunt but, as Mrs Wenthorpe liked to chatter, all that was required of her was to say 'yes' or 'no', or 'indeed' as she plied her embroidery needle. At five o'clock her aunt rose to go to her room and, once the door had safely closed on her, Lydia sped up to the attic and found the trunk Tom had left there. In less than an hour she crept out, dressed in a high-collared coat with rows of frogging, a blue and white striped satin waistcoat and voluminous Petersham cossacks which were so outlandish a new fashion that the sight of her sent Tom into gales of silent laughter. On her head she wore a wig of golden curls cut in the Windswept style. Her eyebrows had been thickened, her cheeks padded, her nose made larger and there was a slight shadow under her eyes which betokened lack of sleep.

'Oh, bang-up,' her brother whispered, as he picked up her portmanteau and carried it downstairs. 'You will take the town by storm.'

'I do not intend to do any such thing,' she hissed back as they reached the hall. 'Do be silent or you'll have the whole household out to see what the racket is.'

Tom had already brought a hackney to the side-entrance and they climbed into it with a sigh of relief. Not ten minutes later they were being admitted to Mrs Burford's drawing-room and the good lady was coming towards the Comte, chins wobbling under her smile, and holding out her hand. 'I am pleased to meet you, Count. Frank has told me all about you. Such a pity you should find no welcome

at Wenthorpe House, but no matter, you are welcome here.'

'Your servant, *madame*,' the Count said languidly,
bowing over her hand. 'We will not talk of things so
un'appy, *non*? It is good that I 'ave a 'ome found
'ere.'

'One of the footmen will take your baggage to
your room,' Mrs Burford said, sitting down and
indicating a chair beside her. 'We will have a
comfortable coze until it is time to dress for dinner.'
She cast an eye over the Count's cossacks as she
spoke and suppressed a smile. 'Frank will be here
directly and he will show you to your room. I collect
you do not wish for a dresser, for I am sure we can
find someone to help you if you do.'

'*Merci, madame*, but me, I like to dress myself.'

Frank arrived at this point and joined in the
conversation, prompting Lydia with leading questions about her family and her life in Canada and
regaling them at some length with all the latest *on-
dit* and offers to take the Count out and about, until,
at last, he suggested taking their guest to his room
so that he could dress for dinner.

'You will stay, Tom, won't you?' Frank said. 'You
do not subscribe to the feud, do you?'

'I cannot understand Agatha,' Mrs Burford said,
as Tom accepted the invitation. 'It is not like her to
bear a grudge.'

'Oh, it is something and nothing,' Tom said
quickly. 'My aunt will be over it in a week, I'll
wager.'

'I do hope so. I do not want any unpleasantness at my ball. . .'

'If *madame* wishes, I will not attend,' the Count said, earning startled looks from Tom and Frank.

'Not come! Why, the ball is in your honour, my dear Count!' Mrs Burford exclaimed. 'There can be no question but you will come.' She rose ponderously to her feet and the young men sprang to theirs. If Lydia was a little slow to do likewise, Mrs Burford did not seem to notice it. 'Now I will go and change.'

As soon as she had gone, Tom and Frank clapped each other on the shoulders, congratulating themselves on the success of the ruse and calling Lydia poor-spirited when she demurred. Frank, in fine good humour, took her up to a guest room on the second floor and left her to change for dinner, saying his room was next door and to shout out if she needed anything. The only thing she needed, she told him tartly, was to wake up and find it had all been a dream. But as her wish was not to be granted she changed into dark pantaloons, grey waistcoat and an evening coat with well-padded shoulders, and went down to dinner.

It was an interminable evening and she found herself having to invent a history for the Count which sounded so false in her ears that she wondered at Mrs Burford's gullibility. Having invented a cache of gold and jewels, she was obliged to elaborate by saying it had been hidden on the de Clancy estate when the family fled and only on her father's deathbed had she learned the hiding place. She planned to go to France shortly to recover it.

'Oh, how romantical!' Mrs Burford cried, and Lydia knew with dreadful certainty that the story would be all over town the following day. 'I wish you may find it and return safely, for I declare France is not the place to be now, what with occupying armies and bands of brigands roaming the countryside.' She heaved herself to her feet. 'Now if you will excuse me I shall retire.'

The young men rose and Tom declared his intention of returning home. 'I promised Aunt Aggie I would not be late,' he said, leaving the room with Mrs Burford.

Lydia turned to Frank. 'Now what am I to do?'

'Do? Why, go to bed, Count.' He smiled suddenly. 'Change back into skirts and creep down as soon as you hear my mother's door shut. I will let you out of the house and Tom will be waiting with a cab.'

When she joined Tom half an hour later, she told him in no uncertain terms that she would not for the world go through an evening like that again and if he thought she would he was very much mistaken.

During the following week the Count, though never seen, became the subject of the latest gossip and Lydia tried, largely unsuccessfully, to put him from her mind and enjoy her Season. She visited the opera and attended a supper party given by one of Aunt Aggie's bosom bows, went to Vauxhall Gardens and for drives in Hyde Park, when Tom allowed her to take the ribbons of the phaeton, and generally was seen by everyone, including the

Marquis of Longham, who kept his promise to call
again and asked her to ride out with him.

Above all else, she loved to ride, and as Tom
spent more time than was good for him at his club
he could never be roused from his bed early enough
to accompany her and she felt starved of her customary fresh air and exercise. Riding with the Marquis
was a pleasure, particularly as he did not seem
disposed to mention their last encounter. She supposed he had delivered his little lecture and had
assumed, like most self-opinionated men, that she
had taken it to heart and was now prepared to
behave in the proper ladylike manner. It irked her a
little that he should be so loftily presumptuous, but
as she had no wish to reopen the discussion she let it
go.

He seemed to know, without being told, that she
would prefer to ride in Green Park rather than the
more fashionable Hyde Park where gossip, rather
than exercise, seemed to be the order of the day,
and they turned in at the Bath Gate with the faithful
Scrivens in attendance. After half an hour, in which
the horses were put through their paces, they dismounted to walk and talk. Lydia had to admit that
he was an amusing and knowledgeable conver-
sationalist, that he had a sense of the ridiculous
which was refreshing and that his smile, when it
reached his eyes, transformed him from a haughty
aristocrat to a gentleman of immense charm. If only
the spectre of the Comte de Clancy did not loom
between them!

His lordship did not seem interested in gossip, the

scandalous behaviour of Caroline Lamb or the latest *on-dit* about Beau Brummel and Lord Byron, but, on being encouraged to do so, told her something of his experiences on the battlefields of Europe, carefully omitting the worst horrors. This led to a discussion of politics, the falling price of corn and his sympathy for the labourers. ''Tis little wonder they riot and break up machinery,' he said. 'Like those of us who should have known better, they expected peace to bring Utopia with it.'

'You do not think we could have a Revolution like they had in France?' she queried.

'There are those who fear it, but I do not think so,' he said with a wry smile. 'The guillotine is a French invention and I doubt the aristocracy of England will be obliged to flee their homes in the way your cousin, de Clancy, did.'

She stiffened. Had he deliberately introduced that name in order to test her? If he had, he had ruined what had been a happy interlude. He was still playing his cat-and-mouse game with her and she would not endure it. 'Goodness, how late it is!' she exclaimed, beckoning to Scrivens to come and help her mount and puzzling Jack, who could so easily have offered his hand to throw her into the saddle. 'I must go; I have a costume-fitting in half an hour.'

Her abrupt ending of their outing must have confirmed his poor opinion of her, she realised afterwards, but she could not have continued their conversation with anything like an easy mind. He remained amiable and pretended not to notice her silence as they rode back to Wenthorpe House,

where he politely refused her far from enthusiastic
invitation to come in for refreshment. 'I shall see
you at Mrs Burford's ball, I hope?' he said, dismounting and escorting her to the door.

'Yes, indeed,' she said, trying to hide her
wretchedness behind a bright smile. 'I am looking
forward to it.'

She was far from anticipating any pleasure at that
function and, though she tried, she could not prevail
on Tom to abandon the masquerade.

'If word gets out I cannot even pay a debt of
honour, then I'll be dunned by every tradesman in
town,' her brother said when she tried. 'We are in
too deep to back out. Mrs Burford is convinced, so
why not Lady Thornton?'

Lydia could see nothing for it but to choose a
costume for the Count which would help to hide her
curves and have it delivered to Burford House in
readiness for the ball. But that would not satisfy
Tom; he insisted Lydia should go with him to pay a
morning call on Mrs Burford the day before the ball
and once again she found herself taking part in a
farce which, in spite of her misgivings, made it
difficult to keep a straight face.

Frank, who was expecting them, was sitting with
his mother in the morning-room when they arrived.
Once the usual greetings had been exchanged and
Mrs Burford had told Lydia how comely she looked
in her yellow and white striped silk gown, and how
well she had managed to match the ribbons in her
bonnet, Frank informed them the Count had been
up half the night playing cards at White's and was

still abed and he would go and wake him. Being nudged by Tom into a reply, Lydia said she had another engagement and could not wait. 'If you wish to stay,' she said to her brother, as she drew on her lemon kid gloves, 'I'll take a chair and leave the phaeton to you.'

A chair was procured and she took her leave while Frank went to rouse the Count. As soon as she had rounded the corner, Lydia dismissed the chairman and hurried back to the side-entrance of the house, where Frank was waiting to let her in. They crept up to the Count's room, where he left her to change while he went back to his mother and Tom. 'Maurice will be down directly,' he told them. 'He is trying on his costume for the ball.'

Lydia had chosen an eighteenth-century costume because its full coat would help to disguise her curves and it was a time when the lavish use of make-up was normal. Working rapidly, she stripped off her gown and sat down before the mirror to transform her face into that of the plump-cheeked, dark-browed Comte de Clancy, adding a liberal amount of white paint and powder and a patch beneath one eye. When she was satisfied with her face, she took the costume from her portmanteau and put on a silk shirt, white breeches and stockings and shoes with high red heels and silver buckles. Flinging back the lace which fell over her wrists, she tied a lace cravat about her neck and tucked it into a flowered satin waistcoat which came almost to her knees. The coat that went on over that was of pale rose with huge silver buttons and lavishly embroidered in silver.

Then, settling a full powdered wig on her own curls and picking up a three-cornered hat, she returned to the drawing-room.

Now she was dressed, her nervousness faded and she began to feel like the actress her mother had been; she became the Count. Her voice deepened and her accent became even more pronounced as she paraded before them to show off the costume. The two young men silently marvelled at the way every movement and gesture proclaimed the man; there was very little that was feminine about the Comte de Clancy, unless it was his unblemished skin and delicate hands. 'It needs just a leetle tuck 'ere, *n'est-ce pas*?' she said, pulling in the waist of the coat.

'Oh, you will have all the young ladies by the ears,' Mrs Burford said. 'So handsome, you are, and such elegant address. I could wish myself twenty years younger.'

There was a great deal more and it took all Lydia's acting ability not to laugh aloud. She agreed that if she should find any of the young ladies to her liking she might very well think of marriage. Then she returned upstairs, re-made her face, changed into the cossacks again and rejoined Mrs Burford with her own clothes done up in the paper in which her costume had been delivered.

'Count, we could have had the tailor come and fetch the coat,' Mrs Burford said. 'There is no need for you to take it back yourself.'

'I 'ave to go out to see my lawyer,' the Count said, bowing over her hand. 'I pass the shop on the way.'

'I'll take you up,' Tom said, bidding goodbye to the Burfords and following the Count to the door. 'I'm going your way.'

They left together and climbed into the phaeton and, as soon as it turned the corner, collapsed into a heap, laughing so much that the horses nearly took fright. They were still laughing when they arrived in Portman Square and drew up at Wenthorpe House.

'Stay here, while I make sure Aunt Aggie is out,' Tom said, wiping tears from his eyes with a lace handkerchief plucked from his sleeve. 'I don't think she would entertain the Count, do you?' He jumped down and went to the door, leaving Lydia alone in the phaeton, in full view of anyone who might happen to be passing.

One of these was the Marquis of Longham, though his intention had not been to pass but to call. Something about the figure of the Count sitting alone in the carriage made him check his stride and then step smartly beind a tree in a neighbouring garden to watch events.

He had just come from seeing his lawyer, a young man who had been in the Peninsula with him and who had returned to take over the practice from his father. Charles Wilmott had confirmed that the land Ernest Grimshaw had appropriated had not been part of the original Longham domain. 'But I don't doubt it belongs legally to the Bellingham family,' he had said. 'There is a rumour that it was won in a wager but I have been unable to find any documents to support this. Without proof, His Grace will find it difficult to turn the man off.'

'I'll be damned if I let that Jack-at-warts make a cod's head of my father, just because His Grace is. . .' the Marquis had paused to find the word to describe his father's state of health '. . .not in plump currant and disinclined to make a push to claim his rights. I will return to Longham Towers and find the proof. In the meantime I have another small commission for you.' He had pulled a fob from his pocket and held it out on his palm, where it sparkled in the sunlight coming into the office through a rather grimy window. It was decorated with a shield-shaped crest in which a stag and falcon were picked out in precious stones. 'I need to find the owner of this.'

Charles had picked it up to examine it more closely. 'Whose insignia is this?'

'That's what I want to discover. It is French, or I think it is, and there is a great deal more — necklaces, armlets, tiaras, rings — a fortune, in fact. Some of it has a design similar to this, but this is the clearest and most easily identified.' He had gone on to tell his friend that he wished to return it to its true owner and received the same advice Tewkes had given him so freely — not to be a ninny and to be thankful for his good luck.

'I would not think myself lucky if I were in his shoes,' he had said, referring to the original owner of the haul. 'He must have been plucked clean and I would give him back his feathers.'

'Some feathers!' Charles had said laconically. 'I will do my best to trace the crest, but finding a living owner might be more difficult. He may have had a meeting with Madame Guillotine, or fled to America, or died on some European battlefield. If the cache was found in a soldier's knapsack, then I'll lay odds it was the latter.'

Jack had left Charles with the problem and decided to walk to Wenthorpe House to pay his respects to Miss Wenthorpe and tell her that he had been called out of town and would not, regretfully, have the pleasure of seeing her at Mrs Burford's ball.

Now, as he watched, Tom came out of the door, spoke to the Count and together they entered the house, and a minute later a servant came out and took the horses and phaeton round to the stables. The Comte de Clancy, if Mrs Burford was to be believed, was not welcome at Wenthorpe House, and yet here he was, going in with every appearance of belonging there. Jack was sure that if he were to knock and ask for the Count the young man could not be produced, not by Mrs Wenthorpe at all events. Tom Wenthorpe was a scapegrace but he was unwilling to believe that Miss Wenthorpe, in spite of the tomboy impression she had given him, was a party to intrigue. Crouching inelegantly behind a tree, watching Wenthorpe House for signs of the Count leaving, he fell to wondering what it was about Lydia Wenthorpe that put her so constantly in his thoughts. It could be the derogatory expression 'Poof!' she had used. It had sounded a warning chord somewhere in his memory and for the life of him he could not place it; as far as he knew he had never met her before that journey to London.

He would have remembered if he had. She was memorable; classically handsome rather than pretty, she was just the right height for someone as tall as he was, though that was of less consequence than her zest for life, her energy, the sparkle in her deep eyes and the way her mouth twitched into a smile, as if life itself was a jest. Was this a jest? He was curious, curious enough to postpone his visit to Longham for a few days and remain in town. He extricated himself from behind the tree and, with a last look at the closed door of Wenthorpe House, turned on his heel and went back to his lodgings.

Lydia took a long time dressing the next evening. It was not that the simple gingham costume of a shepherdess was difficult to put on, for it laced down the front, but she was so nervous, she could not keep still and Betty found herself chasing her mistress all over the room to try and arrange a few flowers in her hair. But at last Lydia succumbed to Tom's entreaties from the other side of the door and, picking up her crook and a muff stuffed to look like a lamb, she joined him and their aunt for the carriage ride to Burford House, meekly enduring her aunt's scold for her tardiness.

Owing to the press of traffic, it was over an hour before they found themselves at the head of the line waiting to be greeted by Mrs Burford, and the dancing had already begun. Their ears were assailed by music from an enthusiastic orchestra, laughter and excited voices and, in a sudden stillness, a stentorious voice announcing, 'Mrs Wenthorpe, the

Honourable Mr Thomas Wenthorpe and Miss Wenthorpe.'

Agatha, panniers swaying, sailed majestically into the room, followed by Lydia whose eyes were dazzled by the colourful scene. There were kings and queens, gods and goddesses, highwaymen, Round-heads, serving wenches, coachmen and harlequins, cossacks and soldiers of every nationality and hue, and dandies so exquisite one could believe them already in costume. In spite of the open windows and the flutter of a hundred fans, the air was made oppressive by a multitude of gasoliers. Since Mrs Burford's room was not over-large, it was, as her aunt had foretold, a squeeze. Even so, Lydia wished there were fewer to witness the masquerade and was almost relieved to note that neither the Marquis of Longham nor the Honourable Mr Douglas Fincham was to be seen.

Frank left his position at his mother's side to bow before Lydia. 'You are in looks tonight, Miss Wenthorpe,' he said, as he led her down the ranks of dancers in a country dance. 'And you have a sparkle in your eyes which betokens mischief.'

'Tis not mischief but terror,' she whispered, smiling to left and right. 'Where is Mr Fincham?'

They parted, she smiled and curtsied to her new partner and took a turn with him, then came to Frank again. 'I pray he will not come.'

He smiled. 'Oh, he will come.'

'I wish the whole thing could be gainsaid. Look at Lady Thorton now, casting her eye about like some predatory animal. She will tear me limb from limb.'

'But she cannot eat you.' He chuckled, bowing as they parted again, continuing when they met again as if there had been no break. 'I fancy you would be a little indigestible. Smile, do; I do not want a set-down from Mrs Wenthorpe for making you cast down.'

She smiled a little woodenly and then stiffened as she saw Douglas Fincham enter the room. He stood, dressed as a Cavalier, looking about him until his eye rested on her, then, as the dance ended and she left the floor on Frank's arm, moved forward to bow before her. There was nothing for it but to take the floor with him.

'You know, Miss Wenthorpe,' he said, leading her towards a set then forming, 'I am persuaded that someone with a countenance as beautiful and a figure as graceful as yours could never be trans-formed into a frog-eating *aristo*. I offered your brother terms so that you would not have to attempt it, but he is not so careful of your reputation as I am. He refused.'

'My reputation is in no danger, sir,' she said, stung to anger, 'but I feel a little unwell and would leave the floor.'

He did not believe her, but he escorted her back to Mrs Wenthorpe who was sitting on the sidelines talking to Mrs Burford and Lady Thornton. 'Miss Wenthorpe is feeling a trifle giddy,' he announced. 'Perhaps some hartshorn might steady her.'

Lydia glared at him and sank into a chair, fanning her face with the lamb muff. 'I think it is the heat,

Aunt, though to own the truth I have felt out of curl all day.'

'Do you want to go home?' Mrs Wenthorpe asked, looking at her niece's flushed face and bright eyes. 'You do look a little ferverish.'

'No, I do not want to spoil your enjoyment. Nor Tom's.' She smiled wanly towards her brother who was flirting outrageously with a young lady dressed as Nell Gwyn. 'Perhaps if I could lie down for a spell. . .'

'Of course.' Mrs Burford beckoned to her companion. 'Jane shall take you to her room.'

Miss Whiting hurried forward and, putting her arm around her, helped her from the room. They moved slowly across the head of the stairs, just as the Marquis of Longham arrived, magnificent in the gold-braided green uniform of an officer of the Ninety-fifth, the elite Rifle Regiment. He handed his shako and sword-belt to a footmen and mounted the stairs. 'Why, Miss Wenthorpe,' he said when he saw she was being supported by Miss Whiting, 'Is something amiss?'

She glanced up at him and wished she had not. She felt the colour flood into her cheeks and for a fleeting moment his hazel eyes seemed to be looking right into her head and she thought she really would faint.

'Miss Wenthorpe felt unwell,' Miss Whiting said.

'Then allow me,' he said, and before she could protest had swept Lydia up into his arms. 'Lead the way, ma'm.'

Ignoring Lydia's feeble protests, he carried her up

to the next floor behind Miss Whiting and gently
deposited her on that lady's bed. 'Thank you,' Lydia
murmured, wishing they would both go away, not so
much because she had to make the transformation
to the Count, but because their sympathy was so ill-
deserved; and not only that, she had suddenly discovered how comfortable it was in his lordship's
arms; she had not wanted him to put her down. 'I
shall be right as ninepence as soon as I've rested.'

'Are you quite sure?' he asked. 'Shall I send for a
physician?'

'No,' she said quickly and a trifle too sharply so
that he looked down at her in surprise. 'Pray do not
concern yourself, my lord. Go back to the ball.'

He looked as if he might like to stay but as Miss
Whiting showed every sign of obeying the invalid's
entreaty he had perforce to follow. 'If you make a
recover before the evening is ended, I shall claim my
reward,' he said with a smile which seemed to say he
did not, for a moment, believe in her illness. 'A
waltz.' Then, seeing Miss Whiting's disapproving
look, he preceded her from the room.

It was guilt and nothing else which made her think
he knew the truth, she decided, and now was definitely not the time to dwell on the last time they had
waltzed. She listened to the murmur of their voices
as they went downstairs; she must concentrate on
what she had to do. She scrambled from the bed and
crept to the door. The sound of music and lively
chatter carried up to her but there was no one about
and she made her way along the corridor to the
Count's room, where she changed into the Count's

costume and carefully made up her face. She took a
last look at her reflection in the cheval-glass, decided
it would do, and, taking her courage in her hands,
went downstairs, where Frank met her at the door
of the ballroom.

'Ah, there you are, Maurice,' he said, beaming at
her and leading her to where Mrs Wenthorpe sat
chatting to Lady Thornton and Mrs Burford. The
latter was making some comment about the Count
being late.

'He is a charming guest,' she was saying. 'I do
hope you will be kind to him.' This last was
addressed to Mrs Wenthorpe, who was obviously
puzzled.

Frank stepped in quickly to make the introduc-
tions. The Count bent low over Lady Thornton's
hand, murmuring, '*Vraiment*, it ees a *plaisir*, my
lady,' and then looked up to find her aunt squinting
short-sightedly at her. She knew a moment of panic
and then her aunt said,

'If you will excuse me, I see Lady Melbourne. It
is an age since I saw her.' And with that she swept
away to have a comfortable gossip with her old
friend.

'That was the cut direct,' Lady Thornton said and
added with a sigh, 'But then Agatha Wenthorpe
never did have any manners. It is to be hoped she
does not give you a disgust for London Society, for
we do not all behave so badly.'

'Pray, think no more of it,' Lydia said, noticing
that Frank had seized the opportunity afforded by
her ladyship's momentary inattention to take her

daughter off to dance. 'They are a 'andsome pair, *n'est-ce pas*?' she said, as Lady Thornton snapped her fan shut in annoyance.

'This is her come-out year, did you know?' her ladyship said, but before Lydia could frame a reply she added, 'She is so much in demand and so innocent that I have to watch that she is not taken in by every rake in town.'

'Monsieur Burford? A rake?' queried Lydia, trying not to smile at the idea.

'Well, perhaps not, but he is not suitable, not suitable at all.' She sighed. 'His mother is one of my oldest friends and so I cannot be blunt about it, but if he does not cease his dangling I shall have to swallow my sensibility and say something.'

'Dangle, what is dangle, my lady?' Lydia asked innocently. 'This word I know not.'

She smiled. 'I had forgot you were not English. It is a silly word meaning he would like to offer for Amelia.'

'Oh, this I comprehend. But Miss Thornton has, perhaps, many offers?'

'Indeed, yes. But her papa is particular whom she entertains; we are, after all, one of the oldest families in the kingdom.' She paused, then went on, 'You, I collect, also come from a very old family. I have heard your story from our hostess, so you need not be shy of telling me.'

'What 'as *madame* said?'

'Why, that you are going back to France to find your fortune.' She laughed in an embarrassed way.

'Not that you need it particularly, for I am told your papa did well in Canada.'

'There is no more to add,' Lydia said. 'You are well informed.'

This seemed to satisfy her ladyship and she smiled, holding out her hand to her daughter who was returning on Frank's arm at the end of the dance. 'Come, Amelia, and meet the Comte de Clancy.'

A moment later, Lydia was leading Amelia out on to the floor, praying that the next few minutes would soon be over and she could escape. She was acutely aware of the eyes of half London Society following her progress and none more than those of the Marquis of Longham, who stood languidly in the doorway, as if wondering whether it was worth his while to continue into the room. Her costume seemed to her to be transparent and her full wig doubly false. She watched him walk over to Lady Thornton and engage that lady in conversation and knew with certainty that the subject of their discourse was a certain Comte de Clancy.

'Such a beautiful couple, don't you think?' Lady Thornton murmured. 'And the young man has prospects, or he will have, once he has been to France to fetch a fortune in gold and jewels from a secret hiding place.'

'If they are still there,' Jack said laconically, regarding the young couple as the dance brought them nearer. 'It must be a long time since they were hid.'

'He is confident of success.' She bowed and smiled as the Count and her daughter went by. 'He is not

wanting in conduct either, considering he is not an
Englishman. A true gentleman, in fact.'

'Indeed, ma'am,' his lordship said in his lazy way.
'I find the young pup a trifle effeminate.'

'That is the sort of remark one would expect from
a campaign soldier who had not been much in
Society himself,' her ladyship retorted.

'Let us hope my taste improves with the Season.'
He smiled. 'I think I will play a hand of faro.' With
a last look at Lydia and a bow to her ladyship, he
left the room, much to Lydia's relief when she saw
him go.

Without the Marquis's eagle eye on her, Lydia
found her taut muscles relaxing and looked down to
find Miss Wenthorpe smiling up at her with corn-
flower-blue eyes twinkling. 'Do not mind Mama,'
she said. 'She will have me betrothed before the
Season is out but you do not have to make an offer
this very night.'

Lydia chuckled; Amelia was far from the insipid,
biddable girl she had at first supposed and it made it
doubly hard to continue the deception, but it was
nearly over; two more minutes and the Count could
take his leave. 'Your *maman* will first wish to be
sure I 'ave my fortune recovered, *n'est-ce pas?*'

Amelia laughed. 'Something like that, and in the
meantime I shall amuse myself and keep her and
everyone else guessing.'

'I see *ma'm'selle* is a young lady of very great
sense,' Lydia said, bowing to Amelia's curtsy as the
dance ended. She offered her arm to promenade the
floor and found herself looking into the amused eyes

of Douglas Fincham. She flashed him a look of triumph as she returned her partner to her mother. She had done it! Tom's wager was safe and it was time for the shepherdess to reappear.

'You will join us for supper, Count?' her ladyship said. 'We make a small party at one of the tables.'

'I. . . I beg you will excuse me.' Everyone seemed to be looking at her and she could not wait to divest herself of the costume and with it her false identity. 'I 'ave to go to France early in the morning.'

'Leaving?' queried Mrs Burford, who stood within earshot. 'So soon?'

'*Je regrette*, I must. An urgent message.'

'How disappointing for everyone,' Lady Thornton said. 'But do promise to call on us the moment you return to England. We shall all be agog to hear of the success of your venture.'

'*Mais oui*. Your servant, my lady. Miss Thornton.' She bowed to Lady Thornton and her daughter and thanked Mrs Burford for her hospitality, and with their cries of '*Bon voyage!*' ringing in her ears hurried off in search of her brother.

She ran him to earth at last in one of the gaming-rooms, where he was about to sit down to a hand with Frank Burford, Lord Thornton—a jovial gentleman, though many said he lived under the cat's paw—and the Marquis of Longham. She acknowledged them briefly and turned to Tom. 'Cousin, I would 'ave a word before you begin.'

'Later, Maurice.' He began shuffling a pack of cards.

'*Maintenant, s'il vous plaît.*'

Reluctantly Tom put down the cards and followed her to a corner. 'Will you never learn?' she whispered. 'What stakes are you playing for now?'

'Counters.' He grinned. 'No more than counters.'

She did not believe him for a minute, but she let it pass. 'As long as it has nothing to do with the Comte de Clancy, because he is about to disappear for good.'

He grinned like schoolboy. 'You've done it?'

'Yes. Witnessed by Mr Fincham, the Count has danced with Miss Thornton and reluctantly declined an invitation to join her and her mama for supper. Now I am going to make an end of the odious gentleman.'

'Odious! I thought him a devil of a fine fellow.' He was suddenly serious. 'Thank you, little sister.'

She turned to leave, only to find Lord Longham at her elbow. 'I'll not be above a minute,' he said to Tom. 'I want a word with the Count on a private matter.'

'*Moi*?' Just in time, Lydia remembered her role. 'I am much in 'aste, my lord.'

'I would like some conversation with you, Count, about your family. I have heard some talk of jewels. . .'

She turned startled eyes on him and for a split-second her guard dropped, but she recovered herself and smiled. 'Jewels, my lord?'

'They were lost in France, I believe?'

Just when she thought it was all over and she had come out of it unscathed, this tall, far too perceptive, far too handsome man had contrived to overset her.

She knew her face betrayed her fear and yet a streak of obstinacy in her drove her to continue the charade. '*Mais oui*. Why do you ask?'

'I was there recently and. . .' He paused, watching her face.

'I go there myself tomorrow,' she said. 'Tonight I leave to catch the packe' for Calais.'

'Forgive me, but is that wise? Things are very bad there still and the old aristocracy are not welcome, especially if they go to reclaim their lands.'

'Poof!' she said, tilting her chin into the air. 'The Comte de Clancy 'as not the fear.'

He smiled slowly, his suspicions confirmed by that one word. 'No,' he said softly. 'I did not think you had.' What, in heaven's name, was she playing at? He looked closely at her. How had she managed to make that lovely face so plump and dissolute, like a man who spent all his nights at the card table and his days in bed? It was unbelievably clever. But it was the height of foolishness too. He felt tempted to tell her so; tempted, too, to put up a finger and trace the outline of her cheek and find the real Lydia underneath the paint, but that would certainly cause a stir. Already the gentlemen at the table were looking at them in curiosity. He turned to go back to them. 'I will await your return with some impatience.'

'You may have a very long wait,' she muttered to herself as she climbed the stairs and opened the door to the room the Count was supposed to have been occupying for the whole of the previous week. She hurried across to the bed where she had left the shepherdess costume behind the drawn curtains. It was over. Laughing softly to herself and unbuttoning her coat, she pulled the curtains back and gasped in surprise to find Douglas Fincham, lounging back against the pillows with her shepherdess costume and the lamb muff draped across his thighs. His supercilious smile sent her newly restored spirits diving into her red-heeled shoes.

'Felicitations might have been in order,' he said slowly, 'had you not cheated.'

CHPTER FIVE

'WHAT are you doing here?' she demanded, too angry to be afraid, though her knees were knocking and her hands shaking. 'Get out at once!'

'And if I don't, will you shout for help?' He dropped her dress and sat up in leisurely fashion. 'Dare you?'

One side of her brain was in a panic, the other side seemed to be coolly wondering what he intended to do, for he had not come simply to congratulate her and admit he had lost his wager. Seduction flitted across her mind, but he had nothing to gain from that. She could try making a bolt for Miss Whiting's room, but he was in possession of her dress and she needed it. 'I insist you leave this room,' she said, marvelling at the coolness of her voice. 'You have lost your wager; let it be an end of it.'

'I do not consider it lost,' he said smoothly, flicking a speck from his sleeve. 'A costume ball where everyone is dressed in ridiculous clothes is not a fair test. You have cheated and your brother's vowels will not be returned to him until the Count has appeared in modern dress.' His dark eyes glittered. 'In truth, I like you so much as the Comte de Clancy, I think you should maintain the imperso-

nation at least until my parents give their own ball
in May for the come-out of my sister.'

'If you think I will do that. . .'

'I should like to see Miss Amelia Thornton accept
the Count as a genuine suitor,' he went on, as if she
had not spoken. 'It should not be difficult; the young
lady has astonishingly bad taste, don't you know?'

Lydia laughed suddenly. 'Oh, has she rejected
you, sir? Are you jealous of the Count? Or perhaps
someone with a little more substance? Who can it
be?'

She knew she had gone too far when he scrambled
off the bed and grabbed her shoulders, shaking her
until her teeth rattled. 'You will do as I say, hoyden,'
he muttered through clenched teeth. 'You will act
the Count until I tell you to stop.'

'And if I don't?' She found her voice at last.

'The world will know the Comte de Clancy for an
impostor.'

'I care nothing for that,' she snapped. 'I intend to
tell Miss Thornton the truth this very night. You had
not supposed I would leave her in ignorance?'

He grinned and released her. 'Neither Lady
Thornton nor her daughter will openly admit they
were gulled by a girl in men's clothes, but they will
certainly be angry enough to confirm the story that
the Count was a young nobody masquerading as a
nobleman in order to deprive the real Comte de
Clancy of his fortune. That is an indictable offence.
You will be called to book and how will my Lord
Wenthorpe view his progeny then?' He paused to let
his words sink in. 'Add to that the fact that Tom

Wenthorpe would rather anything than have the world know he has reneged on a wager. He will sacrifice his sister without a qualm.'

The near-truth of this bit into her anger and weakened her determination to resist him; it was as much as she could do not to let him see it. 'There is no Comte de Clancy and you know it.'

'Do I?' His smile frightened her more than his anger. 'I should not be so sure, if I were you. If the true Count were to arrive on the scene. . .' He left the sentence unfinished and strode to the door, where he turned with his hand on the knob. 'For the pleasure of seeing Miss Thornton fall in love with one of her own sex, I shall make no effort to find him until after my parents' ball.'

The door shut on him and Lydia sank on to the bed. Blackmail! Oh, how foolish they had been to suppose that that odious creature would be content to accept defeat. Now what should she do? The whole charade must be stopped at once and she must find Tom and tell him so.

Fumbling in her haste, she stripped off her costume and put it in the Count's portmanteau, then washed the paint from her face and dressed once again as the shepherdess. With a quick look in the mirror to pat her own curls into place, she hurried downstairs in search of her brother. She could not find him in the card-room and had gone to look for him in the crowded ballroom when Mrs Burford spotted her. 'Miss Wenthorpe, you have made a recovery, I see.'

'Yes, thank you. I was looking for. . .'

'What a pity you missed the dear Count. He has been called away suddenly. News from France, I believe. Perhaps when he returns you will meet him. I do hope so, for he is so young and I do not like to think of him being obliged to sort out his affairs without family or friends to help him.'

'I am sure he has friends,' Lydia said distractedly. 'Have you seen Tom?'

'No. Should you have got up? You still do not look quite the thing.' She caught sight of her son dancing with Amelia a second time and gave a tut of annoyance. 'Look at Frank with Miss Thornton again. He will give the scandal-mongers something to stir in their broth besides sugar and Letty won't like it above half.' The dance ended and she beckoned her son to her. He returned Amelia to Lady Thornton's side and strolled over. 'What is it, Mama?'

'Should you have taken Miss Thornton on to the floor again, Frank? Her mama is already hinting that the Count will be offering for her very soon.'

Frank spluttered and hastily pretended to wipe his face with his handkerchief. 'Really, Mama?' he said, making an effort to suppress his mirth. 'And will she accept him, do you think?'

'Why you should find it amusing I do not know,' his mother said coldly. 'I am grieved to see a son of mine so wanting in conduct, but I will not give Letty the satisfaction of seeing me give you a scold in public. We shall speak of it later.' She paused and looked around her. 'Do you know where Mrs

Wenthorpe is? Lydia is not feeling quite the thing and ought to go home.'

'No, no, I am perfectly recovered, Mrs Burford,' Lydia protested. 'And I want to enjoy the rest of the evening.'

Something in her voice made Frank realise something was seriously amiss. 'Then let us dance.'

She attempted to laugh. 'It will be the second time.'

'So it will. Let it not be said I am not equal-handed.' With that he bowed and led her on to the floor.

'What is it, Lydia?' His voice was full of concern.

'That hateful Douglas Fincham will not accept defeat. He was waiting for me when I went to change my costume. He is threatening to produce the real Comte de Clancy.'

'God! Oh, beg pardon, but is there such a person?'

'I did not think so, but what if there is? He also said he will put it abroad that Tom has turned his back on a debt of honour. Oh, Frank, what a coil we have got ourselves into.'

'We must tell Amelia — Miss Thornton,' he corrected himself hurriedly. 'There is no question of it now. And, whatever Fincham says, the Count must disappear.' He laughed lightly. 'I do not fancy him as a rival, anyway; he is too handsome by far.'

'But what about Mr Fincham?'

'Leave him to Tom and me. Now, you go and find Am. . . Miss Thornton and tell her all.'

'Will she understand?'

'Of course,' he said, drawing her away from the

line of dancers and ignoring the cries which followed them that they had spoiled the set.

Lydia was not so sure of Amelia's forbearance and she dreaded the coming interview. How could she make it sound any less than the despicable, humiliating insult that it was? How could Tom have asked it of her? However could she have contemplated doing it?

She found Amelia sitting with her mother, sipping a cooling cordial, and was made to feel even more of a villain by the young lady's solicitude for her health.

'Oh, I am feeling much better, thank you, Miss Thornton,' Lydia answered, looking into her eyes in an effort to convey the urgency of her request. 'I was on my way to take a stroll on the terrace when it occurred to me you might like to accompany me.'

'Indeed yes, it is so hot in here.' She turned to Lady Thornton. 'May I?'

Her ladyship nodded and the two young ladies went, arm in arm, down to one of the lower salons which they knew led to the garden. Here Mrs Wenthorpe sat with her wig askew, playing loo with three other matrons. She looked up and enquired if Lydia was recovered and, being given an affirmative answer and the information that Lydia was going with Miss Thornton for some fresh air, turned again to her hand. 'Then mind you do not stay out too long and catch a chill,' she said as the girls passed out on to the terrace.

'Oh, this is better,' Amelia said, breathing deeply. 'I do not wonder at your feeling faint.'

They began pacing slowly along the terrace, which was lit unevenly by the light coming from the windows of the first-floor ballroom above it. Lydia was silent, unable to find the words to begin her confession, while her companion prattled on about the different costumes the guests had chosen, the fineness of the night and the brightness of the moon. There was nothing for it but to plunge right in.

'Did you like the Comte de Clancy, Miss Thornton?'

'Why, yes, I find him charming. Why do you ask?'

'I want to talk to you about him. . .'

'If you are going tell me about that silly family quarrel, I have no wish to hear about it,' Amelia said quickly. 'I will not hear a word against your cousin.'

'You have not developed a *tendre* for him already, have you?'

'No, of course not.' She stopped walking to turn towards Lydia. 'If you have come to warn me off him, you may save your breath.'

'But if he were not all he appeared to be?'

'In what way? Not a Count? Not French? Not rich? What care I? I would be the last one to expose him and I hope you may not either.'

'No, I will not expose him. I thought perhaps you might.'

'Why should I? He does me no harm.' Amelia laughed suddenly. 'I am in no danger of losing my head to that young man because, you see, there is someone. . .' She stopped and laughed. 'But it will do Mama good to think I have.'

'What do you mean? Do you know. . .?' She
stopped suddenly because she had heard footsteps
on the paving and looked up to see Tom and the
Marquis strolling towards them, both smoking cigar-
illos. They threw them down and ground them under
their heels as they approached the girls.

'Miss Thornton,' Tom said, striding forward. 'I
searched for you everywhere to claim the dance you
promised me and was so blue-devilled when you
could not be found, I came out to blow a cloud to
console myself. I found his lordship on the same
tack.' He grinned up at the Marquis who was at least
half a head taller than he was. 'He had lost Lydia,
you see.'

'His lordship knew I had gone to lie down,' Lydia
said, trying not to meet Jack's searching eyes.

The Marquis bowed to both girls and addressed
himself to Lydia. 'I learned you had returned to the
ballroom, Miss Wenthorpe, and, if you recall, I had
earlier intimated that I would claim the honour of a
dance.' He sighed theatrically. 'I was told you
seemed to be searching for someone and hoped it
might be me. . .'

'I was looking for Miss Thornton,' she said. 'And
we were having a private conversation.'

'Oh, have we interrupted?' Tom said, gaily. 'But
you girls can have a coze at any time. We claim our
partners, do we not, Jack?'

Jack did no more than smile; he was gazing down
into Lydia's eyes as if he were Dr Mesmer, inducing
such a trance-like state in her, she could not move.
'I. . .' She began and then stopped. What had she

been going to say? I am a fool? I am more than a fool, I am a fraud, not fit to be in polite society, not fit to be noticed by anyone upright and honourable? And my brother, who seems to have made a friend of you and calls you by your given name, is even now doing his best to stop me from blurting it all out. She knew without be able to take her eyes from the Marquis's face that this was true; Tom was fidgeting beside her. Why should he be so concerned, when to all intents and purposes the charade was at an end? He did not know of Douglas Fincham's new demands—unless Frank had told him. But, if he had, Tom would never have agreed to them. Would he? *Would* he? She heard retreating footsteps and knew her brother was taking Amelia away, presumably to go back to the ballroom, and still she stood looking into the dark pools of the Marquis's eyes.

As the moon came out from behind a cloud and lit her face with its soft light, he took her hands in his and held her at arm's length. Her eyes were bright, so bright, he could almost have sworn there were tears on her lashes. That the oh, so level-headed Miss Wenthorpe could be moved to tears was something which affected him strangely. He wanted to take her in his arms and comfort her, to tell her there was nothing so bad they could not overcome it together. The music of the ballroom seemed a million miles away, a background to a moment when time stood still. He did not speak. He did not even smile. Only his eyes conveyed his message, and it was one Lydia did not understand.

She felt as though she was wrapped in a cocoon, a world where nothing and no one else existed. She looked from his eyes to his full mouth and slightly parted lips, over his strong jaw to his throat where a quickening pulse beat just above his stiff uniform collar. She lifted her face and looked once more into his eyes. They were still regarding her as if to commit every feature to memory, drawing her face, line by line, in some corner of his brain to be brought out at a later date, perfect in every detail. Lost to any sense of time and place, she felt as though she was floating, without limbs, floating up into the star-filled sky with nothing to anchor her to the earth but the firm grip of his hands. She clung to them.

They did not kiss; it was not a moment for kissing. He knew that if he bent his head and put his lips to hers he would break that timeless moment. As the strains of a waltz reached them from that far-off other world of harsh colours, loud voices, intrigue and gossip, he slipped one arm about her waist. Slowly, without taking their eyes from each other, they began to dance. With skirts swaying about his long green-clad legs, she allowed herself to melt into him, to become moulded into one being with him. It was as if the music were playing for them alone, and she did not want it to stop; she wanted it to go on forever. But it did, all too soon, brought to an end by the flourish of the orchestra and the polite applause from the ballroom. He stopped and brought her hand to his lips. She shivered.

'Thank you,' he said softly, as if he was thanking her for more than a dance.

She gathered herself together at last. 'I think we should go back indoors.' Her voice was a little shaky. 'Tom and Miss Thornton have returned, and if we are missed. . .'

'We did not come out here together and we need not return together.' He sounded so normal as he tucked her hand under his arm that she believed the moment had been of little importance to him. 'I will escort you to the door and then stay and smoke another cigarillo.'

'Thank you, my lord.'

'You do not mean to disappear again, I hope?'

'Disappear? No, my lord. I am quite recovered.'

'I am glad to hear it. You do not suggest to me a young lady given to fits of swooning.'

'I am not,' she said. 'It never happened before. . .'

He smiled down at her. 'Then it must have been something very serious to make it necessary for you to flee the ballroom earlier this evening. I hope it had nothing to do with my arrival.'

'Good heavens, no!' she said quickly.

'So! You did flee and the headache was false.' He stopped and turned towards her. 'Miss Wenthorpe, if there is anything troubling you, anything at all, I beg you acquaint me with it. If I can be of assistance, I should consider it an honour. . .'

Her trill of a laugh echoed falsely. 'Now, why, sir, should you be forever suggesting something is troubling me? It is not very flattering, you know. There is nothing on my mind beyond choosing which partners to dance with and whether to have the wine or the champagne.'

'Are you so empty-headed?' he asked and then answered himself. 'No, I think it has something to do with the Comte de Clancy. . .'

'The Comte de Clancy.' Did she sound as breathless as she felt? 'What is he to me?'

'Forgive me, but I had thought he was very close to you indeed.'

She thought her shaking hands would betray her and her voice was strained with the effort of keeping it light. 'A mere cousin, and one, I may say, I cannot remember ever having met.'

'He is French, is he not?' he queried, deciding to play her game until he found out the reason for it.

'Yes,' she said, unwilling to say any more.

'But not brought up in France?'

'No, Canada.'

'But I have heard talk of gold and jewels hidden in France.'

'Tattle, my lord, mere tattle.'

'You do not believe there can be any substance in the story, then?'

'What I believe is of no consequence.' Oh, why was he persisting with this inquisition? She did not want to talk about the Count; she wanted to keep everything as it had been a few moments before, when they had been so close, so at one with each other. Now he had introduced a discordant note and spoiled it all.

'But it is of consequence to me,' he said.

She turned on him, angry now. 'Why?'

'Why?' He seemed to be considering the question.

'Because, among several other things, I am concerned for Miss Thornton. . .'

'Miss Thornton!' She stared at him in astonishment and then her heart nearly stopped beating. He cared for Amelia Thornton and was jealous of the Count. And Amelia herself had intimated that there might be someone else. Could it be the Marquis? Was Amelia deliberately trying to make him jealous by allowing the Count to pay attention to her? She had succeeded admirably if she was, more than she realised, for Lydia herself was consumed by the little green monster. It would be laughable if it did not hurt so much.

'She is too young and innocent to be treated so shabbily,' he said.

'By whom, my lord?'

'By the Comte de Clancy. Whom did you think I meant?'

'I am not responsible for the actions of my relatives,' she said, stung to a reply she was immediately ashamed of. 'Do not come to me with your complaints.'

He smiled, but it was the smile of the tiger. 'I would go to the Count himself if I could find him,' he said. 'But he is a very elusive gentleman. Now you see him, now you don't. I had hoped you would put me on his track.'

'I am afraid I cannot help you,' she said coolly as they stopped at the door. In order to give the appearance of observing the proprieties it had been left sightly open and a shaft of light lit the terrace. 'I have no idea where the Comte de Clancy might be found.'

With this whopper, she stepped into the room, where her aunt still sat at the card table with her cronies. She had a pile of coins at one elbow and a half-empty glass of wine at the other. It crossed Lydia's mind that if her aunt had been doing her job as chaperon conscientiously there would have been no ticklish exchange with the Marquis which had put her in such a quiver. But neither would there have been that earlier silent moment, stretching to eternity, and the waltz in the moonlight. She had — though she could not tell exactly when it had happened — fallen head over heels in love with the Marquis of Longham, and the realisation had come almost simultaneously with the knowledge that his affections were engaged elsewhere and he had only been flirting with her. He had no business lowering his famous hauteur and allowing her to see the real man — no business at all; he should have stuck to calling her a hoyden and delivering lectures on her behaviour; that way she would still be heart-whole. Raventrees beckoned to her irresistibly; there she might learn to forget.

The evening dragged on and ended without her being able to speak to Amelia again and Tom seemed to be avoiding her for he had partners for every dance until the time came to take their leave. She could not even talk to him on the drive home because of their aunt's presence, and as soon as they arrived he gave a huge yawn and took himself off to bed. It was not until they met at the breakfast table that she was able to tell him of Douglas Fincham's blackmail and her determination to return home as soon as possible.

Unconcerned, he continued liberally spreading blackberry conserve on to his bread and butter. 'Oh, Lydia, do stop prosing on, there's a good girl. You know you can't go home yet and the evening was a prodigious success. Mrs Burford puts it all down to the mysterious Count. You were exquisite and I have no doubt could carry it off much longer.'

'I could not! And I will not! Douglas Fincham must be silenced. For good.'

He glanced up at her and smiled. 'Murder? Really, Lydia, I had not thought you capable of that.'

'Oh, don't be so idiotish. You know what I mean. Mr Fincham could continue blackmailing indefinitely. . .'

'It will only be another month.'

'And another and another.'

'No. It is double or quits and that will be an end of it.'

'Double or quits!' Her voice rose in a shriek. 'Do you mean. . .? Have you. . .? Oh, no, not even you would behave so shabbily. . .'

'Shabbily, Lydia? Why, it is a great compliment to you. Not even the great Mrs Siddons could do better, believe me.'

'If you were not my brother, I would. . .'

He licked blackberry conserve from his fingers, one by one. 'But think how dull life would be if I were not.'

She could think of no words to express the anger
and frustration she felt. He took her so much for
granted that he could not even conceive that she
would not do as he asked, but this time he had gone
too far. Much too far. She left the table and slammed
out of the room.

She had not cooled down by the time she had
changed into riding dress and taken one of the
mounts from the stables, flung a saddle on it and
galloped out of the mews. Scrivens's cry of 'Wait,
Miss Lydia,' fell on deaf ears.

If she had not been a good horsewoman, she
would have sent more than one pedestrian flying and
entangled herself with several carriages and carts
before she had gone a hundred yards, but she was a
fearless rider and her mount used to her ways, so
that all that happened was that she left the pedes-
trians shaking their fists and the coach drivers shouting abuse, and a few minutes later she turned into
the park, almost oversetting a landaulet which was
coming out of the gate. The carriage was hauled to
a stop by the driver but Lydia could not have
stopped if she had wanted to. It was the last straw as
far as her stallion was concerned; he bolted with her
and she needed all her wits about her to stay on his
back.

With her head low over the horse's neck, the
ground became a blur as it passed under her. The
sound of hoofbeats thundered in her ears and
branches whipped past her face as she fought to
control her mount. On and on they sped, until the
crowds were left behind. She did not see the fallen

tree across the path, nor did she hear the sound of
other hoofs. A warning shout from somewhere
behind her came too late as the horse refused to
take the obstacle; she was suddenly airborne and
then the ground came up to meet her. With a bone-
crunching thump she found merciful darkness.

The first sensation she had when she began to
regain her senses was that she was lying somewhere
soft and warm and that something had touched her
lips, something light, like a leaf or a moth. There
was a mist before her eyes which made everything
indistinct, but slowly the blur resolved itself into the
handsome features of the Marquis of Longham. His
head was so close she could feel the warmth of his
breath on her cheek and he was regarding her with
an expression which was almost like. . . No, she
would not allow herself to go on; he was only
showing concern.

'Oh, you little fool,' he said, but he made it sound
like an endearment. 'Are you hurt?'

She lifted her head and realised he was kneeling
on the ground and she was leaning against his thighs
with her head on his arm. 'I do not think so,' she
murmured, sinking back again, too comfortable to
want to move. 'My lord, how came you here?'

He smiled and brushed a twig from her hair,
steeling himself to resist the temptation to lower his
head and kiss her slightly parted lips a second time;
if he succumbed when she was conscious enough to
know what was happening, nothing would ever be
the same again. She would either think him an
incorrigible rake and never speak to him again or

she would assume that he meant to marry her, and he was not prepared for either interpretation. 'I was returning from a ride and saw you enter the park as if all the demons of hell were at your heels. So did a great many other people, including the occupants of that landaulet you nearly overturned. I collect you owe them an apology.' This was more like the Marquis she knew, giving her a rake-down. 'Don't you know better than to ride like that in traffic?'

'Of course, but my horse. . .'

'He is cropping not two yards away,' he said. 'Once he had rid himself of his burden, he had no inclination to continue. Why were you so foolish as to ride an animal too powerful for you? And where is your groom?'

She could not be such a rabshackle as to let Scrivens take the blame. Reluctantly she sat up. 'I rode out by myself. There is nothing to that, I often do.'

'In Suffolk perhaps it might be allowed, but in town?' His voice was censorious. 'I think not, Miss Wenthorpe.'

'I can do without a jawbation from you,' she said and though she spoke sharply she knew he was right. It was too much to hope that there was no one who knew her among the people who had seen the incident. 'You are not my guardian.'

'If I were,' he retorted swiftly, 'I would make sure you had more care for the safety of your mount.'

She scrambled to her feet and dusted down her habit. 'Oh, there was I thinking you cared that I might be hurt and all the time you were only concerned for the horse. Well, you may save your sympathy for either of us. I shall ride him back.'

'No. His fetlock looks bruised. Tewkes has gone to fetch a carriage to take you home. Besides, you are still too shaken. Do you think you can walk to the end of the path? It is too narrow here for a vehicle.' He took her arm to help her.

She shook herself free, stooped to pick up her hat and strode off ahead of him. Half amused, half annoyed, he shrugged his broad shoulders and followed her. She was the most infuriating female he had ever come across, alluringly feminine at one moment with big soft eyes and tender lips that made a man forget all propriety, and almost mannish the next. She was a bruising rider and had a deft pair of hands with the ribbons of the phaeton, he had noticed, and he would not be at all surprised to learn she was a crack shot as well. He supposed it was being brought up in a male-dominated household. Why her father had not engaged a female companion for her he could not fathom, and as for her aunt. . . He stopped to smile at the vision of Mrs Wenthorpe which came to him; the aunt was so eccentric as to be a positive antidote. How could the poor girl be expected to find a husband? As soon as an eligible male put in an appearance he would either take her for a hoydenish flirt of the kind who abounded in the hazy *demi-monde* on the fringe of polite Society and not treat her seriously or he would be frightened off by her masculine accomplishments. Unless, of course, he could outdo her. Somehow the thought of that amused him.

She turned and noticed his smile. 'I am glad to see my mishap diverts you, my lord,' she said.

'Not at all. I was thinking of something else.'

Or someone, she thought; someone like Amelia Thornton, petite and feminine with big blue eyes and golden curls, who would never put a foot outside the door without a female companion and a groom to accompany her and would never dream of galloping. No wonder he smiled. 'It is hardly gallant to have your mind otherwhere when you are with a lady,' she said, then, unaccountably, laughed. 'But then I am not a lady but a tomboy, isn't that what you said? And now I have convinced you of it.'

'No more than before.' His voice had lost its bantering tone. 'But I can't think why you see the necessity. I liked you best as the gentle shepherdess. Now, there was a lady.'

She was silent. Why did he have to remind her of the ball? Speaking of the shepherdess also brought the Count to mind and she did not want to be reminded of him. For a man who did not exist the Comte de Clancy seemed to be everywhere; he was in her head, in Tom's hopes, part of Douglas's greed and his name was on everyone's lips. She had created a monster and the monster would destroy her.

A closed carriage, driven by Tewkes, came along the path and stopped. Jack hurried forward to open the door and let down the step and, when she had climbed in and the door shut again, jumped up to replace Tewkes on the box. 'I'll drive,' he told him, picking up the reins. 'You walk the horses back.'

As if one scolding were not enough, as soon as the Marquis had left her in the care of her aunt, Lydia was subjected to another. 'Such conduct will not do,' that good lady said, wagging her closed fan at her niece. 'Riding out alone is bad enough to make everyone think you fast, but then to compound that by galloping and falling off. . .'

'I did not fall, I was thrown, and no one saw me except his lordship and I do not believe he will tattle about it.' Lydia smiled in spite of her aching bones. 'The Wenthorpe reputation for horsemanship is still intact.'

'I was not referring to your reputation as a rider,' her aunt cried, throwing up her hands. 'It is your conduct which is at fault. I cannot think what came into you, rushing off like that. Scrivens said you would not wait for him.'

'I was in a hurry.'

'To meet the Marquis, no doubt.'

'I did not know he would be there. I wish it had been anyone but him.'

'Do you, now?' Mrs Wenthorpe said knowingly. 'I wonder why?'

To which her niece responded by bursting into tears. This was so untypical that Mrs Wenthorpe was quite taken aback but as Lydia would not tell her what ailed her she naturally assumed her niece was in love with the tall young nobleman who had brought her home and there had been a lovers' tiff. She smiled knowingly. 'Oh, do dry your tears, child,' she said, putting her arm round Lydia's shoulders. 'You will make your face all blotchy and it is not the end of the world. The young man has invited us to join his party at the theatre tomorrow night and supper afterwards and you can make up your quarrel then. I am sure all can be resolved.'

Lydia sniffed. 'Aunt, if you think I will be seen in the company of that top-lofty, stiff-rumped, odious man, you will have to have second thoughts, for I will not go to the theatre if he is to be there and I will certainly not have supper in his company.'

'Why ever not? What has he done to upset you so?'

'Nothing but hurl insults at me.'

'Insults? He has insulted you? Then, of course, he will apologise.'

'Not he. And I will not give him the opportunity.'

'But Lydia, how did he insult you? I cannot believe he is so wanting in gentlemanly conduct.'

'I won't hear another word on the subject, Aunt, so you may save your breath. Besides, tomorrow I want to call on Lady Thornton and Miss Thornton.'

'You will do no such thing! I will never darken her doors again and neither will you.'

'Why not?' It was imperative that she finish her talk with Amelia and if her aunt had a compelling reason for cutting her ladyship it would make it decidedly awkward.

'I have known Letty Thornton ever since we were girls together but that does not give her the right to criticise me in that sly fashion,' her aunt said. 'She said some very strange things to me at the ball, blaming me for keeping up a family feud when the poor Count is so young and all alone in the world and other such foolish talk which I did not understand but which I am sure was meant to be insulting. Letty Thornton must be going off her head to be taken in by that young man. He is no more the Comte de Clancy than I am the Queen of Sheba and so I told her. I will not stoop to call on her again until she comes to her senses and I will be obliged if you will not call on her daughter either. Goosecaps, the pair of them.' She paused, for Lydia had gone very white and looked about to faint. 'Are you ill, child?' She helped her niece to a chair and pulled the bell-rope by the fireplace. 'That fall has shaken you more than you realised. Why did you not say, instead of letting me ramble on? I must send for the physician.'

'No, Aunt, I am perfectly well. I will lie down until dinnertime.'

A footman arrived and was sent in search of Lydia's maid and when Betty arrived Lydia was placed in her care. 'There is a paregoric in the chest in my room,' Mrs Wenthorpe instructed her. 'Give Miss Lydia a draught and see that she rests until dinner.'

The scolding was forgotten as Lydia was put to bed and cosseted like an invalid. It did nothing to make her feel any less guilty. The hateful masquerade had affected her aunt now and that was the outside of enough. She would confess all and hope for forgiveness. She would do it after dinner when they were comfortably sitting in the withdrawing-room over the teacups.

Even then fate conspired against her. Dinner was

to be *en famille* and at six o'clock she returned downstairs dressed in a green silk gown over an eau-de-Nil slip and made her way across the hall towards the small dining-room, just as a footman announced Mr Burford.

Mrs Wenthorpe had not yet come downstairs and Lydia went forward to greet him. 'We are about to dine,' she said, as he bowed to her. 'Would you care to join us?'

'Thank you, but I am expected at my club. I came for a private word with Tom. And you, too, if I could get you both together without Mrs Wenthorpe.'

She sent the footman to find her brother and then led the way into the library. 'You look very mysterious,' she said, managing to smile now that her decision had been made. 'Don't tell me that odious Comte de Clancy has been giving you trouble.'

'Not exactly.'

She was instantly serious. 'How not exactly?'

Tom came strolling into the room, dressed for dinner except for his cravat. 'I say, Burford, you do choose the most awkward times to come calling. I had half got the wretched thing tied to my satisfaction and had to leave it. I've already ruined three and Barber is losing patience with me. How does Jack Bellingham do it, I wonder?'

'Never mind your neckcloth, Tom,' Frank said, drawing a letter from his coat pocket, while Lydia mused on a mind's-eye picture of the Marquis tying a cravat with long, lean fingers which could be gentle too. 'Just tell me what you make of this. It was addressed to the Comte de Clancy at Burford House.'

Tom took it and read it. 'Oh, I say,' he said, then read it again, while Lydia stood impatiently tapping her foot. 'Oh, I say, what a turn up!'

'What is?' she demanded, snatching it from him. 'Let me see.'

'It has come to our notice that you are trying to trace a quantity of family jewels, left in France,' she read aloud. 'If you would care to call at our offices at your convenience, we may have something of interest to tell you concerning these jewels. Signed Charles Wilmott, Attorney.' She looked up at them. 'It must be a hoax. I'll wager Douglas Fincham is behind it. Throw it away.'

'But what if it's genuine?' Tom said.

'How can it be? We invented the whole story, remember?' She was feeling irritable and miserable enough without Tom acting as if the Count and his jewels really existed. 'If it isn't Douglas Fincham bamming, then someone else is putting us to the test and I will have nothing to do with it.'

'We can't simply ignore it,' Frank put in. 'Wilmott's is a genuine law firm, that much I know, and they would not lend their name to anything havey-cavey.'

'Then return the letter, say the Count has gone to France and cannot be contacted.'

'In that case we should not have broken the seal,' Tom said reasonably. 'And the de Clancy family *was* real; just supposing. . .'

'Just suppose nothing,' she snapped. 'I will not pose as the Count again.'

'But aren't you in the least bit curious, Lydia?' Tom went on implacably. 'After all, we might learn more of Mama's family, might even find real long-lost relations.'

'Then you go, if you are so interested,' she said, refusing to admit that she herself was curious. 'Tell them you are in charge of the Count's affairs in his absence.'

'They are lawyers, Lydia, they will not believe that without written instructions and if the story of the family feud has also reached them they will not divulge whatever information they have to me.'

'They can't have any, there is none.'

'We won't know that unless we go, will we? Oh, come on, Lydia, what harm can it do? If it looks as though he has seen through us, we'll own it all a hum.'

'Promise?'

'You have my word on it.'

'I think we should tell Aunt Aggie.'

'No!' the young men said in unison.

'But she knows more about the de Clancy family than we do. Besides, she is up in the boughs over Lady Thornton's treatment of her and all over the Count. She told me she thought the Count was an impostor. We cannot leave her in ignorance any longer.'

'Tomorrow,' Tom said. 'After we have seen the lawyer, we might have more to tell her. It might be good news. Say nothing tonight.'

Why, oh, why, she asked herself later, did she let him talk her into it? She should have stuck to her guns. The only consolation was that this was not a public appearance of the Count; no one but the lawyer need see her. But even in that she was wrong.

The first person they saw when they left the house next morning was the Marquis of Longham descending from his curricle at their door.

'Good morning, Wenthorpe,' he greeted Tom cheerfully and then looked coolly at Lydia, who became absurdly conscious of her polished hessians and close-fitting beige pantaloons which revealed rather more of her well-shaped legs than she liked. She saw his gaze roam from these up over her full-skirted frockcoat to the cravat at her throat, something which had taken her an age to tie in the latest oriental knot. She felt her cheeks flame as he lifted his eyes to her face. 'Count,' he said. 'What a pleasant surprise to see you here. I had thought you had left Burford House to go to France. I hope this may mean the rift with the family has been mended?' Lydia was conscious of the hint of sarcasm in his voice as she returned his greeting with an inclination of her head.

'It was never a very serious thing,' Tom said quickly before Lydia could speak.

She forced herself to smile and give the Count's light laugh. 'I stay with my cousins at Wenthorpe 'ouse for one day more, then I go to France.'

'Of course.' Jack bowed stiffly from the waist. 'I did not mean to pry. Is Mrs Wenthorpe at home?'

'Aunt Aggie?' queried Lydia, almost forgetting her role. 'You wish to see Aunt Aggie?'

'Well, no,' he admitted. 'It was Miss Wenthorpe I wanted to speak to.' He paused, looking directly into Lydia's eyes and making her wish the ground would open up and swallow her. 'I came to see how she goes on after her. . .her mishap and to apologise for my conduct. We had a slight difference of opinion and I had hoped to make amends. . .'

'Apologise?' Tom queried. 'I am sure no apology is necessary. On the contrary, my sister is excessively grateful for your assistance. Is that not so, Maurice?'

If he had been standing nearer, Lydia would have kicked him. Instead she was obliged to smile at the Marquis and answer. '*Mais oui*, I believe she did say something about the 'elp of your lordship.'

'But I am afraid you cannot see her this morning, Jack,' Tom said. 'She is not fully recovered — the shock, you know. She is so looking forward to the play tonight and would not for the world miss it if she can help it, so she decided to stay in bed until this evening to be sure of being well enough to attend. You understand?'

'Of course,' he said, looking at Lydia. 'Will we also have the pleasure of your company at the theatre, Count?'

'I fear not,' Lydia said. 'I 'ave to travel to Dover tonight. We catch the first tide tomorrow.'

'What a shame!' Jack said with a twinkle in his eye which was not lost on Lydia. 'I had hoped we might have an opportunity for that talk we spoke of.'

Tom looked puzzled, but Lydia smiled. 'Oh, la, I 'ad that forgot. *Je regrette*, it will 'ave to wait.'

'Of course,' he said, touching the brim of his brown beaver with a kid-gloved hand. 'I shall look forward to it.' He climbed back into his curricle and took up the reins. 'Will you tell Miss Wenthorpe I called and that I am looking forward to seeing her at the theatre tonight?' And though he addressed himself to Tom it was at Lydia he looked as he spoke.

'Of course,' Tom said, grinning. 'I am sure she would not for the world disappoint you.'

'Good day to you, de Clancy. I shall look forward to seeing you on your return.' He flicked the reins to set the horses moving. 'Good day, Wenthorpe.'

'What does he want to talk to the Count about?' Tom asked, as they watched him go, then set off down the road, arm in arm like the two young men they purported to be.

'The de Clancy family. He asked to have some conversation with me at the ball.'

'Why? What is it to him?'

'I do not know. Either he has seen right through my disguise or he knows there is no Comte de Clancy and he is playing with me like a cat with a mouse. He says he would like to help me but I think he means to denounce me.'

'Of course he will not. He believes in the Comte de Clancy, as everyone does. Your disguise is perfect. As for what he thinks of Lydia, it is clear the man intends to offer for you.'

'Oh, for goodness' sake!' she said, stamping her foot. 'It is bad enough playing your April gowk

games without being hurled at the head of that. . .
that rake. I have taken an aversion to him and if you
mention his name again I shall refuse to go a step
further.'

'Very well,' he said meekly, having been confirmed in his belief that his sister was in love. 'But
do not stamp in that fashion; it reminds me of
nothing so much as a spoiled young lady and I shall
have to revise my opinion of your ability to sustain
the man.'

'Then let us abandon it at once,' she said quickly.

'After we have seen this lawyer fellow,' he said,
taking her arm and walking her swiftly in the direction of Westminster where Charles Wilmott had his
offices.

CHAPTER SIX

IF TOM had not been with her Lydia would have turned and fled as soon as she found herself in Charles Wilmott's office. It frightened her with its air of legality, its shelves of heavy books, its piles of papers on every available space and its smell of candle wax and ink. A big desk was set in the middle of the room, behind which sat a young man with fair curly locks and broad shoulders. He looked up from studying some papers as they entered and rose to greet them. 'I am Charles Wilmott,' he said, moving forward with hand extended though it was obvious from his puzzled expression that he was not sure which of his visitors was the Comte.

'I 'ave my cousin, Thomas Wenthorpe, with me,' Lydia explained, shaking his hand and bowing. ''E will perhaps 'elp me if I do not understand the Engleesh.'

'Of course. Please be seated.' He pulled forward a couple of chairs and retreated behind his desk again. 'Thank you for coming so promptly.' He paused, shuffling papers, then looked up and smiled. Lydia decided she liked his smile and at any other time might have enjoyed talking to him, but now she could do nothing but fidget and wish herself anywhere but where she was. She forced herself to lean

153

back in her chair and cross her legs in a nonchalant pose.

'I 'ave leetle time,' she said, playing with her quizzing glass. 'I 'ave to go to France.'

'I may be able to save you the journey,' he said. 'I believe you were going there to recover some jewels?'

'*Oui*,' she admitted guardedly.

'Where in France?'

Lydia looked at Tom, but he was busy studying the ceiling and no help at all. She said the first thing that came into her head. 'Fleurry; it is a leetle village between Toulouse and Bordeaux. I 'ave never been there, you understand, but *ma mère* 'ave spoken of it.' That, at least, was true; her mother had often been homesick for the little village where she was born and had told her children that one day she would go back. Sadly the dream had never been fulfilled.

'De Clancy is a very old French family, is it not?'

'Oh, yes,' Tom put in suddenly. 'My mother was very proud of her antecedents, although the family refused to acknowledge her after she became an actress. It caused her great sorrow. She always hoped they might be reconciled, but it was not to be.'

'Is that the reason for this family dispute I have heard about?'

Tom seized the opening thus provided. 'Yes, of course. So silly. What have Maurice and I to do with quarrels which happened before we were born? We are the best of friends, is that not so, Cousin?'

'*Mais oui*,' Lydia said, uncrossing and re-crossing her pantaloon-clad legs. 'But, *pardonnez*, what is it to you, *monsieur*?'

'I come to that. Can you describe the family crest?'

Lydia felt trapped. She looked again at Tom, hoping fervently for a smile and a nod which meant they could reveal their deception, but now he was studying his fingernails. 'I 'ave only seen it once or twice,' she said, remembering a pair of silver-backed hairbrushes belonging to her mother. They had had a design etched on them which might have been a crest. 'I cannot remember *exactement*, but it 'as a stag and a falcon. The falcon 'as its wings so.' She held out her arms. 'Both 'ave coronets.'

'Good. Good. What would you say if I told you I had seen it recently, here in England, on a fob?'

'I should be surprised.'

'Why?' demanded Tom. 'Your father, my uncle, may well have sold pieces when he came to England on his way to America. He would have needed the rhino for the journey and his new life, don't you think?'

'It was not sold in this country,' the lawyer said. 'It was taken from the knapsack of a dead French soldier. We believe it had been plundered. . .'

'We?' queried Lydia, thinking suddenly of Douglas Fincham and his threat to find the real Count.

'My client, a gallant officer and a true gentleman, has asked me to try and restore the find to its rightful owner.'

'A fob?' queried Tom, while Lydia digested the information that it could not be Douglas after all; he had never been a soldier, let alone a gallant one. 'I wonder why he bothers? To the victor belong the spoils and all that.'

'It is more than one piece, it is a whole cache of jewels and gold plate, though, as yet, I have only been privileged to see the fob. . .' He stopped and looked from one to the other, puzzled by their reaction. The Count was showing a decided lack of enthusiasm and the gleam in Thomas Wenthorpe's eye was one of avarice; Charles had seen that light in too many eyes to be mistaken.

Lydia was the first to come to her senses. 'It cannot belong to me,' she said firmly. 'There must be two de Clancy families. *Mon père* took all he 'ad to Canada. 'E left nothing behind.'

Mr Wilmott looked puzzled. 'But the story. . . your visit to France. . .everything I have heard. . .'

'A tale made up to gain entry to the *ton*,' she said.

'You are not the Comte de Clancy?'

'No,' said Lydia and,

'Yes,' said Tom.

Tom looked daggers at Lydia and then turned back to the lawyer. 'What my cousin means is that the title is assumed. The family name certainly is not.'

'Oh, I see.' Charles Wilmott smiled at Lydia. 'But the story of the jewels may be more true than you imagined. All I need is proof of your identity and then I will arrange for you to see the whole collection and you may be able to identify it. Have you papers?

Old letters? Other articles of jewellery which might match?'

'I do not think so. I wish you to forget it, *monsieur*. If our silly game 'as led you to believe we are the rightful owners of the property, then I am sorry. Tell the gallant officer 'is honesty does him credit, but the plunder is 'is.' She almost forgot her accent in her anxiety. 'I wish you would forget the whole affair.' She bent to pick up her beaver hat from the floor where she had put it and stood up. 'I bid you adieu, *monsieur*.'

Reluctantly Tom rose to follow her to the door. He paused and looked back at the lawyer. 'I will talk him round.'

As soon as the front door had closed and they found themselves on the step, he turned on his sister in annoyance. 'Really, Lydia, you are a sapskull; those jewels rightfully belong to us. Our mother was a de Clancy and we would have no difficulty proving that.'

'Not without admitting the Comte is a complete fabrication and involving Papa. Forget it, Tom.'

'You said you wished the Count would come to an untimely end and that is what he will do.'

'Oh, most certainly; at any rate, he must disappear, but that has to be the end of it.'

'But with the Count out of the way. . .'

She managed a faint smile. 'Oh, so we are plotting murder, are we?'

'Don't be such a pudding, Lydia. You talk as if the man were flesh and blood.'

'Oh, don't you see?' she cried, so angry and

frustrated that she had allowed her voice to rise and was receiving some surprised glances from passers-by. 'To everyone else he is real and to inherit what is his you would have to provide proof of his death to the lawyer. How do you propose to do that when he does not even exist?'

'I'll think of something.'

'For two pins I would have told Mr Wilmott the whole truth instead of only half of it. I wish I had now. Tom, what we are doing is criminal and I wish you had never talked me into it.'

'It was you hit on the idea of using the de Clancy name, not me, and you who described the crest. And I ain't letting a fortune like that go begging. Mama was a de Clancy and if there are no other relatives then I am the true heir to the fortune and if I can secure it I will be free of Douglas Fincham and can pay all my debts.'

It was no good; she could not continue to argue with him on the step where they were in danger of drawing a crowd. She clapped the beaver on her Brutus wig and hurried down the street to find a hackney, impatient to return home and throw off the hateful disguise.

He set off after her. 'Think, Lydia,' he said, too self-centred to know when to keep silent. 'Just think what it will mean. You can return to being Miss Lydia Wenthorpe and enjoy the rest of the Season. You have yet to make an appearance at Almack's; I collect Aunt Aggie said vouchers had arrived from one of the patronesses — I forget which but it is of no consequence. And she is moving heaven and earth to get you into one of the Queen's Drawing Rooms and there is your own come-out ball. With the extra blunt we could make it an affair to remember.' He paused, smiling artlessly. 'Longham will offer for you and you will end the year a marchioness.'

'No one will offer for me,' she said bitterly. 'Not that I would have the Marquis of Longham if he did.'

'Why ever not?'

'Because he is. . .' She stopped, unable to put her illogical reasoning into words. 'Oh, you are an unfeeling, insensible thatchgallows,' she snapped. 'And, what is worse, you have made one of me too. I am not fit to be anyone's wife. I shall go home to Raventrees at the earliest opportunity and become an ape leader.'

Unabashed, he grinned. 'If you expect me to believe that tarradiddle, then you must think me a bigger souse-crown than you are yourself. It is obvious to anyone but a complete codshead that you are wearing the willow for Jack Bellingham.'

'I am not! And if you dare so much as mention his name again, Tom Wenthorpe, we will have a serious falling-out.'

He grinned and shrugged his shoulders, but at least she had managed to silence him. If no one mentioned the Marquis, then it might, just might, be easier to stop thinking about him.

The object of their discussion was at that moment driving himself to Chelsea in his curricle, musing on

the strange behaviour of the Wenthorpe brother and
sister. He could, to a degree, understand Tom trying
to gammon his friends for a lark, especially on April
Fool's Day, but what he could not understand was
why Miss Wenthorpe should be a party to the
deception, perhaps even its instigator. It was not the
behaviour one would expect from a well brought-up
young lady in her first Season. He had called her a
hoyden, but he had not really meant it, and now she
seemed determined to prove him right. He was
curious and strangely hurt, as if it was him she were
trying to gull. Nor could he fathom the reason for it.
He promised himself that he would solve the riddle
later and resolutely put his mind to the business
which had brought him to London in the first place
and to Chelsea today. Drawing up at the faded door
of a tall, narrow house, he jumped down and handed
the ribbons to his groom. 'Walk 'em up and down a
bit,' he said. 'I'll not be long.'

Finding documentary evidence of a wager made
half a century before was, he had soon discovered,
more difficult than he had supposed. The records of
the well-known gambling clubs went back many
years and it had been diverting to read in their
betting books of the extraordinary things people
staked their money and possessions on, not just
cards and horse racing, but whether Lord A would
be married before the Earl of B, which of two
spiders would catch a fly in their webs first, or the
speed with which raindrops ran down a window;
even what colour a certain gentleman's waistcoat
would be the following day. Fortunes had been won

and lost in these puerile bets but nowhere was there any mention of the wood on the Longham estate. He had concluded that the wager, whatever it was, had been made at Longham Towers or in its vicinity and he would have to resume his search there.

After his last meeting with Charles, it had occurred to him to ask Littlejohn if he had ever heard anything of a wager. Apart from Tewkes, who went everywhere with his master, Littlejohn, the head groom, was the only one of the Longham servants to accompany him to London. The man had been in the Duke's employ all his working life, as had his father and grandfather before him; if anyone knew any old stories about the wood and those who lived on the neighbouring estate, he would. Jack had sent Tewkes to fetch him from the mews where he lived over the stables.

'It were allus called Harker's Wood,' the groom had said, running his fingers through his sparse gingery hair. 'On account of the family who lived in the house t'other side of it in the old days was called Harker. That was long afore Mr Grimshaw's time, o' course, Mr Grimshaw 'avin' been there only since the beginning of the war. About the time you went away, sir. Sir Bertram Harker was a right crabby old man, used to drive us boys outa the wood with an old sporting gun.' He chuckled at the memory. 'I recall one time it backfired, set his beard afire and knocked him off'n his feet.'

'So the wood belonged to him then. When was that?'

'Oh, fifty year ago, at least. I were a lad o' six or seven.'

'The same age as my father?'

'Oh, aye, he and me did often play together, afore he were sent away to school, that were. Course we weren't s'posed to, him being the old Duke's heir and me naught but the head groom's son.' He smiled again, revealing a broken tooth. 'When he came back, things were different; we hardly met 'cept in the stables.'

Jack could readily imagine that. 'So, the wood changed hands in my grandfather's time?'

'That seems the way of it.'

'Do you know how it came about? Did the old Duke buy it? Or could he have won it with a wager?'

'I can't say as I know for sure, sir, but your grandfather weren't any too free with his blunt and Sir Bertram was known for a gambler. It could be.'

'Were they enemies?'

'Not then. Thick as thieves, they were. Hunted a lot together, went to the races together. Raced each other sometimes.' He paused. 'When Sir Bertram died, the house was put up for sale to pay his debts but it didn' go and had to be rented out, then it stood empty, let go to rack and ruin, 'til Mr Grimshaw took it over in '08 or '09.' He scratched his head again. 'Sir Bertram had a daughter, I recollect, but she married and moved away.'

Jack had been disappointed, not so much at the likely loss of the land but at the thought that Ernest Grimshaw might have bested him. 'It looks as if I must come home by Weeping Cross,' he had told Charles later the same day.

'There may be a note of the wager in the archives at Longham Towers,' Charles had said. 'Or Grimshaw's deeds, though I doubt you'd get a look at those.' He had paused, stroking his chin thoughtfully. 'We must find the daughter. She may know something of it.'

It had taken Charles three weeks to discover that the daughter had died long since, but there was a granddaughter, a widow, who now lived with her son in genteel poverty in rooms above a shoemaker's shop in Chelsea. It was to see Mrs Henrietta Griggs that Jack had driven to Chelsea, with Littlejohn up behind him on the tiger's seat. Tewkes had been left to attend to the laundering of six shirts and a dozen neckcloths, and the polishing of three pairs of boots. He had grumbled, assuming his beloved Captain could not be trusted anywhere without him, but Jack had insisted that clean laundry was essential to his well-being and if he did not look in prime twig at the Drury Lane theatre that night the failure would be laid at his valet's door. And besides, no one but Tewkes knew how to get the mirror shine on his hessians that everyone envied. The flummery had the desired effect and Tewkes had grudgingly allowed Littlejohn to take his place.

Henrietta Griggs, having been apprised of the visit by a letter from Charles, received him politely but coolly. She was six and twenty, or thereabouts, and a little too thin. Her grey cambric dress was very simple, though well-cut, and her stiff white cap with its black ribbons was worn over mousy hair scraped back into a coil at her neck. She would have been plain, but for good bones, fine eyes and a well-modulated voice which soon dispelled this unfavourable image.

'May I offer you refreshment?' she asked, taking his hat and gloves and laying them on a small table just inside the door. 'Tea? Coffee? Some wine, perhaps?'

'Thank you, tea would be welcome.'

She went to a door at the end of the tiny hall and called to someone to bring the tea tray, then led the way into a small drawing-room whose main piece of furniture was a pianoforte in a window alcove. A boy of about five was playing on the hearthrug in front of a tiny fire. At his mother's prompting he rose and went to sit at a dining-table on the far side of the room, which was spread with a cloth and laid out with paper and paints.

'He likes to draw,' his mother said, gazing at him fondly. 'You do not mind if he stays with us? He will be no trouble.'

'He is welcome,' Jack said, realising that the child was to be his mother's chaperon. 'I shall not impose on your time for long. I believe my lawyer has acquainted you with my errand?'

'In part, yes. Do please be seated. I believe there is some dispute about the ownership of some land, though I doubt I can resolve it for you. I have never been to Longham and I never met my grandfather.'

'Did your mother never speak of him?'

'Rarely.' She smiled. 'She had, I believe, expected

a good dowry but her father died about the time of her wedding—I am not sure which event came first—and it was then discovered that not only was there no portion coming to her, but the house and land had to be sold to meet his debts. And even that was not as extensive as she had believed it to be. For someone whose expectations had been high, this was a particularly bad blow. It caused a rift with her husband, my father, which was never healed. He left her a year later.'

'I am sorry to re-open old wounds. . .'

'Oh, they are not my wounds, my lord. I don't remember my father. My mother and I managed tolerably well on our own. She was a fine musician and I have inherited that gift, at least sufficiently to earn a modest living as a music teacher. My father turned up at Mama's funeral but there was nothing for him and I was a stranger to him. He went away again immediately afterwards.'

A skinny little maid appeared with the tea tray, which she put on a small table at Mrs Griggs's elbow.

'Why was the land not as extensive as your mother had hoped?' he asked, watching her pouring tea with long-fingered, delicate hands. 'Could it have had anything to do with Harker's Wood?'

'That was only one of many such disappointments,' she said, handing him a cup of tea. 'My mother told me that when her father died she discovered the land on which the wood stood had been lost in a wager with a neighbour, a horse race

or something of the sort. I am afraid she was
incensed. . .'

'That I can readily understand. But was she sure
that she had no redress? Was anything written
down?'

'My lord, why do you wish to know? It is so long
ago that surely there can be no doubt about its
ownership now? And, forgive me, it is so small a
thing compared to the rest of your. . .the Duke of
Sutton's estate.'

'Oh, it is not the value of the land itself that
concerns me, Mrs Griggs, but the fact that it has
been usurped from under my father's nose. He is
not well, you understand, and I think it was a
dastardly trick to take advantage of that.' He smiled
and set his cup down. 'I need proof it belongs to the
Longham estate.'

'Is there nothing in the estate records?'

'Nothing has come to light as yet.' He smiled. 'My
father is not the best of record-keepers. I had hoped
you might be able to help me.'

'And if you find proof, what then?'

'Why, then we shall turn the fellow off. He is
ruining the wood by indiscriminate felling and not a
new tree has he planted. It looks like a barren desert
where once it had been full of wildlife. We are quite
near the east coast and it had used to shield the
village and the villagers' crops from the gales coming
from the North Sea. Sir Bertram Harker was a
countryman; whatever kind of a scapegrace he was,
he would not have cut down the trees without careful
re-planting and he knew my family would not either.

Now the whole neighbourhood is up in arms and blaming my father for doing nothing about it. *I* intend to do something, Mrs Griggs.'

'But you need to prove your title to the land?'

'Yes.'

She smiled. 'I have a boxful of papers and correspondence between my mother and the family lawyer from the time of my grandfather's death. I do not know why I kept it. I suppose I thought that one day I might read it all and put it into order. . .'

'Mrs Griggs, you will oblige me immeasurably if you will fetch it out and look through it. If you find anything, anything at all about the wood, would you make it available to me?' He hesitated before going on. 'I will recompense you generously for your time and trouble.'

'That is quite unnecessary, my lord,' she said coolly. He realised he had made a serious error of judgement; she would regard payment as an act of charity or the result of a guilty conscience on his part. 'I will do what I can.' She set down her cup on the tray and rose to her feet, bringing the interview to an end. 'If I have any success, I will inform Mr Wilmott.'

Almost reluctantly he rose and took his leave. She was, he decided as he drove back to town, a courageous and independent woman who had shown none of the resentment he had expected. After all, she could have cut up rough and said the land or its price should have been part of her mother's portion; she could have refused to see him, let alone help him. If he should win his case against Grimshaw with her

help, then he would find some way, acceptable to
her, of making amends for the shortcomings of their
respective grandsires.

It seemed that one of his problems looked a fair
way to being solved, so perhaps the other might take
a step forward. Not that the ownership of a haul of
gold and jewels was a particular problem; if Charles
solved the mystery of the crest, then he would
naturally do his best to reunite the owner with his
belongings, but if it were not possible, then he could
console himself that he had done all he could and
accept his good fortune with an easy mind. He began
to feel more optimistic and it was in that frame of
mind he went to his club for nuncheon, had a hand
or two of whist and then returned home where he
found a note from Charles asking him to call because
he had not only traced the crest, but had spoken to
a Comte Maurice de Clancy, who might turn out to
be the true owner of the jewels. He had asked the
young gentleman to provide proof of identity before
proceeding further.

'De Clancy!' Jack lifted his eyes from the letter
and stared into the gilt-edged mirror above the fire
in his library and smiled suddenly at his reflection.
Of one thing he was sure: the Comte de Clancy
could not prove his identity. But why had the
Wenthorpes chosen that name above all others? Had
they known about the jewels? Was it not so much a
harmless prank as a criminal deception to lay their
hands on a fortune? He did not want to believe ill of
either of them, but what other construction could be
put on their behaviour? He could not understand

why other people had not seen through the disguise; it was as plain as a pikestaff to him who the Comte de Clancy really was. And why involve pretty little Miss Thornton? Was she their dupe or part of the plot? He could call on her and try to find out, but how could he do that without betraying Lydia? For some reason he was reluctant to acknowledge even to himself, he did not want to do that.

He could almost see Lydia's reflection beside his in the mirror: her dark hair, curling over her ears, her laughing violet eyes, the upward curve of her mouth, the proud set of her head, her long neck and white shoulders. And what no mirror could reveal: her spirit, her humour, her spunk. He remembered that waltz in the moonlight and his offer of help. She had almost laughed in his face. Furious with himself for his gullibility, he screwed the letter up in his hand and cursed the fate which had made him decide to bury that dead French dragoon before the carrion got to him.

He roused himself as Tewkes came in, carrying a pair of hessians which rivalled the mirror for their shine. 'Here's your boots, Captain,' he said. 'And if you don't stir yourself and change your rig, you'll be late.' He paused when he noticed the letter in his master's clenched fist and his thundercloud looks. 'Not bad news, I hope?'

'What? Oh, no. It seems we might have found the owner of the jewels.'

'Oh.' Then, 'I'm sorry for that, sir.'

Jack sighed. 'So am I, Tewkes, so am I.'

'I did say you should let well alone, now didn't I?

But what's done is done, as they say, so you might as well forget about it.'

But that was one thing he could not do, he told himself, as he went up to his dressing-room to change into evening clothes. He could not forget, nor forgive someone for making a fool of him, not to mention half of the London *ton*. It would serve her right if she were to be exposed.

Lydia herself would not have quibbled at this estimation of her just deserts; she felt beastly. As for facing the *haut monde* from a box at the theatre, it was the last thing she wanted to do. But as Tom patiently pointed out when she said she would not go, who was there to make a connection between Lydia Wenthorpe and the Comte de Clancy?

'The Marquis of Longham,' she retorted.

'Fustian! You are making a Cheltenham tragedy out of nothing at all. You are over-sensitive because you have taken a fancy to him and he to you. . .'

'Don't be so vulgar! And far from liking me he holds me in aversion.'

'Then why did he call this morning to apologise to you and assure himself that you would be at the theatre tonight?'

'Curiosity. He has an idea about the Count and wanted to catch us out.'

'But he didn't, did he? And if he has any suspicions, which, give me leave to doubt, you will not allay them by refusing his invitation after he has taken prodigious trouble to bespeak a box when almost every performance is sold out.'

Lydia could think of no reason that her aunt would believe for her absenting herself from the outing and, besides, she really did want to see the famous Edmund Kean on the stage. Grumbling, she agreed to go and took herself up to her room to change.

She took especial trouble with her appearance and it was over an hour later when she returned downstairs to join her aunt and brother for the drive to the theatre. She had dressed in a gown of deep pink gauze with tiny puffed sleeves over a rose taffeta slip. The neckline and high waist were outlined in tiny rosebuds and seed-pearls and a gossamer scarf was draped over her bare arms. A ruby necklace, pink satin slippers, elbow-length gloves and a mother-of-pearl fan completed an ensemble she knew set off her dark hair and clear complexion to perfection. She did not suppose it would weigh with Lord Longham in the least, but she was determined he should not find her out of countenance tonight. She would show him that she could be as well-bred and ladylike as the best and she would behave with absolute decorum; nothing would evince the slightest need to criticise.

The Marquis of Longham rose to greet them as they were shown to his box a few minutes before the rising of the curtain. He looked magnificent in black satin knee-breeches, a black long-tailed coat and a white brocade waistcoat, across which hung a silver watch-chain and a large fob. Smiling easily, he came forward to take Mrs Wenthorpe's hand and usher her to a seat. Then he turned to perform the same office for Lydia, but the warmth had faded from his eyes and gone was the twitch of amusement from his mouth; there was not even a hint of mockery. He was perfectly civil, perfectly correct, but cold as charity, as he took her hand and bowed over it. Her own smile froze on her face and she uttered an involuntary, 'Oh,' as he straightened his back and she was able to see the detail on the fob he wore. The stag and the falcon were etched there as clearly as they had been on her mother's hairbrushes. She found herself staring at it, her mind so tumultuous with the thought that here was Mr Wilmott's client, the 'gallant officer and true gentleman', she did not, at first, realise he had spoken.

'I beg your pardon?' She sat down heavily in the chair he pulled forward for her.

'I said, I hope I see you recovered from your fall?'

'I did not fall, I was thrown,' she responded mechanically. 'And apart from a bump on the back of my head which ached abominably at the time I am none the worse.'

'I am glad to hear it.' He paused, then to her consternation added, 'I had the pleasure of meeting your cousin, de Clancy, again this morning. I asked him to convey a message to you.'

She lifted startled eyes to his, but his expression was bland and she forced herself to speak calmly. 'Something about an apology, I collect.'

He smiled. 'Yes. I had no right to speak as I did when you had been hurt. In fact, it is not my place to criticise you at all on your conduct or which mount you may ride.'

If that were all he had to criticise she would have been content, but his pointed reference to the Count made her more than uncomfortable. She forced herself to answer him. 'Think no more of it, my lord. I own I was at fault, as my aunt was quick to point out when I arrived home.' She laughed, but it was a cracked sound, without merriment. 'I shall conduct myself with more seemliness in future. I would not want my papa to think my case was hopeless.'

'Oh, never that,' he murmured, as the orchestra struck up the overture. 'I cannot believe the lively Miss Wenthorpe is without offers. . .'

'None that I would entertain,' she said, as the curtain opened and the audience began a frenzied clapping. Let him think on that!

The play was good and Edmund Kean magnificent, but Lydia could not have reported on the plot, nor described the costumes, nor repeated a single line of the dialogue, because her entire attention was taken up with speculating on how the Marquis of Longham came into possession of the fob and whether there was, indeed, more of the same in his keeping. Had he seen through her disguise and invented the jewellery to catch her out? But if that were so, where had he acquired the fob? Had he really found it on a body? She shuddered at the thought and stole a glance at him. Did she imagine it, or did he look darkly brooding, sinister even? He was certainly not smiling, even though the audience was laughing at some droll remark made by one of the players. He was attending to the events on the stage no more than she was.

Long before the interval, she wished the evening
at an end. Of one thing she was certain: any hope
she might have entertained that he might, one day,
come to love her as she loved him was at an end. By
her own foolhardy actions she had put herself far
below his touch.

To the accompaniment of applause, the interval
curtains closed across the stage and the new gas
lamps were turned up to fill the auditorium with
their smoky glow. Jack went to the door to send for
refreshments for the whole party, and Tom, who
had been sitting behind Lydia, leaned forward and
whispered in her ear. 'I say, Sis, have you seen
Longham's fob?'

'Yes.'

'It is, isn't it?'

'I believe so.'

'Then he must be. . .'

'The honest soldier? Yes.'

'Oh, lord, Sis, what now? If I had known it was
he. . .' He stopped suddenly as Jack returned, followed by Mrs Burford and Frank who had been
occupying the adjoining box.

That good lady was her usual talkative self and,
having dismissed the play out of hand with half a
dozen words, went on to say how glad she was to see
them and to know that the family were once again
all in accord. Mrs Wenthorpe, who did not know
what to make of this, replied tartly, 'Why should we
not be in accord?'

'Well, to be sure, I am the last one to dwell on it,'
Mrs Burford said huffily, accepting a glass of cham-

pagne from the Marquis, who was listening in rapt attention, 'even if the Count did leave my house somewhat abruptly. If it was to mend a rift in his own family affairs, then I, for one, applaud it. But I was sorry to see him go.'

'Carrie Burford, just what are you prosing on about?' Mrs Wenthorpe demanded. 'If you are talking about that man-milliner you introduced at your ball as the Comte de Clancy, then you are a bigger sapskull than I took you for. He is a nobody.'

'Oh, then I have mistaken the matter,' Mrs Burford said, colouring to the roots of her hair. 'I should not have mentioned it. But I did wonder if he had received his letter before leaving for Dover. . .'

'How should I know?' demanded Agatha, out of all patience.

'Yes, he did,' Tom put in quickly, seeing that Lydia had been deprived of speech. 'Frank gave it to him.'

'Mama, I told you I had,' Frank said, aggrieved. 'One would think I could not be trusted to carry a letter now.'

'Oh, but you cannot blame me for being interested in the young man,' his mother went on. 'He is such a romantical figure and if he regains his fortune, which was what the letter was all about, for Frank told me so, he will become one of the most eligible bachelors in town this Season, don't you think? Why, Lydia, he might offer for you. . .' She stopped suddenly because the Marquis chose that moment to choke on his champagne. 'Is anything wrong, my lord?'

'No, indeed,' he said, wiping his eyes on a lace-edged handkerchief. 'The bubbles, you know. . .'

To Lydia's immense relief the conversation was brought to a halt by the dimming of the house lights, which necessitated Mrs Burford and her son returning to their own box.

But that was not the end of it. The subject was returned to at supper, which the Marquis had arranged at a hotel not far from the theatre. While they ate soup *à la* Charlotte and fillets of Turbot, removed with glazed ham and ducklings in an orange sauce, Jack, pretending to an idle curiosity, commented, 'Mrs Burford is a great gossip, is she not? Do you think she invents half of it?'

'Course she does,' said Mrs Wenthorpe. 'Caroline Burford is a notable gabble-grinder and a credulous gull to believe everything she is told. Why, she must have known that having a costume ball on April Fool's Day would encourage pranksters.'

He was silent for a moment and Lydia began to hope that he had given up the subject, but when Mrs Wenthorpe turned to speak to Tom he had, out of politeness, to address himself to her, sitting at his side. 'I am persuaded you did not find the play to your liking, Miss Wenthorpe, and for that I am sorry. Perhaps we should have gone to Covent Garden instead?'

'Not at all. I wanted to see Edmund Kean. He is every bit as good an actor as they say he is.'

'You had not seen him before?'

'No.'

'I had thought you might be a frequent playgoer — a connoisseur, in fact.'

Startled, she looked up from the dish of Rhenish cream in front of her to meet his gaze and then looked away again. She would not give him the satisfaction of asking him why he had thought it. She knew and he knew she knew. 'My mother had an interest in the stage,' she said. 'She often talked of it and, of course, we learned some Shakespeare in the schoolroom, Tom and I, hardly grounds for supposing us to be knowledgeable on the subject.'

'Then you were bored by the play.'

'Not in the least, my lord.'

'But you were not paying attention.'

She smiled. 'Perhaps I was overcome by the honour you did us by inviting us into your box. I felt I was the one on display.'

'And very prettily you display, Miss Wenthorpe. I was the envy of every young blade in the audience.'

If she had not felt so miserable, she might have been pleased enough by the compliment to flirt a little, but it did not matter what he said — every word was a barb, every sentence held an innuendo and she knew he was still playing with her in the way a fisherman played in his catch, letting out the line and then, when the fish was exhausted, reeling it in. She might dive and try to swim away, but inexorably he would land her. She applied herself to eating so as not to look at him, but she was acutely aware of his presence beside her, his size and strength, his masculinity, the way his eyes and voice made her

feel weak with longing. She wondered what he
would say and do if she confessed all. She had
already tasted his anger and his sarcasm; his enmity
would be unbearable. But it was inevitable; she had
better make up her mind to that. He had made it
very clear that he disapproved of gamblers, hoydens
and young ladies who behaved without any sense of
propriety. The Count had gone to France, from
where he would never return, but it was too late for
Lydia Wenthorpe to set things right with the
Marquis because of the visit to the lawyer and that
fob. Was it real? Or was it a paste replica made
purposely to trap her?

'How long have you known Mr Burford?' he
asked.

'What?' She came out of her reverie to find him
looking closely at her. 'Oh, Frank? Forever. The
Burfords have been country neighbours of the
Wenthorpes for at least two generations. Why do
you ask?'

'I wondered why the Comte de Clancy should stay
at Burford House, when he is a cousin of yours.'

She fumbled with her napkin. 'You heard the
story.'

'Yes, but your aunt seems very displeased by it
and she does not seem to be a lady to bear a grudge
for long; she is far too sensible. It seemed to me that
the feud might not be between the Wenthorpes and
the de Clancys but between Mrs Wenthorpe and Mrs
Burford? I collect your aunt does not approve of Mr
Burford as a suitor?'

For a moment she was taken aback and very

nearly smiled at the thought of Frank offering for her, but recovered herself to reply haughtily, 'Really, sir, that is hardly a matter that need concern you.'

'Oh, but it does. If Burford's constant escort is displeasing you. . .'

'Displeasing me?' She was genuinely annoyed with him now; what right had he to question her? 'On the contrary, my lord. Mr Burford is a gentleman and he would never do the least thing to upset me. And if I did not like his company, I would choose another's.'

'I beg pardon,' he said, smiling and proving he was not in the least sorry. 'You do right to set me down. I excuse myself on the grounds that my interest is only for your happiness.'

'I assure you I am perfectly happy.'

'Then I must accept that.' He paused and then, as if to bely that by adding to her discomposure, he went on, 'I once offered my help if you should have need of it and, though you declined it, rest assured that the offer still stands.'

'Thank you, my lord, but, even supposing I need any assistance, I should apply to my family.'

He smiled. 'Yes, but families can be the very devil, sometimes.'

'Yours is?' She felt on safer ground by turning the subject.

His smile turned to a rueful grin. 'My father is not in the best of health and he finds attending to matters on the estate sadly wearying. I find I must go home.

I have an engagement in the morning, but shall leave tomorrow afternoon.'

'Indeed, I am sorry.' She tried to convey by her tone that his presence or otherwise in London was a matter of indifference to her, but succeeded only in showing by her heightened colour and slightly shaking hand that she was far from indifferent. If he was out of town, then she would be safe from his all-too-perceptive eye for a little while, but all the same his going would leave a void in her life. It was as if her last bulwark had been removed and there would be no one left to lean on if things got really bad. And she knew from experience how comforting leaning on him could be. Tom, brother or no, would be of little use in a tight corner, and Frank was only marginally better.

'I had hoped to have some conversation with that elusive French gentleman before he left for France,' he said. 'Now it must wait.'

'I do not think he intends to return.'

'No?' He lifted one quizzical eyebrow. 'Mrs Burford seems to think otherwise. And he would hardly abandon a fortune in jewels. . .'

'It was a mistake. The jewels were not his.'

'You surprise me,' he said in all honesty. If the masquerade had not been for the purpose of taking possession of the loot, why had the Comte been conjured up? What devious game was she playing now? 'I thought that was the reason he was in London.'

'And I would wish him in Jericho,' she said. 'If you cannot find a more interesting topic of conversation, we may as well be silent.' She was immediately mortified by her rudeness and stammered an apology.

'No, you are quite right,' he said. 'As a subject of conversation, the Comte de Clancy is a dead bore. Tell me, have you read *The Corsair*? I don't think Lord Byron will ever better it, do you?'

The evening ended with a discussion of the notable literature of the day, but Lydia had little to contribute and was glad when the meal came to an end and their carriage was called up to take them home.

It was a silent journey; everyone seemed to be immersed in private thoughts and disinclined to chatter. Tom, who had seen the strange looks his aunt had been throwing at him and Lydia, especially when the Count was mentioned, guessed that an explanation was about to be demanded, and took himself off to White's as soon as he had seen his aunt and sister safely indoors.

He was right. Instead of allowing Lydia to go straight upstairs to bed, Mrs Wenthorpe required her niece to attend her in her sitting-room where she bade her sit down. 'Now I ain't missing a sheet and I ain't cabbage-green,' she said, sending her dresser away to find someone to bring them hot chocolate. 'There is something havey-cavey going on and I want to know what it is. You and Tom are in a scrape and it's all to do with Frank Burford and that fly-by-night flat-catcher who calls himself the Comte de Clancy. I'm not budging from this chair until you have told me, so you may as well confess.'

Her niece's answer was to throw herself on her knees at her aunt's feet and burst into a torrent of tears. It was some minutes before she was composed enough to do as she was bidden and then she was taken completely by surprise when, instead of the severe scold she had expected, she heard her aunt chuckling with unsuppressed delight. 'Oh, what a Canterbury tale, to be sure,' she said, wiping her eyes. 'And it serves Letty Thornton right and Carrie Burford too. But there's no doubt you've got yourselves into a coil and there's nothing for it but I shall have to help you out of it. Now go to bed, child, and tomorrow we will put all to rights.'

Lydia rose and kissed her aunt, before making her way to her own bedchamber. She felt a great deal better for her confession but whatever her aunt did it would not put things right with the Marquis. He would never love her now. Throwing off her beautiful gown as if it had been no more than a rag, she flung herself between the sheets and wept as if her heart would break.

CHAPTER SEVEN

'YOU will tell Miss Thornton the truth,' her aunt said next day as they drove to Park Lane. 'But I do not think it is in the least necessary to tell her mama. I do not care to have her think I am a flat of the first water. I shall have to swallow my pride enough as it is to call on her.'

'I am sorry, Aunt,' Lydia said for the hundredth time. 'I never thought. . .'

'No, that is just it, you do not think, but I can forgive you, for I am persuaded that it was Tom and Frank Burford who were at fault.'

No, it is not fair to blame them entirely, I was the one who thought of it first.' She paused, but when her aunt did not reply went on, 'What will you tell Lady Thornton?'

'I shall endeavour not to tell her anything but if I have to I shall own the Count is your cousin on your mother's side and I erred in thinking the rest of the family had perished. You have sent him away and we must hope he will be soon forgotten. I have told Tom that I expect him to make a clean breast of all to his father.'

'He will not like doing that.'

'No more he won't, but I believe he will do it.'

'And Mr Fincham? He will call Tom out for a welcher.'

'If he does, it will be one service my scapegrace nephew cannot ask his sister to do for him,' Mrs Wenthorpe said with some asperity. 'It is time that young man stopped hiding behind your petticoats and behaved like the gentleman he is supposed to be. And so I told him this morning. I rose especially early to do so.' She smiled suddenly. 'Not that you are without fault. He has come to look on you as a brother, not a sister, which is hardly to be wondered at when your behaviour is so hoydenish. You will please bear that in mind in future.'

'Yes, Aunt.'

'If we can keep all quiet, then no harm will be done to your prospects of making a match.'

'It is too late; I am sure Lord Longham knows. He has already rung a peal over me about gambling and riding out alone and wanting to drive a high-perch phaeton.'

'How very uncivil of him!' her aunt said, with a chuckle. To her way of thinking it was a sure sign of his lordship's interest. 'But, you know, there are other pebbles on the beach.'

'And there is that fob,' Lydia went on, ignoring her aunt's last remark; now was not the time to explain that other pebbles did not interest her. 'I am sure he decided to wear it last night to catch us out.'

'That is a something else again. If there is a lost fortune, it must belong to someone. Might as well be Tom. Your papa can confirm the de Clancy family history and identify the crest. The rest will be up to the lawyers.'

'That means Mr Wilmott will have to be told there is no Comte de Clancy.'

'Naturally he, above all people, will have to know.'

'And he will tell Lord Longham and. . . Oh, Aunt, I shall not dare to look his lordship in the face again.'

'Fustian! Lawyers are paid to hold their tongues and, as for Longham, whatever you may say about him, he is not a gabble-grinder.'

Lydia gave up. Her aunt had taken command and reduced everything to black and white, right and wrong, but her feelings for the Marquis could not be thought of in those terms. She shut her eyes, remembering the dance on the terrace and the feel of his arms about her waist. Oh, it was too bad of him to make her feel so soft and ready to yield, when he had meant nothing by it. Two minutes later he had been his customary, cold, haughty self.

They arrived at Thornton House without exchanging another word, and were received by Lady Thornton, who was too well-bred to comment on the early hour. 'Do be seated,' she said, then added almost triumphantly, 'I am sorry my daughter is not here, Miss Wenthorpe; she has gone riding with the Marquis of Longham. Will you take tea or coffee?' This last addressed to Agatha who seated herself next to Lydia on a sofa and replied that coffee would be very acceptable.

'I could see no harm in it,' their hostess went on, pulling the bell-rope by the handsome marble fire-place in her morning room. 'Amelia is well-chaper-

oned by her abigail and a groom. Besides, his
lordship is a man of consequence and his address is
excellent, not at all like his rake of a brother, in
spite of what the tattlers say.'

'There is gossip about him?' queried Mrs
Wenthorpe, looking at Lydia with a twinkling eye.
'How glad I am that Lydia has not developed a
tendre for him.'

'Oh, it is nothing to refine upon,' her ladyship said
and then began to do just that. 'He has come back
to England after serving gallantly in his country's
service to find his brother dead and his father missing
a sheet. . .'

'The poor man can hardly be blamed for that,'
Mrs Wenthorpe put in.

'No, indeed. He has a fortune from his mother, so
he is not dependent on his father, which is a good
thing, but. . .' She paused to order coffee from the
maid who had answered her summons. 'Where was
I?' If Lydia had hoped the interruption would
change the subject, she was doomed to disappointment. 'Oh, yes, Longham. He has taken over the
estates and practically made a pensioner of his
father, who may not do a thing or spend a single
groat without his permission. I do not doubt he has
a reason: he must, after all, save the house and land
from ruin, but I feel for His Grace, indeed I do.'

Mrs Wenthorpe murmured something which could
have been assent but could equally have been the
opposite, and Lydia remained silent, wondering why
they stayed, when Miss Thornton was not at home.
But if they left, they would only have to return so

that she might fulfil her errand, but how she wished they did not have to spend the waiting time talking about the Marquis of Longham. Anything would be better than that.

'And the worst of it is,' Lady Thornton continued inexorably, 'there is talk of a court case.'

'Oh?' Mrs Wenthorpe lifted her eyebrows in an enquiry; this was news to her, for she had thought she was abreast of all the latest *on-dit* about the Marquis of Longham.

'There is a Mr Grimshaw who has lately come to town and is by way of being a neighbour of the Bellinghams and he accuses his lordship of all manner of iniquity. I am persuaded he is nothing but a mushroom who has sprung up from nowhere, though he does seem prodigious plump in the pocket. I do not know the whole and would not repeat it in front of Miss Wenthorpe even if I did, but it is most scandalous, I can tell you.' She sighed and went on. 'Bits of muslin I can believe, but to lie and cheat and wrest a person's land from him with threats is something I cannot believe any gentleman of quality would do.'

'No, indeed,' said Mrs Wenthorpe, thoroughly confused.

'And now that he is the Duke's heir, he must needs make a good connection and I have been wondering if I ought to allow him to pay his addresses to Amelia. The Comte de Clancy has left town but Amelia is sure he means to return and she has quite set her cap at him. I am not at all certain that I would be wise to encourage him. After all, my dear Agatha, you repudiated him.'

'So I did,' Mrs Wenthorpe said. 'And very uncivilly, for which I am come to beg pardon.'

'But is the Count who he says he is?' her ladyship went on as if she had not heard her.

Lydia looked at her aunt, who seemed to take a long time answering. 'He is a de Clancy, but more than that I cannot vouchsafe. He is certainly not a gentleman.'

Lydia's amusement at this careful honesty faded when Lady Thornton said, 'Then I shall encourage the Marquis of Longham.'

Her daughter arrived back from her ride at this moment with his lordship in tow, and Lydia, seeing Amelia's sparkling eyes and flushed cheeks, came to the conclusion that the Marquis had been paying her pretty compliments, and once again the little green monster took over and it was all she could do to smile and answer him civilly when, after paying his respects to Lady Thornton and Mrs Wenthorpe, he turned to her with a look in his hazel eyes that was slightly mocking, slightly reproachful, and bowed. 'Your servant, Miss Wenthorpe. I hope I see you well?'

Declining an invitation to stay for the refreshment which was then being brought into the room, he explained he was setting out for Longham Towers almost immediately, and took his leave. Lydia watched him go with a mixture of relief that she would no longer be subjected to his searching scrutiny and desperation that he had gone thinking ill of her and there was no way she could put the matter right.

As soon as the footman had closed the door on him Lady Thornton dismissed the maid and began asking her daughter where his lordship had taken her, what he had said to her and her replies, and whether she found him amiable, so that Lydia was left with the impression that the young lady had found him very amiable indeed.

'Did he say he would return in time for the Countess of Boreton's ball?' her ladyship asked, but before her daughter could reply turned to Mrs Wenthorpe. 'Amy Fincham comes out this year, though she is hardly out of the schoolroom. Amelia will put her quite in the shade, especially if the Comte or Longham comes up to scratch.' Then to Lydia, 'Will you go, Miss Wenthorpe?'

'Of course she will go,' Mrs Wenthorpe put in as Lydia hesitated. 'The invitations arrived days ago.'

'It will be a glittering affair, though it will not surpass our ball,' her ladyship went on. 'We held that early and set the standard, don't you agree?'

'Oh, yes,' Mrs Wenthorpe said with a twinkle. 'The earlier in the Season, the better, when the eligibles have not yet made any offers.'

'Oh, how true!' Her ladyship seemed unconscious of being teased. 'It is not so hot either, and the fashions are fresher. Not that Amelia is not always dressed to a shade. She has a new gown for the Finchams' which is particularly pleasing, enough to make any waverer come to the mark; a heavenly blue, so flattering to Amelia's fair complexion. . .'

'Oh, may I see it?' Lydia asked, being nudged into speech by her aunt's bony elbow. 'Do show it to me, for it would never do for me to dress in the same colour and style.' She turned to Amelia. 'Could we not leave your mama and my aunt to have a comfortable coze together?'

Amelia, who was frequently embarrassed by her mother's pretensions, readily agreed, and the two girls took themselves off to Amelia's bedchamber, where the gown was taken from its tissue and displayed. While Lydia was agreeing that it was, indeed, very fine, her mind was busy wondering how she could set about opening the subject of the Comte de Clancy when Amelia unwittingly helped her.

'Mama thinks that I am being too particular and should have made a greater push to encourage an offer by now. . .'

'I recollect that when we last spoke you told me you wanted your mama to think you had developed a *tendre* for the Comte de Clancy.'

'So I did and you tried to warn me off him. . .' she laughed. 'I am out of all patience with Mama over it.'

'Surely she does not want you to accept the Count's suit? I do hope not because. . . Oh, Miss Thornton, you have been cruelly deceived.'

'Not I.' She laughed. 'Did you think I was fooled? No, Miss Wenthorpe, not above two minutes, though I own I was a trifle miffed. I did not want to make a scene on the ballroom floor — that would have been most improper — and afterwards, when I told F. . . Mr Burford that I was sure my partner had been a woman, though I did not know who it could be, he explained all.'

'Oh, how relieved I am!' Lydia exclaimed. 'Will you ever forgive me?'

'Of course I forgive you, and since I have had time to think about it I admire your cleverness. While Mama is busy watching the Comte de Clancy—what a romantical name!—she does not see what is really happening under her very nose.'

'But she has just said she would encourage the Marquis of Longham, so she cannot have been truly blinded by the Comte.'

Miss Thornton uttered a shriek of amusement and sank on to her bed. 'Oh, Miss Wenthorpe—may I call you Lydia? And you shall call me Amelia. We are to be friends, are we not?' Lydia nodded and she went on, 'I know I should not be disrespectful of Mama but she is truly the most stiff-necked snob in Christendom. It is not as if I need a fortune, for I don't, and I am determined to marry for love.'

'Love? You love the Marquis of Longham?'

'The Marquis? Good gracious, no, though I'll allow he has been very attentive and if his interest has been engaged then I am sorry for it. We should not suit, you know.'

Lydia let out her breath in relief, but as quickly returned to melancholy when she realised that being rejected by Miss Thornton did not necessarily mean the Marquis would turn to her, and she was not at all sure she liked the idea of being second-best. 'But you said there was someone. . .'

'So I did. I shall tell you who it is if you give me your solemn promise not to tell a soul.'

'I promise.'

'It is Frank Burford. We are truly in love, but Mama will not even let me consider him.'

'Why not?'

'She thinks he is too young and irresponsible to settle down. And he has no title. If she were to hear of his part in this masquerade of yours, it would only confirm her low opinion of him.'

'I shall certainly say nothing of it and neither will my aunt.'

'Your aunt knows?' Amelia asked in astonishment.

'Yes, I was obliged to tell her last night. She knew something was wrong, you see, and she made me promise to tell you. . .'

'Then you must think of some reason why you could not do it. Lydia, I do not *wish* to be told.'

'I'm sorry, I do not understand.'

Amelia patted the bed beside her. 'Do sit down and let me explain.' When Lydia obeyed, she went on, 'You know, the arrival of the Comte was a godsend; Mama was beginning to suspect something was in the wind. . .'

'In the wind?'

'With Frank and me. We mean to elope.'

'You are funning me?'

'No, indeed I am not. But everyone will think it is the Comte de Clancy who has carried me off.' She paused, but before Lydia could overcome the aston-ishment which had struck her dumb she went on,

'Oh, pray, don't look so startled, it is simplicity itself. The Count will go to the Fincham ball and just before midnight he will stand up with me. I shall complain of the heat and we will wander into the garden. Mama will not chaperon us too closely. We will slip out of the gate and find the post-chaise which Frank will arrange. He will be waiting for us at the posting inn in Watford where he will have hired a private room. When we have eaten a meal, he will go to see if the horses are ready and you will change back into petticoats and creep back to the coach without being seen. I will join you a few minutes later and then we will be off again. From then on, you will be my companion and we will be travelling under the escort of my brother, Sir David Daventry. The Count will disappear into thin air and if Papa comes after us, for assuredly Mama will make him do so, he will be quite put off the scent.'

'You cannot mean it!' Lydia said, jumping to her feet. 'Whatever made you think I would consent to such a farrago?'

'Why, Frank said you would do anything for a dare. It was his idea and I think it is a prime one. It is foolproof, Lydia, just so long as you continue to play your part.'

'But the scandal when it all comes out. . .'

'No one knows you and the Comte de Clancy are one and the same. I'll wager if any were to suggest it they would be laughed out of court. He is such a top-of-the-trees *man*.'

'And afterwards?'

'The Count will never be seen again, unless you

want him to be, of course, and once Frank and I are married Mama will come about.'

'But you will not be received anywhere,' Lydia insisted. 'Think of your parents, think of Mrs Burford. Oh, the disgrace will be terrible. Miss Thornton—Amelia—you must not do it.'

'Oh, don't be so Friday-faced, Lydia. I thought you would be our friend and stand buff for us. Frank looks on you as the sister he never had; he told me so when I told him I thought he was being too familiar with you.' Every other word was attended by an anguished emphasis. 'It is not so much to ask.'

'It is a great deal. I have been mortified with worry and guilt and so relieved to tell you the truth. . .'

'You only felt guilty because you thought you were deceiving me and that was only proper, but now I am to be a part of the masquerade it is altogether different.' She smiled and drew Lydia down beside her again. 'All I ask is that you become the Count, just once more.'

'But if your Mama knew how much you love Frank, surely she would relent?'

'Not she. If the Count fails to return she will make me marry the Marquis of Longham. You can have no idea what she is like, Lydia. She will refine on and on about my ingratitude, how disappointed Papa will be if I do not make a match, how much my come-out has cost and the humiliation of having a daughter who failed to find a suitable husband when she has every advantage. It will be never-ending. And I shall give in simply to silence her.'

'If Lord Longham knew that, he would surely not offer?'

'He will not be able to stand against Mama either. I am my father's only child, Lydia, and my portion will be considerable. If Lord Longham were to marry me, all his problems would be solved.'

'His problems?'

'His inheritance has been plucked clean by his own father and brother and he must make a good match to come about.' She paused. 'It would be a disaster, Lydia. I should lead him a dog's life and make him dreadfully miserable.'

Lydia smiled wanly at the idea of the Marquis of Longham living under the cat's paw. But she knew her dowry could never match Miss Thornton's, and if that was of prime importance what chance did she have? And Miss Thornton, with her golden curls and blue eyes, was very pretty. She looked up to find Amelia looking at her with a sparkle in her eyes as if she could read her thoughts.

'Oh, I shall have to flirt with him a little because the Comte has gone to France and until you make him come back I must put Mama off the scent. . .'

'That could be dangerous,' Lydia said, remembering the moonlight waltz; that had certainly been dangerous for her peace of mind. 'His lordship is an accomplished flirt and he might take you for a. . .' She stopped, confused.

'How do you know that?' she demanded, then noticing Lydia's anguished look, 'Good heavens! You are wearing the willow for him yourself.'

'Gammon!' Lydia did not normally blush easily,

but now she found her cheeks flaming. 'He is top-lofty and conceited and domineering and uncivil and. . .'

'And you love him.' Amelia laughed. 'You know, if I marry Frank, I cannot be made to marry the Marquis. You must save him from me. If it makes you any easier about it, I will undertake to tell his lordship that I persuaded you to help us and he will not blame you at all.'

'If you do that, he will certainly try to stop us.'

'Goose! I shall say nothing until after we are married and then if he cares for you at all he will do something about it.'

'No, Amelia, it isn't only that. . .' She stopped; better say nothing about the jewels and the visit to the lawyer, though she had a fair idea that the whole of London would know about it very soon.

'It will mean your brother's release from his wager too, don't forget,' Amelia went on relentlessly. 'I should not like anyone's blood on my conscience. . .'

'Blood?'

'Is Mr Wenthorpe any good with sword or pistol? How would you feel if he killed Mr Fincham?'

'Relieved,' retorted Lydia.

Amelia laughed. 'Well, yes. But supposing it was your brother who was killed, what then? Surely you would do anything to prevent that?'

Lydia hesitated. Could she do it? To save Tom? Or the Marquis of Longham from Amelia? 'If I come at all, it will be no further than Watford.'

Amelia smiled. By making her demands so excessive that Lydia was bound to concentrate on those, she had managed to get her tacit agreement to the first and most important part of the enterprise. How very clever Frank was to think of that! 'The first change of horses after Watford,' she said. 'I will engage an abigail there to go on as my chaperon. I have told Frank I would not go without one and he would never compromise me.'

'He will have done that the minute we set off.'

'But we will be married before we return and the whole thing soon forgotten. Please don't fail me now. I shall die if I cannot marry Frank.' She paused and laid a hand on Lydia's arm. 'It is nearly a month to the ball so you have plenty of time to make up your mind. Promise me you will think about it.' Lydia nodded and she added, 'Now let's go back downstairs.'

In a daze Lydia followed her back to the drawing-room where Lady Thornton was still debating the relative merits of the Comte de Clancy and the Marquis of Longham, triumphant that two such eligible men should be vying for the hand of her daughter. It was a conversation which amused Amelia and troubled Lydia and she was glad when her aunt said it was time for them to leave.

'I never met such a noddicock,' Mrs Wenthorpe said of her ladyship when they were safely in their carriage and on their way to Portman Square. 'It is to be hoped the subject of the Comte is allowed to die a natural death now, for I am heartily sick of his name.'

Her aunt was no more sick of it than Lydia herself

and what to do about Amelia's request she did not
know. She told herself over and over that she would
not do it, that Amelia would have thought better of
it by the date of the ball. Eloping was such a direful
step to take and the whole plot would not have
disgraced a Drury Lane farce. Perhaps if she did not
bring up the subject again, then Amelia would
abandon the idea.

But once the Comte de Clancy had been purpose-
fully banished from her mind the vacant space was
taken by thoughts of the Marquis of Longham. He
had obviously decided London Society did not
please him and she was not sure if it was because she
had given him a disgust of her or because he had
received no encouragement from Miss Thornton; or
perhaps there was some other reason entirely.

In the following weeks, Lydia made a determined
effort to pay attention to her social life and the other
young men whom she had barely noticed while the
tall figure of the Marquis was to be seen about town.
She went to routs and breakfasts and once to
Almack's, which was a sad disappointment, drove
her phaeton or rode sedately in Hyde Park with
Scrivens at such a respectable distance that he
thought his mistress must be ailing, and walked in
Green Park with whichever of her admirers fancied
his chances. And one afternoon she and her aunt
drove to Hyde Park in the phaeton to witness a
balloon ascent. Tom, who might have accompanied
them, told them he was going to Manton's to try out
some new pistols, which set her thinking about duels
and bloodshed and quite spoiled the outing for her.

It was a sunny spring day; the sky was blue, and trees green with new leaf and clumps of daffodils glowed in the grass beside the carriageway. Lydia matched the day with a straight gown of primrose-yellow silk, decorated under the high waist with green velvet ribbon. Her chip-straw bonnet was tied on with green ribbon and trimmed with silk prim-roses. Her tall figure was striking enough to draw admiring glances from the crowds who squeezed themselves against the ropes which ringed the area where the colourful balloon was anchored. Behind those on foot, rows of carriages gave their occupants a grandstand view of the proceedings. Half a dozen men had taken most of the morning filling the balloon with hydrogen gas and by the time the Wenthorpes arrived it was almost fully inflated. As they watched, the two men who were to fly it climbed into the basket while dozens of others held the ropes that held it earth-bound. Then, with a roar of flame, the huge silk monster began to strain against the ropes, the anchor man released it and, accompanied by cheers, it soared into the sky. Lydia stood up in the phaeton to watch it as it drifted with the wind over the tree-tops of the park, becoming smaller and smaller until it disappeared from sight.

She was about to sit down again when, at the edge of her vision, she caught sight of the Marquis of Longham standing near the roped-off enclosure. She turned to look more closely. He was wearing knee-breeches and top-boots and a frockcoat of tan cloth with brown velvet facings. But it was not his clothes which surprised Lydia but the fact that a young boy,

in nankeen breeches and duffel-coat, was sitting
astride his lordship's shoulders with one hand firmly
planted on the crown of his lordship's beaver and
the other waving at the disappearing balloon. He
was obviously happy and comfortable on his perch,
held securely by his lordship's hands about his
ankles. Beside them stood the slim figure of a young
lady, neatly dressed in pale blue and white striped
cambric with a matching pelisse and a plain straw
bonnet tied with a blue ribbon. She was undoubtedly
the child's mother and on familiar terms with the
Marquis, for she turned and spoke to him and they
looked at each other and laughed.

Lydia's knees buckled and she subsided on to her
seat in a daze. She remembered Lady Thornton's
reference to 'bits of muslin' and wondered why she
should be so surprised that this particular piece of
gossip should be true. She stole another glance at
the Marquis's companion. She looked respectable,
and whoever heard of a bit of muslin who took her
child with her on an assignation with her lover? They
seemed more like a happy family group, and more
dangerous to her peace of mind for that. When the
balloon could be seen no more, he lifted the child
down and all three began to walk towards the gate,
the man and woman with the child by the hands
between them. The sight of them was too much for
Lydia. With a strangled sob, she grabbed up the
reins.

'Have a care, child,' her aunt remonstrated, as the
horses turned sharply in the mêlée of departing
carriages and they found themselves wheel to wheel

with a yellow-painted barouche containing Lady Thornton and Amelia. The occupants of both carriages exchanged greetings and, as neither could move in the tangle of traffic, all but the brooding Lydia chatted about the balloon ascent.

'As a form of conveyance it is worse than useless,' Lady Thornton said. 'All the morning in preparation and then a carriage needed to get one from the point of descent back to civilisation.'

This seemed unanswerable, and the conversation progressed to future engagements and the Fincham ball in particular, which was now only three days away.

'Have you heard from the Comte de Clancy?' Amelia asked Lydia, leaning towards her with the smile of a tiger.

'No.' Lydia cast a terrified look at her aunt; it was too much to expect that she had not heard, for Miss Thornton had spoken quite clearly. She tugged on the reins but it served no useful purpose; they were stuck until the carriages in front of them had moved.

'I have. He has written to say he will be returning in time for the Finchams' ball and hopes to have the honour to be my escort. I do believe he has been successful in his venture into France, for he tells me he has something particular he wishes to impart to me. Can it be that he has recovered his fortune and means to propose, do you think?' She smiled wickedly. 'Shall I accept him?'

'You should not put any great store on what he says,' Mrs Wenthorpe said waspishly, looking daggers at her niece. 'Lydia knows better than most how little he can be relied upon.'

'There!' Lady Thornton said to her daughter. 'Did I not tell you you would be better fixing your attention on Longham? At least he is an Englishman.'

'If the Comte does not return, then I shall,' Amelia said, looking hard at Lydia. 'His lordship is certainly a very handsome man and a marchioness is superior to a countess, after all.'

'Perhaps his affections are already engaged,' Lydia said, fighting to control her own feelings as well as the frightened horses; she was furious with her so-called friend and almost in tears over the Marquis parading his *cher-amie* for her to see. 'Or perhaps he is secretly married. I perceive him over there.'

'Where?' Amelia twisted in her seat.

Lydia pointed with her whip, her unhappiness making her voice unnaturally high. 'There, with the young lady and the little boy. A pretty picture they make, do they not?'

'Oh.' Amelia studied his lordship's companion for a moment. 'She is hardly *haut ton*. She looks like a soldier's wife.'

'I collect the Marquis was a soldier,' Lydia said.

'Oh, I know he is not married, he told me so, and if that is one of his barques of frailty then it is very ill-judged of him to be seen with her here. I have a good mind to call him over and ask to be introduced.'

'You will do no such thing!' her horrified mother exclaimed. 'You will not even notice him.'

'Too late, Mama, he has seen us.'

Lydia took her attention from her horses in order to confirm this and in that instant the greys saw a narrow opening between the barouche and a tilbury and started through it, jerking the reins from her grasp. They managed to squeeze through the space but the phaeton became stuck and before Lydia could recover the ribbons they were rearing and neighing and passing on their panic to the other horses until a mass stampede seemed imminent. Drivers and grooms yelled at each other while their passengers cried out in terror; carriages banged together and wheels locked. Into the pandemonium rushed the Marquis of Longham. In no time he had positioned himself between the heads of Lydia's horses, grabbed their snaffles and calmed them sufficiently to have them standing still. Then he picked up the reins, put them back into her hands and closed her fingers over them, holding the grip for seconds longer than he needed if all he wanted to do was ensure she had regained control of the greys. His touch sent a shiver through her from finger-tips to toes. It was like fire, followed by ice, and she nearly cried out. She wanted to throw herself at him, to ask him to climb up beside her and take her away, anywhere where they could be alone together and she could explain herself. Ashamed of her weakness, she jerked away from him, almost upsetting the horses again.

'Hold 'em!' he commanded, and turned his atten-

tion to disentangling the tilbury from the barouche
so that their respective drivers could take them
away.

'Are you hurt, my lady?' he asked, coming to the
side of the barouche. 'Miss Thornton?'

'A little shaken, that is all, my lord,' Lady
Thornton said, looking towards Lydia who was now
apparently holding her two greys quite calmly. 'If
you had not been near by I believe we should have
been overturned and it is no thanks to that silly chit
that we were not. She is incapable of doing anything
without making a mull of it and should never be
allowed to drive a phaeton.'

'Oh, I do not think you should blame Miss
Wenthorpe,' he said, making Lydia's cheeks flame
with embarrassment. 'Something frightened the
horses.'

'I am glad to see you returned to town, my lord,'
Amelia put in loudly enough for Lydia to hear. 'I do
hope that means you will be coming to the Fincham
ball.'

'Yes. And hope to have the honour of standing up
with you, Miss Thornton. Will you save me a waltz?'

She gave a trill of laughter. 'Why, yes, if the
Comte de Clancy does not claim them all. He will
be returning especially to escort me; did you know?'

His hesitation was only momentary. 'No, I did
not, but I shall look forward to meeting him again.'
He bowed to both ladies, Lady Thornton nodded to
their driver and the barouche moved slowly out of
the crowd, followed by the tilbury. He stood and

watched them thoughtfully for a moment and then returned to Lydia.

The smile with which he had favoured Amelia faded and he looked at her with a hard glint in his eyes which made her tremble. Tom had been putting off going to Raventrees and their father could not have communicated with Mr Wilmott or the Marquis, so it could only be that her tormentor had guessed the identity of the Comte and was furious that he intended to reappear. But why did that make her feel so illogically angry with him? She busied herself with the reins and avoided looking at him.

'The cattle are calm enough now,' he said, addressing Mrs Wenthorpe. 'I would drive you home but. . .'

'Oh, do not trouble yourself,' Lydia put in quickly. 'I can manage easily. Please return to your friend; she is looking quite lost.'

He turned to look at Henrietta, who was standing uncertainly a little way off. Lydia flicked the reins and before he could turn back again she had put the phaeton about with a dexterity which would have drawn an admiring comment if his lordship had not been too preoccupied to notice it. In a minute she was bowling out of the gate.

He returned to Henrietta and offered his arm to walk her back to the road where he might find her a hackney.

'Was anyone hurt?' Henrietta asked.

'No, not at all,' he said, then lapsed into silence

and she was too sensible to interrupt his thoughts
again.

He had returned from Longham after talking to
his father and wading through a mountain of papers
and documents, none of which had been put into
any sort of order. One year the wood was not
included in the estate accounts and the next it was,
but there was no record of a sale having taken place,
nor of it having been handed over as the stakes in a
wager.

His father had been foxed most of the time and
out of temper and told him curtly not to waste his
time on pin-pricks when finding an heiress would be
more to the purpose. He was growing old, he said,
and he needed to see a grandson before he finally
stuck his spoon in the wall. Edward had been on the
point of proposing to the Earl of Winton's eldest
when he'd wound up his accounts and if Jack did not
make haste and procure himself a wife he would find
himself having to take his brother's leavings. 'And I
am persuaded you would not like her,' he had added
maliciously. 'She has a face like a horse; comes of
living on the back of one, I suppose. The only good
thing about her, apart from her dowry, is her seat
on a hunter. And *that*, I can tell you, is broad
enough.'

'I will find my own bride, sir,' Jack had told him
stiffly. 'And it makes no difference to my intention
of bringing Grimshaw to book. There is something
very havey-cavey about that man.'

His father's continual nagging was enough to drive
the most dutiful son away and there was nothing to

keep him in Essex; he'd returned to London to find
a note from Charles telling him that he had heard
from Mrs Griggs. She had enclosed a letter from her
grandfather to his agent which instructed him to
change the boundary fence of the manor grounds to
exclude the wood because the land had been
acquired by the Duke of Sutton. Jack had lost no
time in going to see Charles and examining the
letter. Here was the proof he needed and he gave
the lawyer instructions to proceed with an injunction
against Grimshaw. Then he had gone to see Mrs
Griggs to offer his thanks and, if he could prevail
upon her to accept it, some recompense.

'I am glad the letter was of some use,' she'd told
him, showing him into her tiny drawing-room and
offering him refreshment. 'But I could not accept a
reward.'

'Your grandfather lost his wager and the land was
handed over, but. . .' if she thought there had been
dishonesty, then she might reconsider '. . . I, too,
have found evidence. . .'

'Then you did not need mine?'

'Oh, indeed, I did. This concerns the wager itself.
It was won, no doubt of that, but. . .' he paused
'. . .there are ways to slow a horse down.'

'No, my lord.' A bright pink spot had appeared
high on each cheek. 'It all happened too long ago. If
you really wish to make restitution, then you should
leave the land to Mr Grimshaw.'

'No. You see, my father is not well enough to
fight his own battles and I am sure Grimshaw's
encroachment would not stop at the wood. If I had

not returned when I did. . . But you do not want to hear about that. The whole thing must be distasteful to you. But I must make amends. . .'

'You do not care about the land or the wager at all, do you?' she had said suddenly. 'It is only the thought of losing you cannot stomach.'

He had laughed at the uncomfortable truth. 'I have offended you.'

'Not at all.'

'Then let me do something for the boy.'

She would not accept money and that was how he'd come to suggest the outing to Hyde Park to see the balloon ascent. He had not stopped to look into his motives or he would have realised that it was his annoyance with his father and, to some extent, Lydia, and not his innocent grandfather which had prompted his generosity. How could he take a bride when the only woman he wanted for a wife was embroiled in some devilish plot to relieve him of his plunder? It wasn't as if he wanted the jewels; he was doing his utmost to return them to their rightful owner. He smarted under a dual grievance—his father's insistence on him marrying and Lydia's perfidy.

He had taken Miss Thornton out riding to discover if she was a party to the deception but she had chattered on to him about the Comte de Clancy in such a way that he had been convinced of her innocence. Poor child! What would she do when she learned the truth? It would serve Lydia Wenthorpe right if he were to cut the Count out with Miss Thornton and put an end to her capers but he knew the dangers of that. He would lay himself open to an attack from Lady Thornton on behalf of her daughter. He had considered the idea of offering for Miss Thornton only as long as it took him to think of Lydia in his arms. Damn his father! He had never taken the slightest interest in his younger son before the death of the elder, who had been cast more in his own mould, and now he demanded instant obedience. He had a good mind to propose to Mrs Griggs to spite him! She was cool and restful and undemanding. And not at all like Lydia Wenthorpe!

He had just decided it would be grossly unfair to her even to think of such a thing when he espied the tall figure of Lydia standing up in her phaeton like some golden Greek goddess in a chariot, standing out from the lesser mortals who surrounded her. He had watched her until the boy's insistent cries of, 'Look, sir, look!' had forced him to remember his duty.

Later he had seen the two carriages, side by side, with Lady Thornton and her daughter speaking animatedly to Mrs Wenthorpe. Lydia, he had noticed, sat silently beside her aunt, as if impatient to be gone. And then her impatience had overcome common sense and she had tried to leave — impossible in that crush, of course; he could not imagine why she had attempted it. As soon as he had helped to free the carriage, she had driven off and left him staring after her like some gauche schoolboy given a put-down. She was unpredictable, perverse, wilful and utterly infuriating, and he loved her to distraction. There was nothing for it; he would have to confront her and *make* her tell him the truth; someone had to show her the folly of what she was doing.

Mrs Wenthorpe was, at that moment, doing her best to do just that. 'I am very displeased, Lydia,' she said, as soon as they had taken off their bonnets and gone into her sitting-room. 'I hope you can enlighten me as to how Miss Thornton is still under the impression that there is a Comte de Clancy. And how she came to receive a *letter* from him. I cannot understand her Mama allowing her to receive letters from gentlemen.'

'That was a whisker, Aunt. There was no letter. She was bamming me.'

'Why?'

'I. . .' She paused, remembering her promise of secrecy. 'I think she may be displeased with me.'

'You may be sure it is nothing to my displeasure. You have let me down sadly, Lydia, and your dear papa too. As for your coming out and making a good marriage, I think that is out of the question now. I have come to the conclusion that I must own my failure and send you home at once.'

Lydia had been thinking the same thing, but she could not bear the thought of her father's hurt if she went home in disgrace. 'Oh, Aunt, it would break Papa's heart. I want to go home, indeed I do, but if I go suddenly without saying why everyone will gossip, you know they will. Can we not think of a reason for me to go which will not cause any raised eyebrows?'

'The announcement of your engagement is the

only thing that will serve, my child, and that seems as far away as ever. I never met such a contrary miss when it comes to the social graces. Don't you know how to attract a man?'

'It seems not,' Lydia said, thinking of Jack Bellingham. If she had tried just a little harder, if there had been no masquerade, if Tom had not persuaded her to visit the lawyer and made matters ten times worse, would he have come to love her? It was a question she could not answer and it did no good even to think about it because what was done was done and there was no undoing it.

'Is that what you truly want?' Her aunt peered closely at her niece and saw the pallor of her complexion and the bleakness in her eyes, and her annoyance turned to compassion. 'It would not be a clanker to say you were ill,' she said. 'You do not look at all the thing.'

'I have the headache. It was the noise and the horses trying to bolt and. . .'

'The Marquis of Longham. You have been a fool, girl, don't you know that?'

'Yes,' said Lydia miserably.

'Then you will go home where the country air may do you good. If a certain person has anything in his cockloft at all, he will come after you.'

'I do not wish him to come after me,' Lydia said, regaining some of her spirit. 'He seems perfectly happy with what he has and I will not be one of those wives who turns a blind eye to her husband's peccadilloes simply because he has bought her on the marriage market. I would rather remain single.'

Her aunt laughed, knowing she was thinking of his lordship's companion in the park. 'Gammon! You will come about. Now, before you set off for Suffolk we must decide what to do about this fiction you have perpetrated.'

'I'll put an end to the Count myself, Aunt,' Lydia said, suddenly making up her mind. 'He'll disappear, I promise. Please give me a few more days.'

She did not tell her aunt how this was to be achieved, but she was still so full of an inexplicable and ungovernable rage with the Marquis and annoyance with Amelia, not to mention worry about Tom and Douglas Fincham, that she could not think beyond her desire to do something utterly crazy. There was no hope for her now, but if it was to be the end then she would go out not with a whimper but a bang!

CHAPTER EIGHT

MRS WENTHORPE made no move to persuade Lydia
to attend the ball and, believing her niece intended
to have a quiet evening at home and go to bed early,
she had decided to visit her friend, Mrs Davies. She
was expected to return about half-past nine, by
which time Tom and the Comte de Clancy would
have left for the Finchams' mansion in Kensington.
But Lydia was taking so long dressing, Tom had
come to her bedchamber door. 'What are you doing
in there, Lydia?' he called. 'Aunt Aggie will be back
any minute.'

'I'm almost ready.' She sat on her bed to put on
white dancing pumps with silver buckles.

She had decided to dress entirely in white—white
stockings, white satin breeches fastened below the
knee with white ribbons; white brocade coat
trimmed with white braid; a white satin waistcoat
embroidered with silver thread and a pristine shirt
and cravat in which nestled a single diamond pin.
'No one will forget Maurice, Comte de Clancy, after
this night,' she murmured, going to the mirror. Her
reflection showed her a rather pale, dissolute young
man with plump cheeks and the shadows of sleep-
lessness about the eyes. She smiled and, placing a
white silk high-crowned hat at an elegant angle on
her golden wig, she opened the door to her brother,

213

who stood and stared at her with his mouth hanging open.

'So?' she enquired in the Count's voice. ''Ow do I do?'

He walked slowly round her. 'So this was what all the secret shopping was about. You will stand out like a beacon.'

'So I 'ope.'

'I trust you know what you are about,' he said. 'But I begin to think this mummery has addled your upper works.'

'If Mr Fincham wants a show, he shall have one,' she said in her own voice, handing him a small valise and leading the way downstairs. 'Has the hackney arrived?' They dared not involve the servants by taking their own carriage and Betty, assured that her mistress was going to bed early to catch up on the lost sleep of the previous weeks, had been given the evening off. The rest of the indoors staff were below stairs and the hall was deserted.

'I mean to go home to Raventrees tomorrow and put it all before Papa,' he said, stealthily opening the side-door. 'So if you want to cry off. . .'

'I do not want to cry off,' she told him. 'I started it and I shall finish it.' She marched ahead of him to the gate and on to the road where the carriage waited. 'I shall finish it in a blaze of glory. And tomorrow I'll return to Raventrees. My Season is finished.'

'Oh, Lydia, I am truly sorry; it's all my doing. . .'

She gave the jarvey the direction and settled herself on the seat beside her brother. 'It is of no

consequence. I never liked the idea of the Marriage
Mart anyway. I shall stay quietly at home with Papa
and become an ape leader.' She smiled suddenly.
'But I shall have a night to remember, a night when
I fooled the whole *ton*, a night when I helped two
people in love to attain their dream. . .'

'And lost your own,' he said miserably. 'I think I
shall tell Bellingham.'

'You will do nothing of the sort!' she rounded on
him. 'It is nothing to do with him.'

'Nothing?'

'Nothing.'

There was no more to be said and they continued
without speaking again until they were just short of
the Earl of Boreton's mansion where a lonely figure
stood on the corner, muffled in a huge overcoat.
Lydia ordered the driver to stop and silently handed
over her valise.

'You are late,' Frank said. 'I was afraid you had
changed your mind.'

'No, though I'm not sure I shouldn't,' she said.

'Make sure you are not late; the chaise won't
wait.' He paused. 'I am counting on you to bring
Amelia safely to me. Tell her. . .tell her I love her.'

'Tell her yourself,' she said, laughing, then to their
driver, 'Carry on.'

The Earl of Boreton who, with his wife, son and
daughter had been standing at the head of the stairs
to greet their guests, had decided there would be no
more latecomers and they might as well join the
dancers, when Lydia and Tom arrived. They turned
back and all four stood transfixed at the sight of the

white-clad Comte de Clancy as he handed his hat to
a footman, crossed the marble-floored hall and made
his way up the magnificent curved staircase with his
cousin at his side.

Douglas was the first to recover. Smiling silkily,
he moved forward and bowed before the Count and
introduced him to his parents and sister, all of whom
said how pleased they were that the Comte had
honoured them with his presence.

Lydia made an elegant leg. 'The *honneur* is mine,'
she drawled in the Count's affected accents. Then
she stepped into the ballroom and stood just inside
the door, surveying the scene through her quizzing
glass in a languid pose. It was between dances and
everyone was either promenading round the ballroom in pairs or standing in little clusters talking,
but as soon as the Comte de Clancy was announced
all conversation died away and the whole assembly
turned to look at this vision of pristine manliness.
Deliberately she scanned the sea of faces, looking
for one particular one, but could not see him.
Supposing he did not come? Would that make the
evening any easier to live through? Or harder?
Could she go back to Raventrees on the morrow
never having seen him again? It seemed she must.

'A real out-and-outer,' Douglas whispered,
coming to stand beside her. 'If you last the night
out, then I fear I may have lost my wager.'

She turned and lifted one dark arched brow to
him. 'And will you then concede defeat?'

'Naturally.' The bet had lost its appeal as far as he
was concerned. He was more interested in a cache

of gold and jewels. Mrs Burford, being the gossip that she was, had set the whole of London talking about the Comte's visit to the lawyer and everyone knew that a soldier had brought the de Clancy jewels back to England in his knapsack. Highly exaggerated stories were being spread about their worth and how the matter had come to light. Douglas had his eye on the prize. He could denounce Lydia as an impostor but then she would blab about his blackmail and it would not guarantee that he would end up with the loot. Judging by her lavish costume and that diamond pin, it had already been handed over to her and his best course was to relieve her of it; she could hardly make a furore over its loss. How to do it was the thing most on his mind as he stood beside her watching the men taking their partners on to the floor for the next dance. He smiled suddenly as he spied Lady Thornton making a beeline for them, pulling Amelia by the hand. 'Here comes your great test, my dear. For your own sake, I hope you succeed.'

'Count,' Lady Thornton said breathlessly. 'How nice to see you here. And looking so magnificent.' She turned to her daughter. 'Do you not think so, dearest?'

'Yes, Mama. Top-of-the-trees.'

Lydia bowed.

'And Amelia is in looks, don't you think?' Lady Thornton demanded, ignoring her daughter's discomfiture.

'I 'ave never seen a lady more *ravissante*,' Lydia said, then, before her sense of the ridiculous could overcome her, she added, '*Mam'selle*, will you do me the *honneur*?'

Amelia dropped a curtsy and bent her head, more to hide her laughter than in modesty, and then allowed herself to be led on to the floor. I am glad to see you in such outstanding twig,' she whispered. 'The scandalous Comte de Clancy will be easily described.'

'I wish he had not come. Every minute I expect to be exposed.'

'Fudge! You are magnificent. Now I shall make sheep's eyes at you and you must try to look like a man in love.'

As soon as the orchestra began to play, Lydia realised it was a waltz, and though she had been practising she found the man's steps very difficult and they could hardly keep from bursting into hysterical laughter. 'I think we had better take a stroll before we let the cat out of the bag.' Amelia said at last.

Lydia was glad enough to agree and put up her arm to escort her partner from the floor. They found a couple of chairs beside a potted palm, out of sight of everyone, and sat down. 'Shall I do the agreeable for appearances' sake and fetch you some lemonade?' Lydia asked.

'Later. I want to talk.'

'You have changed your mind?' Lydia asked, more in hope than expectation.

'Not at all. Did you see Frank?'

'Yes, he says all is arranged. The chaise will be ready at midnight at the side-gate and we must not be late. For my part, the sooner we can leave, the better — before Lord Longham arrives.' It was not possible to think about what she was doing without that peer coming into her mind and sticking there like glue despite all her efforts to oust him.

'What has it to do with his lordship?'

'You have heard about the jewels, haven't you?'

'Everyone has. What is that to the point?'

'He has an interest in the Comte de Clancy. . .'

'But not in Miss Lydia Wenthorpe.' Amelia laughed. 'Oh, dear, how mortifying for you. But I promised to tell him everything and I shall keep that promise, though as he has not come I doubt he can be really interested.'

There must be some truth in that, Lydia thought, admitting to herself that all the time she had been dressing she had been thinking of his possible reaction when he saw her not merging into the background in black pantaloons and tailcoat but in gleaming white from head to foot. Surprised? He might well be. Full of admiration for her acting? Perhaps. Regretful? What might he regret? His top-lofty attitude towards her? His invention of the jewels? He *had* invented them, she told herself over and over; the story of finding them on a dead French soldier was too far-fetched to be believed. If his fabrication was meant to be the answer to hers, it had failed, because she had no intention of claiming his loot. But there were other things he might be sorry for. Was he sorry he had come after her when her horse bolted? Had he taken advantage of her insensibility to kiss her and now wished he had not?

And there was that waltz and the disturbing way he
had looked at her. Above all, had he regretted that?

If the Marquis of Longham regretted anything, it
was not the dance on the terrace, nor the kiss he had
given her when she'd lain unconscious in his arms;
her closed eyes and slightly parted lips had been too
tempting to resist. Would it have made any difference if she had known about it? he asked himself, as
he dressed for the ball. Would she have confided in
him? By hedge or by style, he intended that she
should do so tonight, even if he had to beat it out of
her — or kiss it out of her. If she told him everything,
then they could go forward in a relationship he knew
would be stormy but which would be entirely
delightful. If she persisted in playing the Comte,
then it would be an end of all his hopes and he might
as well marry the Duke of Wilton's horsey daughter.
He sighed heavily and picked up his cravat just as
Tewkes knocked and put his head round the door.

'There's a lady called to see you, Cap'ain. . .'

'Lydia,' Jack murmured, because she filled his
thoughts and he could think of no one else.

'No, sir. Mrs Griggs. I told her you weren't
receiving, but she won't go away.' He paused. 'The
lady's in what you might call a quake. Got her lad
with her too. I put her in the drawing-room.'

'Very well. Tell her I will be with her directly.'

Tewkes disappeared, and Jack finished tying his
cravat in greater haste than such an operation normally demanded and hurried down to greet his
visitor.

She was sitting on the edge of one of the Chippendale chairs with her hands clasped in her lap. She wore a dark cloak with a hood which had fallen back from a face so pale, he thought she might be about to swoon. Beside her stood her son. 'I am sorry to come here like this,' she said, springing to her feet as soon as he entered the room. 'But there was no one else I could go to.'

'Please sit down again, ma'am,' he said, with every appearance of patience though he was far from feeling it. Lydia's disgrace could be complete by now and he nowhere on hand to prevent it. 'Tell me what has happened.'

'I had a visit from Mr Grimshaw this afternoon. He is the most objectionable man I have ever come across; the things he said about you I cannot repeat. . .'

Jack smiled grimly. 'I can imagine.'

'He told me I must withdraw my support in your forthcoming lawsuit or I would be sorry I had ever meddled in his affairs. He said. . .' She stopped and took her son's hand. 'He hinted the boy would be harmed. My lord, I am sure he means it. I came to ask you to drop the case.'

Jack paced up and down while Tewkes poured two glasses of wine, one of which he took over to Mrs Griggs. She was about to refuse, but then changed her mind and took it, gulping at it gratefully.

'I'm sorry, I cannot do that,' Jack said slowly. 'It would not end there, you know. It would only make him think he was invincible and he would go on, adding insult to injury.' He stopped his pacing to take a glass from Tewkes and stand opposite her. 'But I promise you no harm will come to you or to the boy. I will put a stop to Mr Ernest Grimshaw's antics if I die in the attempt.'

'You will not call him out? Oh, please, my lord, don't do anything so foolish.'

'I will do whatever is necessary, ma'am,' he said coolly. 'Now, I suggest you return home. . .'

'My lord, I dare not go back. I am sure he has set men to watch me and I am afraid. . .'

'Then he will know you came here.' Heaven help me, he thought, if her visit gets out, I might have to offer her marriage after all. Aloud he said, 'Give me a moment to think.'

'Cap'ain, you could take Mrs Griggs to Wenthorpe House,' Tewkes said. 'Mrs Wenthorpe can be trusted to look after her until you can make other arrangements.'

Jack turned to him. 'Does Mrs Wenthorpe not go to the ball?'

'I believe not, Cap'ain, nor Miss Wenthorpe neither.'

'But I'll wager the Cómte de Clancy is there,' Jack murmured under his breath, and then aloud to Henrietta, 'Will you allow me to take you to Mrs Wenthorpe while I seek out Grimshaw. . .?

He stopped suddenly as Tewkes, who was on the point of leaving the room again, coughed. 'My lord. . .' Tewkes only used his employer's title when he knew he might receive a severe put-down. 'My lord, the man is not a gentleman; you cannot call him out. It's not done and you know it.'

'No, but. . .'

'But there is more than one way to kill a rat,' Tewkes went on. 'I know something what might make the devil scuttle back to his hole. . .'

Jack eyed him suspiciously, while Henrietta looked from one to the other; the Marquis seemed to allow his servant a great deal of freedom and yet she could not doubt the respect each had for the other. 'Out with it, man.'

'Certain bits of paper have come into my possession. . .'

'Fetch them.' He paused. 'No, tell Littlejohn to bring the coach to the door first. The *closed* coach,' he added. 'And then fetch the papers.'

Tewkes scuttled away and soon returned, handing a sheaf of crumped papers to his lordship. 'The coach will be at the front of the house in five minutes, Cap'ain.'

By the time the carriage was ready, Jack had acquainted himself with the gist of the documents he had been given, which consisted of orders, invoices, bills of lading and dunning letters. 'So that's where the timber went,' he said. 'He was selling it to the dockyards at a huge price as seasoned wood.'

'But not all to our dockyards,' Tewkes said. 'You'll see most of it went to French ports; Napoleon's new fleet was built with English oak. In my book that's treason.'

Jack smiled. 'Not the whole fleet, my friend, but more than enough. This puts a whole new complexion on Master Grimshaw's activities. Bellingham grievances fade into insignificance.'

'And that's not all,' Tewkes put in. 'He was owling.'

'Owling,' repeated Henrietta who had been sipping her drink while she watched the two men. It was almost as if she had been forgotten. 'You mean catching owls?'

Tewkes laughed. 'No, ma'am, owlers were people who smuggled wool to France during the war. Did you know half the French military uniforms were made of British wool?'

'But that's dreadful!' she said, suddenly understanding what she had got herself involved in. 'No wonder he did not want to be brought to court over a little piece of land.'

'And here's something else,' Jack said. 'A message. "Latour. Hollesley Bay, midnight. 6th March. Three flashes to come in, six to abandon." Doesn't say which year, though.'

'Latour's a French name,' Tewkes said, stating the obvious. 'I reckon he was harbouring spies. His house is not far from the coast, only the other side of that wood.'

Jack looked up from his reading. 'I assume I am not supposed to ask how you came by these?'

'Why, Cap'ain, they sort of fell into me hands. I was looking for something about the wager. . .'

Jack grinned; he had a fair idea that his servant had been doing a bit of housebreaking while they were at Longham Towers but he would not force him to lie by asking him. 'Why did you say nothing before now?'

'It seemed to me I was the best one to deal with that thieving cove, my lord, not being so perticlar as you about doing the honourable. . .'

'I never heard anything so. . .' Jack stopped, remembering Mrs Griggs. 'I will deal with you later. Now we must hurry.' He turned to Henrietta. 'I have an engagement this evening but, if you permit it, I will take you to Mrs Wenthorpe first.'

She was reluctant to go, but even more reluctant to return to Chelsea, and they set off for Wenthorpe House in the old coach. He smiled as he helped her into it; he had told Lydia he might yet find a use for it and now he had—to convey a lady secretly from his lodgings. He hoped sincerely that she had not been seen arriving and that Tewkes was right when he said Mrs Wenthorpe would help them.

Agatha, who had only a few minutes before returned to the house, belonged to the old school— nothing ever surprised her. She sent for a servant to prepare two adjoining rooms and something for her guests to eat, filling in the waiting time with incon-sequential chatter which did nothing to disguise the fact that she was more than a little distracted. As soon as Mrs Griggs had taken her son up to their rooms to put him to bed, she turned to the Marquis.

'Why did you take Mrs Griggs to Hyde Park, you foolish boy? Don't you know what people are saying about it?'

'I can guess,' he said laconically.

'Lydia is convinced you are a rake. It is because

of that I think she is going to make a thorough cake of herself. I dread to think what the outcome will be.'

'What is she going to do?'

Mrs Wenthorpe drew a deep breath. 'She left me a note saying she was going home to Raventrees tonight.'

'Tonight!' He had been sure she was going to the ball and was more than a little taken aback. 'How can she have gone tonight? Who has she gone with and how? She would never go alone, would she?' He paused. 'Would she?'

Mrs Wenthorpe sighed. 'I would put nothing past Lydia, my lord. When I first read her letter, I thought perhaps she had persuaded her brother to take her, but I know Tom intended to go to the Fincham ball and remove to the country tomorrow. . .' She stopped to gulp from a glass of brandy which stood on a small table at her elbow. 'I believe she has gone to the ball dressed as. . .'

'The Comte de Clancy.'

'So you did see through her disguise.' She smiled crookedly. 'She was sure you had. I never saw it myself so I do not know how good it is.'

'Very good indeed,' he said, then added, 'Except to someone who knows and loves every single feature of her capricious face.'

'Oh. So you do love her, then?'

'Can you doubt it? In spite of the fact she has set me up as a complete flat. What I do not understand is how she came to hear about the jewels before I had ever said a thing about them myself.'

'That looks bad, I own, but you must believe she didn't know about them, not until your lawyer wrote to her. . .to the Comte, that is. She never meant to involve you. It was a prank that got out of hand and nothing to do with you.'

'Then why, in the name of heaven, did she choose the name de Clancy? I did not even know it myself until my lawyer traced the arms.'

'It was her mother's name. Part of the story she told was the truth. There was a de Clancy family and they did live at Fleurry, but as far as I know all but Nanette—Lady Wenthorpe, that is—perished. I believe she only escaped because she was such a good actress; she left France through Spain dressed as a French soldier. It was where she met her husband; his lordship was on a diplomatic mission at the time. If there were other survivors, I never heard of them. Lydia was sure you had somehow come by the fob and invented a cache of jewels to catch her out.'

'No, there is a substantial fortune. If I had known Lady Wenthorpe's name was de Clancy. . .' He paused. 'I will give the find to Lord Wenthorpe when I take his daughter home.'

Mrs Wenthorpe's expression brightened. 'And about time too. Now, why don't you go and find her and put her out of her misery?'

'I intend to. Are you sure she has gone to the ball as the Count? You don't think she may have found some means of leaving town?'

'No, she went to the ball, I'll stake my oath on't; though what was afoot I do not know. She gave her

maid the night off but Betty's beau let her down and
she came back early. She saw Lydia and Tom getting
into a hackney and came to tell me the minute I
came in. Oh, if only I had stayed at home, I could
have stopped her. I was about to order the carriage
to take me to Kensington when you arrived, though
what I could do to save the situation I have no
notion. I suppose I should have tried to shield her
by pretending I believed in the Comte de Clancy.'
Her lined old face suddenly creased into a wicked
smile. 'I must confess it would give me a great deal
of satisfaction to gull Letty Thornton, but not at
Amelia's expense, nor yours, my lord.'

'It appears that your niece does not have the same
scruples, ma'am,' he said laconically. 'But in spite of
that she must be rescued from the bumblebath she
has fallen into.' He smiled and added, 'Though not
before she has confessed the whole to me.'

'Are you so cruel that you want to see her
squirm?'

'No, but I wish her to be open with me or there
will be no dealing together.'

'She is stubborn.'

He laughed. 'I know that, ma'am. But we must
waste no more time. Will you leave all to me?'

'Yes, and glad to.'

He thanked her for sheltering Mrs Griggs and
hurried back to the coach. 'Horse Guards,' he
ordered Littlejohn, climbing in beside Tewkes. 'And
spring 'em.' The next minute they were lurching
through the streets at breakneck speed, considering
the amount of traffic still about.

'Ain't you going to the ball?' Tewkes asked, hanging on to the strap.

'Later. First we pay a visit to the Colonel.'

The Colonel under whom both had served in the early part of the Peninsula campaign was now working at the Department of Military Knowledge at the Horse Guards, but at that time of night it took some time to run him to earth, which they did eventually at Watier's, a club notorious for its deep gambling. He was reluctantly prised from the gaming table and came to an ante-room ready to give the rightabout to anyone who had the temerity to call him from so important an activity. Seeing the one-time officer whose gallentry he had so often commended, he forgot his annoyance, greeted him warmly and asked him to join the play, which Jack politely refused before losing no time in putting the evidence of Grimshaw's traitorous dealings into his hands.

'Latour,' he murmured. 'So that's how he came and went.' He looked up at Jack. 'He was well-known to us as a spy and we knew he had come to England on several occasions, but we could never catch him. He covered his tracks too well. If this Grimshaw fellow was his contact, then he has a great deal to answer for.'

'What will you do?'

'Arrest him. I'll send the Runners after him.' He paused. 'Unless you want the pleasure of bringing him to book. . .'

'Thank you, sir, but no. I am unforgivably late for an engagement. I will leave it to you. . .'

The Colonel smiled and tapped his nose. 'A lady, heh? Nothing else would keep you from the chase.'

Jack grinned. 'I must go. May I suggest you act swiftly, sir? He may miss those.' He pointed to the papers in the Colonel's hand. 'If you need me again, I shall be at your service.'

'But not tonight, heh? Oh, well, you are not in the army now, so I cannot detain you. Be off and enjoy yourself.'

Jack came smartly to attention, bowed and hastened back to his coach. 'Earl of Boreton's,' he ordered Littlejohn, jumping in the coach and settling himself beside Tewkes. 'Now for the Comte de Clancy. Let us pray we are not too late.'

It was past the hour when even latecomers were usually admitted and there was only a footman, half asleep in a chair by the door, when they arrived. Jack threw his hat into the man's lap, making him wake with a start, and bounded upstairs unannounced.

He had hardly been in the ballroom five minutes, searching for the figure of the Count, when he was accosted by Lady Thornton. 'There you are, Longham,' she said, tapping his arm playfully with her closed fan. 'You are prodigiously late.'

'Yes,' he said, peering round over her head for Lydia among the crowds of colourfully clad dancers. 'But I am here now.'

'And a good thing too. The Comte has gone a good way to stealing a march on you and has already danced twice with Amelia. Have you seen him?'

'Not yet,' he said grimly.

'Then you are in for a surprise. I declare I have never been so startled.'

'Oh?' Jack lifted one eyebrow in enquiry, wondering if she had seen through Lydia's deception, but decided she had not, or she would not have continued to refer to Lydia as the Comte. 'How so?' he asked, mildly.

'You'll see.'

'But that is just it, I cannot see her. . . I mean Miss Thornton, of course.'

This slip of the tongue persuaded her ladyship that the Marquis's mind had been on her daughter all along and she felt suitably gratified. 'La!' she said, tapping him again with her fan. 'Your head is so full of *l'amour* you are paying no attention to me. And why not? I give you leave to go and find her.'

He bowed and hurried away. After ten minutes he had established that the Comte was not in the ballroom and widened his search to the supper-room and the conservatory. Had she left? Had she gone to Raventrees after all? Who would take her? Not her brother for he was dancing and apparently enjoying himself in the most unconcerned fashion. If he had not been so preoccupied with finding Lydia, Jack would have dealt him a facer; he was sure that young man had been the cause of all the trouble.

He found Lydia at last, sitting on a sofa in the window of the book-room, lost in thought. She had not seen him and he stood in the doorway a moment to watch her. The room was lit by a single candle which she had probably brought there herself and

she looked almost ethereal in that sparkling white
costume; her face was uncommonly pale and her
eyes seemed darker than usual, more deep-set and
misty. Definitely misty, he told himself; she was on
the verge of tears. Good God, that would give the
game away if anyone saw her. He took a step nearer.
'Lydia.' His voice was no more than a murmur, but
she started up as if she had been shot and her hand
flew to her face in a very feminine gesture.

'Oh, my lord, it is you,' she said, forcing herself
to be calm. To be discovered was bad enough, but
to be discovered by the Marquis was enough to
throw her into a panic. After Amelia had left her to
dance with the other young hopefuls who had filled
her card, Lydia had danced and flirted and danced
again and been the centre of a galaxy of young
ladies, but after her second dance with Amelia her
bravado had deserted her, and she had scuttled away
to hide herself until the time came to claim her
partner for that all-important supper dance. 'You
'ave me taken with surprise,' she said, sinking back
on her seat and reverting to the character of the
Count. 'I did not know you 'ad arrived.'

'Evidently not,' he said, seating himself beside
her. 'Would the Comte de Clancy have come himself
if he had known?'

'Why should 'e not?' She was amazed at her
coolness considering he was sitting very close to her
indeed and she could feel the warmth radiating from
his muscular torso. It would be so easy to lean
against him, to put her head on his shoulder and
turn traitor. ''E 'ad the invitation.'

'You are not afraid of being exposed?'

Her hands were shaking so much she could not keep them still. She thrust them into the pockets of her coat and leaned nonchalantly against the sofa-back. 'Exposed, my Lord Longham? I do not know what you mean.'

'Oh, I think you do,' he said. 'What I do not know is the reason for it.'

'For what?'

'Perhaps this is what you are after?' He unclipped the fob from his waistcoat and dangled it in front of her face. 'This and all that goes with it.'

'No!' she said, shrinking back from the jewel swinging like a pendulum before her eyes. 'Keep your spoils, my lord, I have no interest in them.'

'Not interested in a fortune! Now I had heard that was why the Comte recently went to France — to find a fortune in jewels which was all the time in this country.'

'The jewels do not exist,' she snapped. 'And if they did, a man as supposedly on his uppers as you are would not scruple to keep quiet about them and not try to return them. I do believe you invented them.'

'There is no need for me to invent,' he said, then smiled as if cajoling a child. 'You have done enough inventing for both of us. And I am glad you have decided to spit out those cheek-pads and drop that ridiculous accent.' He put the fob into his waistcoat pocket. 'In truth, there is quite a cache of jewels but they shall go to Lord Wenthorpe and he may do with them what he wishes.' He paused, watching the

look of consternation cross her face, to be followed
by another of sheer obstinacy. 'Now we have disposed of that irrelevance, will you please tell me just
what your game is?'

She blinked away her tears; tears were for women
and children and the Comte de Clancy was a man;
at least he would remain one until she reached
Watford.

'I am waiting,' he said.

She looked up at him, her misery plain on her
face, but she managed a cracked laugh. 'As you say,
a game, my lord, no more than an April Day jest.'

'This is May, and you will forgive me if I say it is
no jesting matter but a cruel deception. I thought at
first it was aimed at me, but now I discover it is Miss
Thornton who is the butt of your humour, and that
is worse. Miss Thornton is a gentle person, a delicate
young lady. . .'

'And I am not?' she retorted with some heat. 'Oh,
I know you think I am a hoyden of the worst order,
so you do not need to deny it.'

'I have no intention of denying what is so patently
true.'

'There are worse things than being a tomboy. . .'

'Indeed there are. Footpads and highwaymen,
pickpockets and flat-catchers. . .'

'I am not a criminal!' she cried, stung to anger and
quite failing to see the light of amusement in his
eyes. 'And you are a fine one to talk of deceiving
people. You pretend to be the pick of the
Season. . .'

He laughed. 'I have no such pretensions.'

'Do you deny you are looking for a wife?'

'Most certainly I deny it,' he said, smiling at her. 'I have found the woman with whom I wish to share my life.'

'Oh.' She was silent for a moment, thinking of Amelia. Would he be very disappointed when he discovered he could not have her? 'Does she know you have your little bit of muslin tucked away for your amusement when the honeymoon is over?'

'Little bit of muslin? Now where can you have learned such a term?'

'You forget, I am so like a man that everyone takes me for one.'

'Yes,' he said softly, resisting the urge to put up a finger and trace the outline of her troubled face. 'I had forgotten because you don't look at all like a man to me, not even in that rig.'

'Don't change the subject!'

'Ah! The subject. What was it now? Something to do with why you have been gammoning Miss Thornton and half the world with this wretched masquerade.'

'No, we were talking of you.'

'And my little bit of muslin. Really, my dear, you must learn to be a little more discreet. . .'

'And so ought you. Fancy bringing her to Hyde Park and showing her off in front of everyone! It is not as if she is anything special.' It seemed as if the little green monster was sitting on her tongue and speaking with her voice and she could not stop him. 'She looked very ordinary to me.'

'Mrs Griggs is very special,' he said, getting to his

feet and making an effort to control his anger and keep his voice low. 'She is a true lady. And if I were not a gentleman, I would. . .' He paused, thinking of how he would enjoy a rough and tumble with her. She might kick and scratch but she could be tamed.

'Call me out, *monsieur*?' she queried, cocking one eyebrow up at him and adopting the Count's voice again. 'I would 'ave to choose pistols for, un'appily, I 'ave not the skill with *l'epée*.'

'I should put you across my knee and spank you and make you apologise to Mrs Griggs, except that I would certainly not want her to know what you had said of her.'

'Why did you not bring the lady to the ball?' she demanded. 'Does she know of your intentions towards Miss Thornton?' She laughed harshly because he was looking at her with a strange expression on his face which betokened an outburst of anger beyond anything she had ever provoked in her father and she found herself suddenly very afraid. 'Which one of them are you deceiving most?'

'Neither.' He ground the word out from clenched teeth.

'You need not flatter yourself that Miss Thornton will accept you,' she went on, unable to stop. 'She agrees with me that you are the most odious, the most disagreeable, the most unprincipled man she has ever met.'

He disconcerted her by throwing back his head and laughing aloud. 'How glad I am to know that!' Taking her shoulders in his hands, he pulled her to her feet and gave her a shake. 'Now stop trying to put me off the scent with talk of Mrs Griggs. If you want to know where the lady is at this moment, she is at Wenthorpe House, enjoying a comfortable coze with your aunt.'

'Aunt Aggie!' Was there no end to the surprises he could spring on her?

'Yes.' He paused. 'Your aunt was about to come here when I called. . .'

'But she thinks. . .'

'You are on your way to Raventrees. No, she doesn't; your maid saw you leaving the house and was concerned enough to tell Mrs Wenthorpe how you were dressed. I persuaded your aunt to allow me to come in her stead.'

'Oh,' she said miserably. She might have known he would not have come on his own behalf.

'So you see I am not here because of Mrs Griggs or Miss Thornton but because of you and this charade of yours.'

'Aunt Aggie told you?'

'She did not need to. Were you foolish enough to think I would not recognise you?'

In spite of herself she was curious. 'When did you realise it was me? Was it at the fair?'

He laughed. 'No, it was dark, if you remember, and I was feeling too bruised and knocked about the head to think of anything except my bed.'

'Why did you fight? Tom said it was because you are a devil-may-dare like me.'

'Is that what you call it? Yes, perhaps you are right. But perhaps I did not wish to see your brother beaten to a pulp. . .'

'So you took the punishment instead. How very magnanimous of you!'

'You do not believe me?' he queried, tilting his head on one side to look at her with a crooked smile.

'Of course not. Why should you do such a thing?'

'What would you have said if your brother had taken a thrashing and you knew I could have stopped it, but held myself back?'

'Oh, do not gammon me into thinking you did it to please me. Why, as far as you knew, I was not even there!'

'If I had not been there,' he said, 'if your brother had taken up the challenge, what would have happened?'

'I dare say he would have given a good account of himself,' she lied. It was far more comfortable talking about Tom than about the Comte de Clancy and she found her taut nerves beginning to relax. She pulled herself up sharply; that way lay disaster.

'Perhaps. But if he had been beaten, would that have put an end to the Comte de Clancy? I've often wondered.' He paused to smile at her. 'Without Tom there would not have been a Comte at all, would there?'

'No, I suppose not.'

'Why did you do it?'

She looked up at him defiantly. 'It was a challenge.'

He laughed. 'Like riding in my coach?'

'Yes.'

'But far more dangerous. You risked your reputation and your future for an hour or two's excitement.'

'I do not need you to ring a peal over me for it,' she said sharply. 'I am not unaware. . .'

'Then why go on with it? If it is not for the de Clancy jewels, what can have induced you to come here tonight? And in that rig. You might as well have put a notice in the *Morning Post*.'

'Oh, do you not like it, my lord?' she asked, flicking a speck of dust from her pristine white sleeve. 'Now, I thought it just the thing for going courting.'

'Let me take you home. At once.'

'No.'

'Would you prefer that I denounce you, here and now?'

'You wouldn't.'

'Try me.'

He would, she decided. 'I. . . I cannot go with you.'

'Why not?'

'I cannot tell you; it is not my secret. Oh, please say nothing. We are harming no one. . .'

'We?'

She hesitated then went on, speaking slowly and hoping to convince him, 'I cannot tell you anything except that after tonight the Comte de Clancy will disappear for good and, please God, he will be forgotten. You must trust me.'

'I seem to recollect asking you to trust me, but you found you could not. Why should I oblige you now?'

She risked looking up into his face and had a
moment of indecision; he was gazing at her with an
expression that was more of pain than of anger. Was
there hope for her after all? Would he understand?
Could she make him see she had to go through with
the masquerade just once more, just for tonight, to
please someone else, even if it meant displeasing
him? She looked into his eyes and felt as if she was
drowning in a warm sea. He was silent, watching
her, refusing to save her. And the next moment she
was in his arms and his mouth was on hers.

She tried to push him from her but he held her
fast and then as his lips parted hers and the kiss
deepened she ceased to struggle and forgot everything in the pleasure and the pain of it. She felt soft
and yielding and would have fallen in a heap at his
feet if he had not been holding her upright. She
found herself clawing at his back, pressing herself
against his muscular torso, feeling his thighs against
hers. It was madness, but she did not want it to stop.
While he held her like that nothing could come
between them. 'Let me take you home.' His voice
was low and sensuous; it caressed her.

'I don't want to go,' she murmured.

'Why not? Surely you do not want to go on with
this charade now?'

The change in his tone brought her to her senses.
Could she confide in him? Dared she? But he would
put a stop to the elopement if she did; Amelia would
never forgive her and Frank would be waiting in
Watford. He had said he was counting on her to
deliver Amelia to him safely and he would be

beside himself with worry. 'I cannot. Frank is expecting. . .'

'Frank! You mean Frank Burford?'

'Yes.'

'What a clunch I have been!' He pushed her from him. 'I've been blind.'

'No!' She looked up at him in despair; whatever she said, she made matters worse. 'You do not understand. . .'

He looked down at her from his great height and his lip curled. 'Oh, I understand very well. I understand there is to be an elopement. You must have thought me a prime jobbernot.' He bowed. 'I wish you happy, Miss Wenthorpe.'

'Oh, you. . .' The case clock against the wall struck midnight and put a sudden stop to whatever it was she meant to say. It was too late for explanations; it had always been too late. 'I have to go. Perhaps one day, my lord, you will find it in your heart to forgive me.' Before he could stop her, she had darted away, leaving him staring after her.

CHAPTER NINE

THERE was no time to think of the consequences of that strange conversation or that heartbreaking kiss; she had to put Jack Bellingham from her mind, now and for always, and find Amelia. She hurried back to the ballroom, forcing herself to behave calmly. A new dance was about to begin and Amelia was busy staving off the attentions of two would-be partners. Seeing Lydia, she smiled and hurried to join her.

'Where have you, been, Count?' she cooed. 'I thought you must have forgot we were engaged for this dance. Now I do believe the sets are all made up.'

'Then let us walk, *ma chère*,' Lydia said, smiling and offering her arm. 'It is 'ot in 'ere, is it not?'

They forced themselves to walk slowly towards the door and down to the ground floor. People were milling about down here too, so their stately promenade continued until they were in the garden and out of sight of other strolling couples, when they began to run.

'If the coach has gone, I shall never forgive you, Lydia Wenthorpe,' Amelia said as they reached the side-gate. 'And neither will Frank.'

The travelling chaise stood on the corner. The driver was already up on the box ready to leave. ''Bout given you up,' he muttered, as they scrambled

242

inside. ''Arf a minute more and I'd ha' bin gorn.'
He cracked his whip and they set off through the
night-dark streets at a ruinous pace.

'Do you think anyone will come after us?' Amelia
asked. 'How long before we are missed?'

'With luck, not until the ball ends at dawn, and it
will be an hour or two after that before they realise
what has happened and organise a pursuit.' If the
Marquis of Longham does not put a spoke in the
wheel, she added, silently, sitting back in her seat
and closing her eyes. She would say nothing to
Amelia of her encounter with him; it would only put
her into a panic and there was nothing to be done
about it. Besides, she was still shaking from that
devastating kiss and she did not want to talk about
him.

He thought she was eloping with Frank and,
thinking about it now, she remembered him quizzing
her before about Frank, and her evasive answers. If
only she could have stayed to explain, if only she
could have told him she loved him, but it would
have made no difference; he did not return her love.
She was everything he most disliked in a woman; he
had kissed her only to punish her and oh, how
bitterly, how sweetly it had hurt! Amelia, white-
faced and apprehensive beside her, was more to his
liking, petite and graceful and so very feminine.
When Amelia and Frank were married he would
know the truth, and what would he say when he
realised she had been instrumental in helping the
elopement and taking Amelia from him? It would

be one more thing to add to her crimes as far as he
was concerned.

The paved streets and mansions of the rich gave
way to humbler brick homes, strung out on either
side of the road, and then they were travelling in
open country between hedges and fields and
occasional wooded areas. Amelia was silent and
Lydia was consoling herself with the thought that
tomorrow she would be safely at home in Raventrees
when the crack of a pistol and a shout startled them
both.

'Surely it cannot be Papa already,' Amelia whispered, looking paler than ever.

Lydia leaned forward to look out of the window
as their driver hauled their team to a stop. They
were being held up at gunpoint by a rider in a thick
black coat with a kerchief over his mouth and chin.
His accomplice, who was unmounted, was a rough-
looking fellow in fustian breeches and a thick leather
jerkin, with a wide-brimmed hat pulled down over
his eyes. He was aiming a pistol at their driver.
'Would you believe we are being held up by toby
men?'

It was like a set piece and, drained of all emotion,
she watched with a kind of uncaring detachment as
the man in the cloak dismounted and approached
the carriage. Her first thought was that Lord
Longham had followed them and decided to teach
them a lesson by frightening them out of their wits.
She would give him a rake-down if he had. But no,
this man was too short and somewhat plump. 'Your

jewels!' he demanded in a grating voice. 'Hand 'em over or I let fly with this.'

In true ladylike fashion Amelia gave a little cry and fainted across Lydia's lap; the Marquis would have appreciated this evidence of femininity, Lydia decided; she had never felt less like swooning. 'You 'ave frightened the *ma'm'selle*,' she said calmly in the Count's voice. 'She 'as fainted clean away. Put up that pop gun.'

'This is no jest,' he said, pointing the pistol at her. 'Hand over the jewels or you die.'

While Lydia was wondering whether to defy him, Amelia moaned and opened her eyes. 'What happened?'

'This gentleman of the road wishes for our jewellery, *ma chère*.'

'Oh, then we must give it to him.' She sat up to undo the clasp on her pearl necklace. The man grabbed it from her and turned to Lydia. 'Now you.'

'I 'ave only this.' She took the diamond pin out of her cravat and handed it to him.

'That will not do. I want the de Clancy jewels.'

After the initial surprise at this demand, Lydia looked up and laughed at him. 'Surely, *monsieur*, you 'ave not been 'oaxed by that — 'ow do you say? — Banbury tale?'

She wondered what he would say if she told him that not only were there no jewels, there was no such person as the Comte de Clancy, that she was a woman and that Lord Longham was, even now, denouncing her to Lady Thornton. Before many hours had passed Lord Thornton or his agents would be on their trail. She had only to keep him talking until help arrived. The idea of aiding an elopement had flown right out of her head. 'You have ridden post for a pudding,' she said, trying to sound unconcerned. 'I advise you to abandon a quest which can only lead to the gallows.'

Infuriated by her apparent lack of fear, he pulled open the door and dragged her from her seat, then reached in and grabbed Amelia's arm. 'You too.'

Amelia, sobbing now, tumbled out beside Lydia and they stood and watched helplessly as he took their cases from the boot and emptied the contents over the road. When that revealed nothing he started on the carriage, pulling out all the cushions and looking under the seats. 'You will find nothing,' Lydia said. 'You are a fool to believe gossip about fortunes that do not exist.'

He turned angrily towards her. 'Oh, they exist. Now pick that up and put it back.' As they bent to obey, he added, 'Everything. I want no clues left behind.' When they had done he returned the baggage to the boot and flung the cushions back into the coach. 'Now, get back in.'

'Will he let us go?' Amelia whispered as they obeyed.

'I doubt it. We can identify him.'

'Then he will surely kill us.' She began to sob hysterically.

'He hasn't the courage.' She smiled and patted Amelia's hand. 'They haven't found the jewels and now they cannot agree what to do with us. Listen to them arguing like a couple of fishwives.' She looked past Amelia to the other side of the road. It was still dark but she could make out a ditch and a hedge and beyond that a field. 'We could get out this side and make a run for it while they are making up their minds.' She unfastened the door carefully. 'Tell me, what are they doing now?'

Amelia overcame her fear sufficiently to look out on the nearside. 'Talking. The big one in the jerkin is climbing on to the box. The other is pointing his pistol at our driver. Oh, he will shoot him!'

They heard his voice. 'You. Get down. You can go home by shanks's pony.' Their driver lost no time in obeying, but before Lydia could persuade Amelia to put her plan into action the cloaked man had hitched his horse to the back of the carriage and joined them. No sooner had he taken his seat than the chaise gave a lurch and they were on their way again, driven by the accomplice.

'Where are you taking us?' Lydia asked, while Amelia sat hunched beside her, unable to speak. 'I doubt you mean to convey us to our destination, but I would be very much obliged if you would.'

'If you do not have the jewels, then you are going to meet someone who has. Wenthorpe, perhaps, or the Marquis of Longham. It makes no odds.' There was something about his cracked laugh that was familiar.

'You think we are going to meet Longham?' She forced a smile; if only it were true; if only his lordship were somewhere at hand. 'You could not be more wrong.' She leaned forward and whipped the cloth from his face, then laughed at his consternation. 'You are the biggest souse-crown in Christendom, Mr Fincham,' she said. 'You, above all people, should know why the Comte de Clancy's jewels were invented. I needed the story of a fortune to play the part properly.'

'Oh, but they are real. I heard your welcher of a brother telling Frank Burford so. If you do not know where they are, Tom does.'

'Then find him and ask him. I promise you we are not going to meet him. All you have done is tumble upon an elopement, no more, no less. Are you not afraid someone will come after us? I assure you Miss Thornton is. If you stay with us, you will be caught. . .'

'Two women eloping!' He went into gales of maniacal laughter.

'I am glad you enjoy a jest,' Lydia said. 'Now, stop the coach and let us go. We will say nothing of this night's work, if you do.' She made a dive for the pistol in his hand but his grip tightened and he pushed her roughly back on to her seat.

'If you try that again, I shall be obliged to shoot you,' he said. 'I have nothing to lose, after all.'

'And will your accomplice agree to that?'

'Jake? He will do as he is told.'

Lydia was not so sure about that; the big man had seemed the more nervous of the two, but she kept her thoughts to herself and the coach tumbled on through the night. Dawn was turning the eastern sky a rosy hue and the dark shadows on either side of the road were taking on the definite outlines of trees, hedges and haystacks when they turned off the high road on to a narrow lane. After several minutes they turned again on to what was little more than a cart track and they found themselves being thrown from side to side as the wheels slid into muddy ruts. Lydia decided it was time to take possession of their abductor's gun. She would need to be careful he was not given the opportunity to use it, either on them or to alert the driver who was cracking his whip and urging on the horses with a choice selection of epithets.

Before she could do anything the coach stopped suddenly; throwing her forward. She made to grab the gun, but Douglas was alert to his danger and knocked her back against the door which had not been properly closed. It flew open and she tumbled out into the ditch which ran alongside the lane.

The air was suddenly pierced with Amelia's screams. Douglas slapped her hard to silence her and jumped down to examine the inert figure.

'You've killed her,' the driver said, scrambling down from his perch. 'I didn't come into this to do no murder.'

'Fustian!' he said. 'She's only stunned. Help me take her inside.' He turned to the now silent Amelia, who peered down from her seat, looking faint enough to fall into the road beside her friend. 'Get down, Miss Thornton, and go indoors.'

Slowly she turned her head and saw that they had come to the end of the lane and a small farmhouse stood not twenty yards away. She watched in a trance as the two men picked Lydia up between them.

'Go on,' Douglas said. 'Go in front and open the door. And no tricks.'

Now her hysteria had subsided, Amelia had become numb. She walked unsteadily to the door and pushed it open. The room they entered was very simply furnished. There was a table, four chairs, a sideboard and a settle on which they put the unconscious Lydia. Amelia ran to kneel beside her.

'Look after her,' Douglas commanded her, and, to his accomplice, 'Pen and paper, if you have such a thing. I must write a letter.'

The cottage was apparently Jake's home; he went to the sideboard drawer and found writing materials before turning to stir up the fire and set the kettle on the hob. Douglas sat down and wrote quickly. 'That should do the trick,' he said, folding the paper and putting it in his coat pocket. 'Stay and guard them till I come back. And keep an eye on the tall one.' Then he strode out of the house, unhitched his horse and rode back down the track.

Jack had stayed in the library after Lydia left him. He was furious with her, with Frank Burford, with Tom Wenthorpe, but most of all with himself for allowing his feelings to overcome his sense. How blind he had been! How easily fooled by the depths of those violet eyes into thinking she might care for him. He had been right the first time: she was a hoyden, an eccentric, too mannish for words, beyond consideration. Burford was welcome to her. His thoughts ran on in this vein for some time, but he could not convince himself. Belittling her did nothing to ease his hurt or help him to forget the taste of those soft lips. She had wanted him then, he could have sworn to it; she had responded to the pressure of his mouth, had kissed him back with all the passion of a woman in love. But what did he know about women in love? Nothing, he told himself, nothing at all. None of the women he had known — and some had been skilful lovers — had been in love with him, nor he with them. Damn them all!

It was some time before he remembered Mrs Wenthorpe; he had promised to extricate Lydia from the coil in which she had embroiled herself and instead had behaved like a clod and made her run from him. Whatever he felt about her or his own foolishness, he must rouse himself and do what he could to keep his word. Reluctantly, he returned to the ballroom.

Lydia was nowhere to be seen; neither was Miss Thornton or Frank Burford. The only actor left in their little drama was Tom Wenthorpe waltzing with Amy Fincham. And that young man's unconcern incensed him even more. He forced himself into a languid pose, though anyone who knew him well would have realised that his hazel eyes missed nothing.

'Well, did you find her?' Lady Thornton appeared at his side just as the music came to an end and Tom offered his arm to his partner for the customary promenade around the room.

'Yes, my lady, but now I have lost her again.' He gave a rueful smile, aware of the irony in his answer.

'Pity. I would much rather it had been you and not the Comte.' She paused, idly watching Tom and Amy. 'I saw them go out into the garden. It was some time ago now. They may still be out there. If you want to cut the Frenchman out, you had better do something about it.'

'Yes. Will you excuse me, my lady?'

'Of course.' She tapped him with her fan. 'Call tomorrow. I'll make sure Amelia receives you.'

'Thank you.' He bowed and hurried across to Tom and Amy. 'Your pardon, my lady, I need a word with your partner.' He grabbed Tom by his sleeve and propelled him into a corner.

'I say, Longham, that's a bit much,' Tom said, aggrieved. 'You were monstrous rude to Lady Amy and you are pulling my coat out of shape.'

'It's nothing to what will happen if you do not tell me where your sister is.'

'Lydia? At home, in bed, I shouldn't wonder.'

'You know she is not. She was here earlier as the Comte. Now where has she gone?'

'How should I know? She don't tell me everything.'

'She's gone to meet Frank Burford, hasn't she?' He shook the young man angrily. 'Hasn't she?'

'Yes. But with Miss Thornton. . .'

'Where?'

'Watford, I think.'

'Has your travelling coach been repaired?'

'Yes, but you are surely not going after them in that?'

'No, you are going home to Raventrees in it as soon as you leave here.'

'Why should I?'

'If you want to come out of tonight's adventure with a whole skin, that is what you will do. You will also ask your aunt to call on Lady Thornton and set her mind at rest; her daughter is safe and sound at Raventrees with Miss Wenthorpe where you took them on leaving the ball. She is to say she has confronted the Comte de Clancy who has admitted he is an impostor and has prudently decided to disappear. Do you understand?'

He refused to listen when Tom tried to justify himself, and went into the garden. An exhaustive search revealed no sign of Lydia or Amelia, though a small side-gate was banging back and forth as if someone had failed to close it properly. He went on to the lane which ran beside the mansion. There were fresh wheel marks and hoofprints in the mud as if a carriage and horses had been standing some time. He smiled ruefully and returned indoors to fetch his hat and take leave of his hostess, then he called for his carriage and returned home. Half an hour later he had been shaved and changed from his black brocade evening coat and pantaloons into buckskins and brown coat and was heading north in his curricle accompanied by Tewkes.

It was almost dawn by the time they left the town behind and were dashing through open country, past meadows and farms, over bridges and through villages, at a rate which made even the normally placid Tewkes cry out for him to have a care. To begin

with it was easy to track the chaise the girls were
using simply by describing the Comte's distinctive
dress at the tolls they passed through. Why Lydia
should have taken Miss Thornton with her and
arranged to meet Frank at Watford he did not know,
nor did he intend to tax his brain with it, any more
than he would waste time wondering why Lydia had
gone as the Count and in that white rig. It was either
an act of extreme recklessness or there was some
deeper reason for it. He was trying to make up his
mind which it could be when the trail went cold. The
coach had passed through the toll at Barnet but the
next tollkeeper could not remember a young man
dressed in white, though he had let two or three
carriages through.

'She could have put on a cloak or an overcoat,' he
said to Tewkes. 'We'll carry on to Watford.'

There was a coach standing in the yard of the
Green Man when they arrived in that town but it
belonged to a fat alderman and his wife on their way
to Dunstable. They went into the inn and found
Frank Burford in the back parlour, pacing backwards and forwards in a ferment of worry and
indecision. The look of relief on his face when the
door swung open changed to dismay when he saw
Jack. 'Longham! What are you doing here?'

'I came to stop you making a fool of yourself and
ruining a lovely young lady. Where is she?'

'She isn't here,' Frank said morosely. 'She must
have changed her mind.'

'No, she did not do that,' he said grimly. 'The

ladies left as arranged. Are you saying they have not arrived?'

'They're not here, are they? They should have come hours ago. I thought her mama must have discovered what was afoot and kept her close or persuaded her. . .'

'Wait a minute,' Jack said slowly. 'Did you say her *mama*?'

'Yes. Lady Thornton. She does not approve of me, you know. . .'

Jack suddenly threw back his head and laughed. 'Of all the sapskulls. . .'

'I beg your pardon.' Frank said stiffly. 'There ain't no call for you to say that. I might not be a pink of the first water, but. . .'

'Oh, not you, my dear fellow, I was referring to me.' He was grinning like a schoolboy. 'I thought it was Miss Wenthorpe who was eloping.'

'Lydia! With me? Good lord, what a comical idea!' He paused. 'You said they left as arranged?'

'They might have been a trifle late.' He smiled. 'I am afraid I detained Miss Wenthorpe.'

'And you did not pass them on the road?'

'No.' He turned to leave. 'We must go back and look for them.'

'You don't suppose Lord Thornton followed them and has taken them home?'

'No, I do not.'

'Then they must have lost their way. Or over-turned or been waylaid. Oh, I should never have let them come alone. . . If anything has happened to them. . .'

Jack stopped to look back at him. 'Well, are you coming or not?'

'Of course I'm coming.' He followed Jack into the yard, but just as they were about to get into the curricle the innkeeper came hurrying out to them, waving a piece of paper. 'Beg pardon, sir,' he said, addressing Jack. 'Are you the Marquis of Longham?'

'Yes.'

'This came for you about half an hour ago, my lord. I was busy in the back room getting breakfasts for the next stage and didn't see you arrive. I was told to give it to you personally.'

'How did anyone know you would be here?' Frank asked, watching Jack unfold the letter and skim through its contents.

'Someone evidently does.' He turned to the innkeeper. 'Who brought this?'

'A boy. Said he'd been paid a sixpence by a man who stopped at the toll on the edge of town. Would there be anything else, my lord?'

'Nothing, thank you.' The innkeeper went back inside and Jack handed the missive to Frank. 'Here, read it.'

'"Miss Wenthorpe and Miss Thornton will be returned to you unharmed in exchange for the de Clancy jewels,"' Frank read. '"If you do not have them with you, you are to send for them and wait at the Green Man for instructions."' He looked up. 'What do we do now?'

Jack's appearance of calm belied the tempest of worry and anger inside him. His imagination painted a thousand lurid scenarios of the two girls in the clutches of unscrupulous scoundrels. How would they cope? Lydia would not panic, he decided, but she might attempt something foolish to free them and force their abductor into violence. If that happened. . . He stopped himself; thoughts like that would not help. 'Their coach must have been halted between the last toll and here,' he said. 'The horses would have been pulled up sharply and may have marked the road. The villains—I doubt there was only one—would have been waiting somewhere in hiding, behind a hedge or among trees, and almost certainly mounted. They may have abandoned the carriage or taken it with them. We must look for signs.' Then as Frank seemed disinclined to stir himself he added, 'Come on, man! I am not staying here to wait on a kidnapper's convenience.' He sprang into the curricle and turned to Tewkes. 'You wait here in case there are more messages.'

Ignoring the servant's grumbling at being left out of the chase, they set off, driving slowly and stopping frequently in order to examine the road at every point where a vehicle might have been halted or to ask at dwellings if anyone had seen the coach with its distinctive occupants.

'This is going to take all day,' Frank said after getting down for the third time and finding nothing of significance. 'Perhaps we should have waited at the posting inn as the letter said.'

'You think I should pay the ransom?'

'The ladies are surely worth a few paltry jewels.'

'Oh, they are worth every grig and groat, but. . .'

'The de Clancy jewels do not exist, then?'

'They exist, and I accused Miss Wenthorpe of masquerading as the Comte to get her hands on them.'

'What a mull! Amelia will never marry me now.'

'And you will be well served, sir. You are an incompetent bungler. I could almost wish the Comte had been a real person and taken her from you.' He checked himself suddenly and smiled. If Lydia were a man it would be his loss. 'Why, in heaven's name, did you cook up such a crank-brained scheme?'

'Lady Thornton would not countenance me. It was all on account of my wild behaviour as a student, pranks and so forth. Made a bit of a reputation. All behind me now, of course. I have a decent income, a country estate and a town house and every prospect of settling down, but her ladyship would not have it. I had to think of something or Amelia would have been forced into a marriage she hated. Maybe with you.'

'Impossible,' Jack said laconically, as they climbed back into his curricle. 'But why involve Miss Wenthorpe?'

Frank's expression momentarily lightened. 'She made such a capital fellow.'

'It was your idea?'

'Well, yes, but I wouldn't have thought of it if Lydia hadn't puffed herself up to play the man. And she thought of the name herself.'

'You had better tell me the whole. From the beginning.'

Before they had gone another mile, Jack was in

full possession of the facts. Poor Lydia! To have been forced into the masquerade and then to have him scolding and misunderstanding her on top of everything, it was no wonder she had run from him. But what courage! What resourcefulness! And what a fool he had been! He could not wait to tell her so and a great many other things beside. Pray God she was safe; that they were both safe. 'You may thank providence I am fully occupied in tooling this pair,' he said when Frank had finished. 'I am mightily inclined to draw your cork, and if anything has happened to either of them I most certainly shall.'

'Lydia will look after them both.'

'She is not a man, for you to put such a burden on her,' he said furiously. 'She is a woman, strong-willed and capable, it is true, but a woman for all that—beautiful, graceful, capricious but entirely delightful.'

Frank looked at him in surprise. 'Good God! You. . .'

'Yes, and if one hair of her head is harmed you shall answer to me for it.'

Frank had nothing to say to that and they rode on in silence until Jack pulled up at a hedge tavern which was set a little off the road with a yard and a tumbledown stable beside it. 'We'll ask here.'

They left the carriage and went inside. It was low-ceilinged and dirty. 'This ain't fit for pigs, let alone young ladies,' Frank said, as if the kidnapper would take account of that. 'Good heavens! Fletcher!' This last was addressed to a man who was eating break-

fast in the taproom though it was nearer noon than
breakfast-time.

'Mr Burford!' he said, rising.

'This is my coachman,' Frank explained to Jack
before turning back to his servant. 'Where is Miss
Thornton and. . .the young man?'

'I don't know. The high toby took them. They had
guns; I couldn't stop 'em. They took me coach and
left me to walk. I've tramped leagues, and what with
me boots plaguing me and me empty stomach rum-
bling I couldn't go no further. "Martin," I sez to
mesself, "You ain't goin' another step 'til someone
comes along with a vehicle to take you up." So, here
I am.'

'Do you know which way the coach went?' Jack
asked.

'Straight up the road.'

'Then come along and show us where it
happened.'

Reluctantly the coachman left his ham and eggs
and followed them out to the curricle where he
clambered up behind them and once again they
turned in the direction of Watford.

'I shall soon know every blade of grass on this
stretch of road,' Frank said. 'If there had been any
signs we would have seen them before now.'

Twice Fletcher stopped them and assured them it
was the spot and twice he owned himself mistaken,
but a third descent from the carriage revealed hoof
and wheel marks and, more significantly, a scrap of
white lace and a silver shoe buckle. Their spirits rose
as they walked beside the horses, following the

tracks to where they turned down a lane. From there they followed the scent like bloodhounds, picking out a particular hoofprint until they found themselves on a very bumpy track at the end of which they could see a small house and a wisp of smoke.

'We had better approach on foot,' Jack said. 'There's no telling what they might do if they see us coming.' He turned to Fletcher. 'Draw the rig into that field and wait with it. We may need to leave in a hurry.'

Douglas, watching from an upstairs window, cursed. He had not expected to be found so quickly. He should have shot that driver and not listened to Jake, but it was too late for that now; he had to get the women away. He crossed the room to the back window. There was a garden and beyond that a field and across the field was another road. He ran downstairs.

The two girls were sitting side by side on the settle. Amelia was calmer and Lydia was fully conscious. She thanked providence that the muddy water in the ditch had cushioned her fall, though she had a lump on the back of her head which was throbbing unmercifully. Her beautiful suit was ruined but that was of little consequence; she had come to hate it.

'Come on, both of you,' Douglas said. 'We're leaving.' He turned to Jake. 'Tie their hands and gag them and be quick about it.'

'So, someone is coming,' Lydia said, guessing the reason for his haste and wondering who it might be. She opened her mouth to shout a warning but before she could make a sound a dirty cotton handkerchief had been forced between her teeth.

As soon as both girls had been securely tied, Douglas ordered Jake to destroy all evidence of their stay. 'You ain't never seen us,' he said, flinging half a dozen sovereigns on to the table. 'Act the innocent.' Then to the girls, 'Come on. This way. And make haste.' He pushed them in front of him out of the back door and across the yard.

He took Lydia's arm, knowing Amelia would follow, and hauled her, stumbling, along an overgrown track alongside the field. By the time they reached the road on the far side, Lydia was fighting for breath and her wrists were hurting. She kept grunting in an effort to make him realise her predicament.

'I'll untie you if you promise to behave,' he said.

She nodded.

He took the gag from her mouth and untied her. 'I'll have my pistol handy and I won't hesitate to use it if you try anything.'

'Now what are you going to do?' she asked, wishing she could have a drink to clear the taste of the filthy handkerchief from her mouth.

He ignored her and released Amelia. 'Now, both of you, walk ahead of me that way.' He pointed with the gun.

'Where is he taking us, do you think?' Amelia whispered as they obeyed.

'I do not know. I don't think he does either. He didn't expect visitors.'

'Who was it, do you think? Could it have been

Frank? He'd be out of his mind when we didn't arrive.' She paused. 'Or Papa perhaps?'

'Perhaps.'

'If it is, will that man Jake tell?'

'I doubt it. He won't want to hang for his part in it.'

'Stop talking.' Douglas's voice came from just behind them. 'Just walk.'

'You have cooked your goose now,' Lydia told him without looking round. 'You will be on the run for the rest of your life.'

'With your ransom I can afford to go abroad. So, we will find another hiding place for you until I can collect it.' He chuckled. 'You will write a letter to Longham begging him to comply with my instructions.'

'Lord Longham! Don't be absurd!' Was he being absurd? Would the Marquis have followed them? She could think of no reason why he should; she had been so upset when he found her in the book room and even more so when he kissed her that she had hardly known what she was doing, but surely she had not let slip anything about an elopement, had she? Would he have followed? She could not imagine that proud, implacable man doing the bidding of a kidnapper, especially to help her, whom he despised. On the other hand, his lordship had not denied he had a *tendre* for Amelia, so perhaps he would hand over the jewels for her sake. But did they exist? She had only his word for that.

They heard a carriage coming up behind them and

Douglas stepped into the road and held up his hand for it to stop.

A portly red-faced man in a green frock coat put his head out of the door. 'What's afoot?'

Douglas walked round to speak to him. 'Our coach lost a wheel and we started to walk, but the lady can go no further.'

'Where are you making for?'

'St Albans.'

'This ain't the road for St Albans.'

'No. Ninny that I am, I thought it was a short-cut and now we have lost our way. I'd be much obliged to you, sir, if you would take us up.'

The portly man looked thoughtful as if the request needed a great deal of consideration, but at last he said, 'Very well, get in. But make haste.'

The girls were only too glad to comply. Riding was infinitely better than walking and if there was some way they could let the man know their predicament then he might help them.

'I must thank you, sir,' Douglas said when they were settled in their seats and on their way. 'I do not know what we would have done, if you had not come along. My name is Brotherton, by the way.'

'I mean to stop in Watford for a change of horses, Mr Brotherton. 'I'll put you down there.'

'Oh, that will be wonderful,' Amelia said, thinking of Frank. 'Of all places it is the best.'

'I do not advise Watford,' Douglas said calmly. 'The horses there are nothing but skin and bone. I'd go on to St Albans if I were you.'

'How can you say that?' Lydia put in. 'The Green

Man 'orses are as good as any to be 'ad.' She turned
to their rescuer. 'Your beasts look done for. It would
be a sin to ruin them for an extra few miles.'

'You are right. Watford it is.'

Lydia gave Douglas a triumphant grin; he scowled
back at her and the coach rumbled on. Everyone
was silent.

'I have it now!' Amelia exclaimed suddenly. 'It's
Mr Grimshaw, isn't it?' He looked startled and she
added, 'We met at Lady Winter's soirée. Don't you
remember?'

He smiled humourlessly. 'You have the advantage
of me, I am afraid.'

'Miss Thornton,' she said. 'I was with Mama.'

Silently he cursed. 'Lady Thornton, to be sure.'
He turned to Lydia. 'Then who are you?'

'The Comte de Clancy,' she said promptly. If
anyone was on their trail, then that name should
help them.

'De Clancy,' he murmured. 'I've heard that name
somewhere.'

'Everyone 'as,' she said. 'It is a fine French name.'

'French, of course,' he said thoughtfully, wondering where the young pup's loyalty lay. He was
probably an *aristo* and a man-milliner at that, useless
in a tight corner.

'Are you making a long journey, *monsieur*?'

'Scotland. I have friends there.' He laughed suddenly, remembering how badly he had misjudged
Longham and that woman, Griggs. He had felt sure
they were lovers, especially when she had rushed off
to the man's rooms the minute he had delivered his

ultimatum. If his men had not been on their toes
and warned him of the visit to Horse Guards, he
would, even now, be in custody. How Bellingham
had learned about his wartime activities he did not
know. Flight had been his only recourse; there were
people north of the border who were not so loyal to
the English crown who would shelter him. And after
all that to be sharing a coach with someone who
recognised him! 'Needed to get away from town for
my health's sake,' he went on, telling himself not to
panic.

As they passed through the toll on the edge of the
town, Douglas smiled easily. 'I should be mightily
obliged, sir, if I could prevail upon you to let us
continue with you to the next stage. We will not
delay you here by leaving the coach.'

Grimshaw had been thinking hard and his
thoughts had been running along the same lines; if
the Runners were close behind him, then the presence of his passengers might be providential. He
would make the man get out and see to the changing
of the horses, while he stayed hidden. 'My dear
fellow, of course,' he said. 'I am rather gouty and
would welcome your help in making sure we have
good horses and they are changed swiftly. If I can
prevail upon you. . .'

'Delighted to be of service, sir,' Douglas said.
With luck Jake would have delayed Longham and
Burford and they would not yet be back in Watford.
That they would return when their search proved
abortive he did not doubt. It was their only link with
the girls. He could leave a note for Longham and

then find somewhere to hide his prisoners while he sent someone to collect the ransom. Perhaps Grimshaw. That was it; he would make use of the man. He had heard of him; if the rumours he had heard were true, he had no liking for the Marquis of Longham and would welcome an opportunity to do him down.

They drew into the yard of the Green Man, which was bustling with activity. A stage had just drawn in and the passengers were passing into the inn while the ostlers and grooms set about changing the horses. As Douglas jumped down, Lydia went to follow him, but he turned and pushed her back into her seat. 'Stay there. We have no time to waste.' He smiled at Grimshaw. 'The Count fell into a ditch, as you can see, and he can think of nothing but his spoiled looks. If he gets out he will delay us by taking a room so that he can change his clothes. Such vanity! I pray you detain him or we shall lose valuable time.' He disappeared, leaving the girls facing Grimshaw.

Lydia tried to rise but he reached out and grabbed her arm, forcing her back into her seat. 'You heard what the man said. You must stay here quietly with me.'

She sank back on to her seat and stared at him. Had they jumped from the frying-pan into the fire? She did not like the look of his little button eyes which glinted at her with a menace which was far more frightening than Douglas's juvenile threats.

'Please let us go,' begged Amelia. 'We are being held against our will.'

'Is that so?' He smiled a pudgy, humourless smile. 'It makes no odds.'

The horses were changed, Douglas returned and they were on their way again in a matter of minutes. Lydia's spirits sank to their lowest ebb since their capture. Now they were leaving any chance of rescue behind them for no one would have expected them to have gone beyond Watford.

Amelia began to cry.

'Stop that!' Douglas snapped, pulling out his pistol. 'I cannot abide watering pots, and that sniffling will make me lose all patience. Would you have me use this?'

Grimshaw, seeing the gun, looked startled and then he began to laugh. He laughed so much his fat belly wobbled and tears streamed down his round cheeks and lost themselves in his many chins. 'Oh, dear,' he said, wiping his eyes on a large green kerchief. 'This is a pretty kettle of fish.'

Douglas, who hated being the object of such merriment and whose nerve was already at breaking-point, turned the weapon on him and told him to shut his maw. 'It's no laughing matter,' he added. 'And you, too, will do as you are told.'

'By you?'

'Yes.'

Grimshaw smiled. 'Then I should inform you that I know for a fact that the Runners are not far behind us.'

'Runners?' Douglas repeated in dismay, but recovered himself quickly. 'Surely they did not send

Runners after the silly chits. They were trying to elope, you know.'

'They're not after them, my dear fellow, but me. I only took you up to give me some cover if we should be stopped and questioned. If I'd known we were, as you might say, in the same boat, I might not have been so willing.'

It was Lydia's turn to laugh. 'Why, *monsieur*, what 'ave you done?'

He smiled across at her. 'Nothing but try to keep what is mine and make a living, not easy in these troubled times, harder still in wartime.'

'What kind of living?' Douglas asked.

He laughed. 'Importing and exporting.'

'Contraband,' Lydia said, correctly interpreting his euphemism. 'And in wartime. Is that not treason?'

'Depends whose side you are on,' he said. 'You are a Frenchman, you should understand. I'd have done all right and none been the wiser if the Marquis of Longham hadn't died. . .'

Lydia's heart missed a beat and then began to thump so fast she could hardly breathe. She thought she might faint. 'Dead?' she whispered, as the colour drained from her face. 'He can't be. . .be dead.'

'You knew him?'

She nodded, hardly aware of the others in the coach, that Amelia had cried out in dismay and Douglas had uttered a furious oath. Her life seemed to have stopped right there and then, in a coach halfway between Watford and St Albans. On either side of the road the life of the countryside went on as if nothing had happened. Men continued to work in the fields and the birds still sang. But they did not exist for her. She remembered the feel of his lips on hers, warm and alive. How long ago had that been? A lifetime and yet only a few hours. What could have happened in so short a time? 'How?' she asked in a whisper, forgetting her accent.

'Took a fence. Jug-bitten, he was, though that was not unusual. Head hit a rock. You must have heard about it. . .'

'Drunk!' she cried. 'I do not believe it. He was perfectly sober when I left him last night.'

'Last night!' He laughed suddenly. 'I ain't talking about the present Marquis. I meant his brother. Died three months ago. Jack Bellingham is a different kettle of fish altogether. He ain't like his father, nor his brother; he don't turn a blind eye for a little golden grease.'

Lydia found herself shaking like an aspen. Of all the silly mistakes to make, but it had served to bring her to her senses. He was alive! She would not give him up for want of a word. Please God, if she came out of this bumblebath safely, she would go to him; she would find him and try to make him understand. 'Was it the present Marquis who sent the Runners after you?' she asked, forcing herself to smile.

'Probably. It was only by chance I heard of it.'

'And will he come with them?' Oh, let him find us, she prayed; make him see that I am not a hoyden past redemption, that I am a woman with a woman's heart and as effeminate as he could wish. Oh, let it not be too late.

'Maybe, maybe not.'

'No,' said Douglas suddenly. 'He ain't with your Runners, Mr Grimshaw, that I promise you.'

'Good, then we are allies,' Grimshaw said, settling back in his seat. 'Now we'd best put our heads together and decide how to proceed.' He would find somewhere on the road where he could persude them to get down, a lonely spot where their bodies would not be found for a very long time. His coachman would help him; he was in too deep to refuse. There was too much to lose to be squeamish now.

CHAPTER TEN

JACK tooled his curricle into the yard of the Green Man behind Frank's coach, which was being driven by Fletcher. The man they had found at the farmhouse had been difficult at first and denied all knowledge of any abduction, but a search of the house and outbuildings had soon revealed Frank's hidden travelling chaise. Faced with this evidence and with a little persuasion, he had told all he knew, but that was little enough and certainly did not include what the kidnapper meant to do next or where he was taking the ladies. He had simply been hired by a flash cove, whose name he did not know, to help him lift a haul of gold and jewels, but there hadn't been any and all he had out of it was a paltry four guineas. It certainly wasn't worth risking the nubbing cheat for. If Jack had thought for a minute that a thrashing would have extracted any more information, he would have administered one, but he was fairly sure the man did not know. He gave him a severe set-down with a warning of the peril he was in by consorting with criminals and, because he did not want to be put to the trouble of taking him into custody, had left him where he was. There had been nothing for it but to go back to Watford and wait for the kidnapper's next communication.

It had already arrived and was given to them as

they crossed the yard, but it told them nothing, except that the young ladies were safe and they were to wait until they heard from the writer where to take the jewels. The innkeeper had not seen the man who left the note; he had been far too busy. Questioning the ostlers and grooms produced no further information; all swore they had had their hands full seeing to the several coaches that had called. Jack went in search of Tewkes, for surely he had been on the look-out, but he was nowhere to be found, either in the inn or the yard. His absence was puzzling; it was not like Tewkes to go off like that without a word.

'What now?' Frank asked.

'I need fresh horses.'

'I bespoke a team for the coach, you may as well have them,' Frank said, morosely. 'I won't need them now.'

While the horses were being changed, they went into the dining-room of the inn and Jack ordered pork chops and a glass of porter each.

'You're never going to booze and peck while Amelia and Lydia might be in mortal danger,' Frank said.

'Supper was a hellish long time ago,' Jack retorted. 'And they are in no danger as long as we stay calm. The man wants his ransom, don't forget.'

'You've done nothing about sending for the jewels.'

'He doesn't know that.' It was important to stay cool, if only to counterbalance Frank's tendency to panic. 'I wish I knew what had become of my man.'

'Oh, I say, there he is,' Frank said, catching sight of Tewkes through the window. 'And he's riding my bay.' He left the table, followed by Jack, and hurried into the yard where Tewkes was dismounting. 'That's my mount,' he said to him in aggrieved tones.

'Yes, sir, sorry sir.' He turned to his employer. 'I was in the yard, keeping a watch like you told me, and this here shay arrives and who should get out of it but Mr Fincham.' He paused, but neither interrupted. 'I thought it was queer seeing's he was at his sister's ball last night. He was in a rare hurry and ordered the horses to be changed in double-quick time; very free with his blunt, he was. I was goin' over, careful, like, to see if he was alone when the landlord called me back to ask where you were. He had another letter, said the fellow in the shay had given it to him, but by then it had gone. Then I remembered where I'd seen that coach. . .' He stopped, his eyes alight with triumph. 'It was at Longham. It was ol' Grimshaw's.

'Grimshaw's. Are you sure?'

'Yes, Cap'ain.'

How, in heaven's name, had those two come to be in partnership? Would Grimshaw have kidnapped the girls to ensure his freedom from arrest? It put a whole new complexion on things. Grimshaw was dangerous, far more dangerous than that young pup, Fincham. Jack swore imaginatively and at some length, which made Tewkes smile; this was more like Captain Bellingham of old.

'There weren't no riding horses except the one Mr Burford had come on,' Tewkes said. 'So—begging his pardon—I took it and rode after them to see where they went. I'll swear they're making for St Albans. I've found a short-cut that'll bring us out ahead of them, if we go now.'

'Then why are we wasting time?' Jack said. 'Let's be off and God help you if you are wrong.'

All three ran to the curricle but they could not get out of the yard because the mailcoach was coming in and blocking the entrance. Two men jumped from it almost before it stopped.

'I'll eat my hat if they ain't Runners,' Tewkes said.

'Thornton would never have sent Runners after Amelia, would he?' Frank said.

'No, I am sure he would not.' Jack knew he could trust Mrs Wenthorpe to play her part to prevent that. These men were hunting a different prey, but he wished that Lydia and Amelia had not become part of the chase, which would undoubtedly become public knowledge; he had hoped to avoid giving the scandal-mongers anything to stir their broth with. He jumped down and hurried over to the new-comers. 'Are you looking for Ernest Grimshaw?'

'We are indeed,' one of them said, eyeing Jack up and down. 'Who are you?'

'The Marquis of Longham. I set the authorities on to the man.'

'Then you can identify him when we catch up with him,' the man said. 'We thought he'd be making for the south coast to join his French friends, but no, he runs north.' The man smiled and tapped his nose. 'But we're two downy birds and hedged our bets.

Trouble is we lost him when he turned off the main road. Nothing for it but to keep stopping and making enquiries. He'd have to change his horses somewhere or run them into the ground.'

'He changed them here,' Jack said. 'If you come with me, I think I can promise you will have your man in the space of a few hours.' He paused. 'But there is something you could do for me in return.'

'Depends,' the man said.

Jack explained what he wanted and five minutes later the curricle containing Jack and Frank, with Tewkes up behind, left the inn, followed by Frank's travelling coach, driven by Fletcher and with the two Runners as passengers.

The occupants of Grimshaw's carriage were heartily sick of each other's company and no one had spoken for miles, but Lydia's mind was busy with escape and discarding one plan after another. They were travelling too fast to consider jumping out and she could still feel the bump on her head from falling from the other coach, and that had been practically at a standstill. Besides, Amelia would not consider doing anything like that and she could not leave her. Nothing could be done until they arrived at their next stop, the Peahen in St Albans.

'I 'ave the 'unger,' she said, as they rattled into the town. 'Do you think we may 'ave something to eat while the 'orses are changed?'

Douglas had felt pangs of hunger himself and agreed on condition the girls did not speak to anyone and did nothing to attract attention to themselves, though he was doubtful about the Comte's filthy white suit. 'Perhaps you should change,' he suggested.

''Ow?' she asked. 'We left our baggage behind in the other coach.'

'Then wear my cloak.' He took it off and draped it round her shoulders as they came to a stop in the yard of the posting inn. 'Remember I have my pistol and I shall be right behind you.'

'And I shall take care of your fair friend,' Grimshaw said, as his coachman came round to open the door and let down the step. But it was not the coachman.

Amelia gave a little scream and flung herself into Frank's arms, nearly knocking him off his feet. Lydia, who had not seen who it was, thought this was another of Douglas's tricks and turned in her seat to try and take the gun from him. While they struggled, Grimshaw took the opportunity to jump down on the opposite side. He found himself face to face with the Runners who seized his arms and hauled him away. True to their promise to the Marquis, they did not interest themselves in who else might be in the coach, though there was an interesting commotion coming from its interior.

Lydia was kicking and clawing, fighting with all her strength, her fury making her glassy-eyed and deaf to everything except her own laboured breathing. She did not hear anything of what was happening in the yard. She wanted that pistol and she meant to have it. Someone shouted and grabbed her legs. She kicked out and heard a grunt of pain.

'Damn you, will you come out of there?'

She was hauled out backwards and set on her feet.
'Let me be!' She turned on her assailant, arms
flailing. 'You. . .you. . . Oh!' She stopped and
stared. Jack was standing with feet apart, ruefully
stroking his chin where a red weal was already
appearing.

He smiled. 'You've a kick like a mule, Monsieur
le Comte. I would not for a minute envy anyone
who tried to hold on to you.'

She was speechless. She had been longing for him
to come, and now he was here, all he could do was
laugh at her and address her as the Count. And
there were dozens of people in the yard, all crowding
round and agog with curiosity, assuming she was one
of the criminals and enjoying her humiliation. It was
not at all how she had imagined their reunion would
be. She pulled herself up short. But of course it was
typical of him not to take account of her feelings and
she was as big a ninny as ever. Nothing had changed.
'You should mind your own business,' she snapped,
covering her distress with words. 'I nearly had his
gun and now he's getting away.'

This was true. Douglas had taken advantage of
the situation and had turned Grimshaw's coachman
off the box and climbed up there himself. He flicked
the whip, but the inn's staff had already begun the
routine of changing the horses and all that happened
was that they broke away from the shafts and trotted
up the road without him. The spectators enjoyed the
joke hugely and even Lydia found herself smiling as

the Runners took him into custody and appropriated the coach to take their prisoners back to London.

'Let him go,' Jack told them.

'Let him go?' Lydia could hardly believe her ears. 'After what he has done? You can't mean it.'

'Indeed I do.' He smiled and those hazel eyes of his bored into hers, making her heart beat in her throat and almost stopping her breath. She felt like screaming and stamping her foot and beating his chest with her fists, anything to let loose the confused emotion she felt and stop him looking at her in that searching way of his. He knew how she felt about him, she could not disguise it, so why did he not have pity on her and turn away? And after all she and Amelia had been through he proposed letting that evil Fincham go free!

'Why? You surely do not condone what he did?'

'Certainly not, but can the Comte de Clancy afford the ignominy?'

'Poof!' she said, and stared in bewilderment as he threw back his head and laughed aloud. 'What have I said that is so comical?'

'Poof! Do you know the Comte de Clancy and Miss Wenthorpe say that in exactly the same way? Now, I wonder why that is?'

So that was how he knew! 'You've been playing a game with me all along, haven't you?' she said. 'You knew right from the first and yet you said nothing until last night. I hate you for that. Do you hear me? I hate you, hate you.' It was a terrible effort to hold back the tears.

'It is you who were playing the game, my dear

Count, and you would not have thanked me for spoiling it, would you?' He smiled. 'Please don't look so down-pin; it is all over now.'

'Yes, I suppose it is,' she said dully, looking across the yard to where Frank and Amelia sat on a bench, completely absorbed in each other. Oh, if only she and Jack could be like that! 'What will they do now? It's surely too late to go on with the elopement.'

'Elopement!' he exclaimed. 'How can you have come by that extraordinary idea? No one here would be so foolish as to risk a scandal by eloping, would they?'

'Then what. . .?' Oh, he was infuriating but she did not doubt he had managed all.

The crowd was thinning; there was little more of interest to see. Jack moved closer to her and took her arm, much as a man would take the arm of another man for a stroll. His touch was enough to set her quivering with desire and yet he seemed not to notice it. 'You were magnificent and brave, a valiant soldier,' he said, guiding her towards Frank and Amelia. 'Now we must set all to rights. Be patient, our time will come.'

She looked up sharply but he simply smiled in an enigmatic way and spoke to Frank. 'What reason did you give for not going to the Fincham ball?'

Frank looked up, surprised at the question and not a little annoyed at the interruption. 'I said I had been sent for on an urgent matter to do with my country estate.'

'It's near Hertford,' Amelia said. 'We were going there after we were married.'

'What kind of business?' Jack continued to press Frank.

'I don't know.'

'Think about it. It's important you can tell people what it was.'

'There has been some unrest among the labourers on the Home Farm, so it could be that, though my steward is certainly capable of taking care of it. What has that to do with anything?'

'Everything. It is time you faced up to your responsibilities if you want Lady Thornton to change her mind about you.'

'She will never do that now. I have made a complete mull of everything.'

'She will come about if you behave like a responsible suitor and not a young scapegoat,' he said. 'I think you should go home at once and see to your estate, show yourself as a caring landlord and employer. If anyone should enquire, you went there yesterday and have been there ever since.'

'What about Amelia?' He took her hand in his. 'We should be married.'

'So you should, but not in this havey-cavey way. Take your coach and go home.'

'You must think me a prize rake-shame if you think I will abandon Amelia. . .'

'You are not abandoning her. You are putting her into my care.'

Lydia looked from one man to the other; surely the Marquis was not, even now, hoping to take Amelia for himself? Was that what he had meant

when he had said 'our time will come'? Why couldn't
Frank see the danger?

'I can't let you take her home to face her parents
without me.'

'I'm not taking her home, I am going to take both
young ladies to Raventrees.' He heard Lydia gasp
behind him and turned to smile at her. 'Miss
Thornton is going to stay with Miss Wenthorpe for a
se'enight or two. Tom is already there, together with
the Wenthorpe coach. As far as the world is concerned he took her and Miss Thornton there
immediately after the ball ended. There never was
any question of an elopement. The flight was
planned between you to frighten Lord and Lady
Thornton into listening to their daughter's wishes.'

'Who will tell them that?' Lydia asked.

'I am persuaded Mrs Wenthorpe has already done
so.' He smiled. 'Of course none of them knows
about the kidnap, which is why I did not want
Fincham detained. With luck he will see the error of
his ways and go abroad for a long tour and there will
be no gossip. But we must waste no more time.
Burford, say your goodbyes to Miss Thornton and
be on your way. I'll see what I can do to persuade
Lady Thornton that you are a changed character,
but it will have to wait a se'enight or so, for I've
business of my own to see to.'

Lydia watched as Amelia went with Frank to his
coach, then turned back to Jack, undecided whether
she ought to be grateful or angry. She was glad for
Frank and Amelia, of course, but Jack, because of
the capable way he had handled everything, had

made her seem so helpless. And that, she supposed, was what she did not like; it proved how weak she was, how incapable of playing the man when it really mattered. She might have fooled Lady Thornton and one or two others, but she had failed none the less. Why, then was he still addressing her as if she were the Comte?

'You arranged all this before you left London,' she said. 'While we were talking, while you were. . .' She stopped and blushed crimson, remembering that kiss. 'Of all the unwarranted interference, the conceit of it. . .'

'Yes, my darling, someone had to save you from your own folly.' He smiled, knowing what she was thinking and understanding her completely. 'Do you know, I have never much liked the Comte de Clancy? I really do not wish to kiss him again and yet, I fear, I shall have to if you stand there like that.'

'Like what, my lord?' Had he truly called her 'darling'?

'Tousled and troubled, bright-eyed and beautiful beyond anything a man could ever be. Certainly too lovely for my peace of mind. And let us have no more "my lord"; my name is Jack.'

Her heart began to sing. 'Jack,' she said softly, making it sound like a caress.

'Oh, Lydia, if you do not want me to make a complete ass of myself, go away.' He laughed suddenly and there was no steel in his eyes now. They were liquid pools of light, drawing her towards him. And yet he had told her to leave him.

'Go away?'

'I took your valise from Frank's coach. You will find it in room three. Go and change before I forget myself completely.'

Joyfully she found a chambermaid to show her to the room and quickly changed into a cambric slip striped in light and dark shades of blue topped with an open gown of pale blue muslin, over which she wore a matching pelisse, embroidered with roses. She had packed it because it was the sort of dress she could wear in the country and it was to Raventrees she had intended to go today. But to be going there with the Marquis! Oh, if only. . . He had called her 'darling' and gazed at her with a soft look in his eyes; there had been no contempt, nor aversion in them. It was almost as if he loved her. Could it be true? But he had looked at her like that before. Had it meant anything then? Did it now? She hurried her toilette, thankful that her hair was easily brushed into shape; delay in rejoining him would be unbearable. She had to know the truth, once and for all.

He was waiting for her in the inn's back parlour, which was miraculously empty of patrons. She hesitated in the doorway, unsure of herself. He stood with his back to the fireplace and watched her. How could anyone mistake this vision for a man? He smiled and took a step towards her. 'Lydia once more. All woman. *My* woman.' He took a step towards her. 'Come here, my love.'

Her feet seemed to fly as she ran into his arms to be enfolded against his broad chest and held there so tightly, the breath was almost driven from her body. 'Don't do that again,' he murmured. 'Don't ever give me a fright like that again. If Fincham's pistol had gone off. . .' He stopped to hold her at arm's length, looking down at her with dancing eyes. 'And I never went to see the Comte de Clancy again, do you hear me?'

She could not answer because he had covered her mouth with his own and the joy of it spread through her from the top of her head all the way down to her toes. This man, this big, handsome, infuriating man, was all she wanted, would ever want. He let her go at last, simply because neither had any breath left. She laughed suddenly.

'Share the jest,' he commanded.

'I was remembering the Comte creeping about the corridors of Burford House, trying to be in two places at once. You thought I was fainting and carried me to Miss Whiting's room, remember?'

'How could I forget?'

'I wanted to tell you the truth then. All along I wanted to tell you. That was the night I realised I loved you. When we danced on the terrace. . .'

'Oh, I fell in love with you long before that. It was the first time we met. You were so practical and matter-of-fact and not at all concerned that you might have been killed when the coach overturned. I knew you were no ordinary young lady.'

'No, you said I was a hoyden.'

'I am sorry, my darling. Will you ever forgive me?'

She reached up and pulled his face down to hers and kissed him again. 'Is that answer enough?'

'And now will you answer me another question?' He held her away from him to look down at her. 'Will you do me the inestimable honour of becoming my wife?'

'Oh, yes, yes, my darling. You must speak to Papa at once.'

He laughed. 'I already have. Two weeks ago. He told me if I thought I could tame you, then I was welcome to try, for he had never been able to.'

'What a whisker!'

'It's the truth, I swear it. And I shall tame you like this.' And he kissed her forehead, her cheeks, one by one, her ears, her throat and her lips, and he kept on kissing her until Tewkes came in and told them bluntly that if they did not let the landlord have his parlour back right away they would have to buy the whole place.

Laughing, they made their way out to the curricle where Amelia waited for them. There was little room for three, but they squeezed in beside her, Tewkes climbed up behind and they pulled out of the yard, heading towards Raventrees and home.

MILLS & BOON

Experience the thrill of *Legacy of Love* with 4 romances absolutely free!

Experience the trials and the tribulations, the joys and the passions of bygone days with 4 gripping historical romances - absolutely FREE! Follow the path of true love and bring the past alive. Then, if you wish, look forward to receiving a regular supply of 4 *Legacy of Love* romances, delivered to your door! Turn the page for details of how to claim more FREE gifts.

An irresistible offer for you

We'd love you to become a regular *Legacy of Love* reader. And we will send you 4 books, a cuddly teddy bear and a mystery gift absolutely FREE.

You can then look forward to receiving 4 brand new *Legacy of Love* romances every month for just £2.50 each. Delivered to your door, along with our regular Newsletter featuring authors, competitions, special offers and lots more. Postage and packing is FREE!

This offer comes with no strings attached. You may cancel or suspend your subscription at any time and still keep your FREE books and gifts. It's so easy. Send no money now but simply complete the coupon below and return it today to:-

Mills & Boon Reader Service, FREEPOST, PO Box 236, Croydon, Surrey CR9 9EL.

— — — — — — **NO STAMP REQUIRED** — — — — —✂

YES! Please rush me 4 FREE *Legacy of Love* romances and 2 FREE gifts! Please also reserve me a Reader Service subscription. If I decide to subscribe, I can look forward to receiving 4 brand new *Legacy of Love* romances for just £10.00 every month - postage and packing FREE. If I choose not to subscribe, I shall write to you within 10 days and still keep the FREE books and gifts. I may cancel or suspend my subscription at any time simply by writing to you. I am over 18 years of age.

Please write in BLOCK CAPITALS

Ms/Mrs/Miss/Mr _____ EP60M

Address _____

_____

_____ Postcode _____

Signature _____

Offer closes 31st March 1994. The right is reserved to refuse an application and change the terms of this offer. One application per household. Offer not valid to current Legacy of Love subscribers. Offer valid only in UK and Eire. Overseas readers please write for details. Southern Africa write to IBS, Private Bag, X3010, Randburg, 2125, South Africa. You may be mailed with offers from other reputable companies as a result of this application. Please tick box if you would prefer not to receive such offers. ☐